Whispers

Second chances unearth long-buried secrets

...

Wongan Creek Series
Book 1

Juanita Kees

Published by Juanita Kees (Kees2Create)

eBook ISBN: 9781763632417

Paperback ISBN: 9781763632424

Cover Design Copyright © by Paradox Book Cover Designs & Formatting.

Whispers
Juanita Kees

Second chances unearth long–buried secrets ...

Travis Bailey has his hands full managing his canola farm while taking care of his orphaned niece and his elderly neighbour who is battling the onset of Alzheimers. He doesn't have time to fall in love.

Social worker, Heather Penney, knows what it's like to care for someone with a debilitating illness. She lost her mother to Motor Neurone Disease. Initial blood tests show she might carry the same gene so her future isn't guaranteed. Travis and Casey are fast winning her heart, but the small gold mining town of Wongan Creek holds sad and dangerous secrets. Travis' twin sister drowned under suspicious circumstances and the town bully he suspects of her murder has turned his attentions to Heather.

About the Author

Finding hope in country towns with dark secrets ...

Juanita escapes the real world to create emotionally engaging stories steeped in crime, suspense, mystery, and intrigue. Her books are set in dusty, rural outback Australia and on the NASCAR racetracks of America. Her small-town USA and Australian rural stories have made the Amazon bestseller and top 100 lists. Juanita also likes to dabble in the ponds of fantasy and paranormal with Greek gods brought to life in the 21st century.

Juanita graduated college with distinctions and a diploma in Proofreading, Editing and Publishing in 2011 and started her freelance writing business, Kees2Create Words. As a developmental and structural editor, she assists writers to polish their manuscripts for submission. In 2012, she achieved her dream of becoming a published author and now has multiple novels on the market.

When she's not working, writing, editing, or proofreading, Juanita enjoys travelling to discover new worlds for inspiration. Mother to two handsome heroes and partner to a car enthusiast, Juanita also has a passion for fast cars and country living.

Juanita loves to talk books with readers and would love to connect. Contact her via:

Amazon Author:
https://www.amazon.com/author/juanitakees
Website:
https://juanitakees.com/contact/
Kees2Create Words Editing:
https://kees2createwords.com/
BookBub:
https://www.bookbub.com/authors/juanita-kees
Newsletter:
https://kees2createwords.substack.com/embed
Goodreads:
https://www.goodreads.com/author/show/6454477.
Juanita_Kees
Book Love Book Club:
https://www.facebook.com/groups/607880523038543

Chapter One

Travis Bailey tucked the oily rag in his hands into his back pocket, dragged the hat off his head and wiped the sweat from his forehead with his sleeve. Casey needed new school shoes, the bloody tractor had thrown a piston and old man Murchison had stolen his own sheep — again.

'Where did you see them last, Harry?' he asked, thinking how much more bowed his seventy-two-year-old neighbour's back had become in the last few months.

'Down by the creek. I'm sure I put them there this morning. I betcha some bastard's stolen them again.'

More like he'd herded them out to pasture and forgotten where he'd put them. 'Are you sure they're not in your back paddock?'

Travis put his hat firmly back on his head and

squinted at the sun. The school bus would be along in another hour or so and then Casey would be home. The rest of his day would be taken up by peanut butter sandwiches minus the crusts, and reading homework. He didn't have enough time to go looking for sheep that were likely not missing in the first place.

'Any chance you didn't put the sheep out to pasture this morning?'

These days his good friend could barely remember a conversation he'd had five minutes before. But, he couldn't rule out the possibility that someone had played a prank on the old man.

'They're trying to scare me off my property, I tell ya.' Harry leaned on his cane.

Now there was a possibility he couldn't ignore. Mine shareholder cum property developer and all round arsehole, John Bannister was trying to snap up property to expand mine operations wherever there was so much as a hint of gold.

Still, Travis couldn't risk being late for the bus and leave his niece to wait at the side of the road, especially not with their social worker due for her routine visit.

His application for adoption had raised the level of assessment in their case, put more focus on his parenting skills and Casey's welfare as an orphan, but he knew deep down it was what his sister would have wanted. And what he wanted too.

On the bright side, it brought the lovely Heather

Penney out to the farm, and Travis didn't mind that at all. New in town, pretty and already a hit with the locals, Heather was breaking hearts all the way from Collie to Kalgoorlie. Lucky his heart wasn't available for breaking, but at least he could enjoy the view.

'All right then,' said Travis. His day had turned to shit and he wouldn't get another thing done without his tractor anyway. 'Let's go over to your place and see if we can find them. We need to hurry though, I need to clean up and put the toilet seat down before Heather Penney arrives.'

'You're a bloke. We have a right to keep the toilet seat up or we piss on it and then the missus complains anyway. Who's Heather Penney?'

'You need a filter on that mouth, Harry. Heather is my case worker. Doc Benson will be enrolling you in the welfare department's care program soon if you keep forgetting where you put your sheep. Anyone would think you're losing your mind,' Travis teased.

Harry growled under his breath, the irony of the truth not lost on him. 'Sounds like one of those government people who come in and tell you how to run your life.'

'She is. Kinda. Except she's really nice about it.'

'What's a bloody social worker going to do about my sheep anyway? Find them a foster family? I don't need a social worker, I need a friggin' policeman and Riggs can't handle the whole damn town on his own, so it will be days before he gets out here to do something about it.'

Travis sighed. He and Harry had this same conversation so often he didn't even have to think of a response because it came naturally. Harry never remembered anyone other than Riggs running the small town's police station which, until the opening of the Wongan Creek gold mine ten years ago, had been a one-man show. Now they had five cops in town and if things got out of hand when the boys let loose in the pub, they'd call in reinforcements from one of the closest towns — which added at least one or two more to the town's head count.

'Come on, Harry. Since my tractor is shot to hell, we'll take your ute. I'll drive.'

He steered the old man across to the firebreak along the fence line where Harry had parked the ancient, rusty vehicle — if you could call it parking. More like stopping inches before he drove right through the perimeter fence. Travis made a mental note to check it for damage later.

Riggs would have a fit if he knew Harry was driving. He'd taken his licence off him last winter when Harry had almost driven into the flooded creek and couldn't remember how he got there. It might be time to hide the keys, although the old bugger would probably just hot-wire it instead.

'I can drive,' Harry insisted.

'You don't have a licence.'

'I can still drive,' he grumbled.

'And I wouldn't be a good neighbour if I let you. Now, keep an eye out for those sheep. We'll do a quick drive past the creek and then back up to your place. I'll have to let Heather know what's happened and try to delay our appointment otherwise I'll run out of time.'

'Who's Heather?'

Travis bit back a grin and turned the key in the ignition. The engine coughed to life and rattled loudly as he drove along the fire break to the road. It wouldn't be long before Harry's ute joined the other rusting carcasses in the back paddock on his property. That could only be a good thing for Harry's safety.

Travis turned left out onto Crossman Road and drove the five kilometres to the creek that ran through Harry's property. As he drove over the old steel bridge, he looked but couldn't see any sheep. Not that he'd expected to.

Harry muttered and cursed in the seat next to him. 'Nope, nothing. Bloody mongrels.'

'Nothing here, Harry. I'll have to come back and look again after I've picked Casey up from the bus stop.'

'Yeah, yeah, righto. How's the kidlet doing at school?'

Travis glowed with pride. There was only room for

one girl in his life and that was the almost six-year-old Casey. 'She loves it. Come right out of her shell.'

'That's good. Poor kid. To lose her mum like that ...' Harry's voice trailed off.

The glow Travis felt turned to a dull ache. It had been two years since his twin sister drowned in the same swollen creek they could have lost Harry to, and he felt the horror of it as if it happened yesterday. If he'd been home when she went missing that day, he might have been able to find her, save her, avoid the horrible suspicion surrounding her death, silence the rumours that it might have been suicide. Guilt and regret danced a tango in his gut. He only had himself to blame for the selfishness that took him away that day.

He'd needed — wanted — an escape from the terrible silence that had taken hold of their family. He'd thought trying out as the next Australian Buckjump champion was the perfect opportunity to ride off the anger and frustration, and the need for revenge that gnawed at his gut. Every time he'd looked at his sister, he'd watched her retreat a little more. So he'd packed his bag and headed to Newman to scratch the itch that ate at his soul. His father had warned him against it.

Grow up, son! Stop chasing pipe dreams. You belong on the land in Wongan Creek, doing things that won't break your legs or injure your spine and destroy your future.

Travis grimaced at the irony of his father's words. His actions had destroyed their futures.

His mother had begged him not to go. Tracy had called him a frigging idiot — the last of the few words she'd spoken since the party at the Bannisters' place that changed their lives forever, the catalyst for the situation he now found himself in. He should have listened. The twelve hundred kilometre drive home with Tracy's death on his conscience had been the longest two days of his life.

'You've done well raising that kid, son. Tracy would be proud of you. I'm bloody proud of you.' Harry's quietly spoken words pulled him back from the memory.

'Yeah, cheers, mate.'

Travis let silence hang heavily in the air as he turned into the bumpy driveway of Murchison's Run. Pride was all well and good if you'd earned it, which he hadn't. The result of his actions had driven his parents out of Wongan Creek. Even though his mother had denied it, his father's stony silence had confirmed it. The blame for what happened to Tracy lay squarely with him. If he'd stayed home, she'd still be alive.

His mother had said they were ready to leave the farm to him, but he knew the truth was that they couldn't live with the sadness of how much they'd lost that day. They couldn't look at Casey and not be reminded of their own little girl they'd buried too soon, or the circumstances they suspected his niece had been conceived in.

The thought that the truth might come out one day as to who Casey's father was scared the shit out of him. He didn't doubt for a moment that if that happened, she'd be torn from him in an instant and thrown into a family who didn't know the meaning of love.

But, there were days when his life felt as desolate as Harry's rundown farm with its rusting sheds, patched fences and empty paddocks. He wondered why he stayed on his own farm with all the memories while his parents travelled the country trying to escape them.

He sighed. He knew the answer as well as he knew every inch of his paddocks and the creek below them. He loved his farm out here in the south-eastern corridor of Western Australia. The land was a beautiful, rough and challenging mistress. He could never be cooped up in a city apartment, or even in one of the sprawling suburbs where the houses were so close together you could hear your neighbour fart. And he owed it to his family to stay. He owed it to Tracy to give Casey a loving home and a good, stable upbringing.

He might have to reconsider their future when Casey got to high school age. Even though Wongan Creek had a perfectly good high school, he wanted to explore the best options for her education. He wasn't sure he could bear to send her away to a boarding school, but if that's what had to be, he'd just have to man up and do it.

As he pulled up outside Harry's old weatherboard house, he spotted the white four-wheel drive with the Wongan Creek council logo on the door and the coppery mane of the loveliest girl in town. Heather Penney.

Sunshine chased away the gloominess of his thoughts. Her pretty face and wide smile would take the edge off, but his stomach took a dip at her presence on Harry's farm.

He hadn't had a chance to call her yet, so why was she here already? Please God don't let her have come to take Harry, not before he'd had a chance to secure the old man's future.

Heather Penney watched the rusty old ute rattle up the driveway. Sergeant Riggs should slap a yellow sticker on it and declare it unroadworthy. Harry Murchison should not even be driving. Hadn't his licence been suspended only six months ago?

Damn the stubborn, grumpy old codger. It would serve him right if she had the old rust-bucket towed away and carted him off into a care facility.

Unofficially, she was keeping an eye on him at Doc Benson's request. More to make sure he was eating and managing around the house on his own, but so far it seemed his neighbour had the situation under control.

Doc knew the incidents of forgetfulness were on the

increase, and that something would have to be done sooner rather than later. With some extra time on her hands before her visit to the Bailey farm next door, Heather had stopped in to say hello and have a cup of tea with Harry.

Her heart did a little flutter as she noted it wasn't Harry behind the steering wheel. Travis Bailey — eligible bachelor — fancied by every woman in town who didn't need assisted-breathing apparatus and a walking cane.

Even the ladies of the Country Women's Association were knitting jumpers and scarves for him. Travis — with his easy smile, twinkling eyes and big heart — was the kind of man you wanted to marry and nurture.

It seemed there wasn't a single person in Wongan Creek or the surrounding areas who hadn't been on the receiving end of his help at some stage or another. All you had to do was drop his name at a CWA meeting and they'd wax lyrical for hours on his generosity.

Heather ignored the swarm of butterflies partying in her belly, smoothed her ponytail and adjusted the broad-brimmed hat designed to keep the bite of the sun off her face. No way would she join the Travis Bailey fan club or try to snag his attention.

She sighed as Travis pulled to a halt behind her four-wheel drive, turned off the engine and opened the door. The man was so very sexy with his jeans worn in all the right places and his work boots covered in red dust. And oh lordy, that crop of thick, dark blond hair when he pulled off his hat like he was doing now ... she just wanted to run her hands through it and get her fingers tangled. Heather shivered against the heat that tickled her spine. Lovely to look at, but no hope to hold because she was a professional assigned to his case and his arms were a no go zone. Not that she was interested. No way.

His green eyes twinkled with humour below the shock of gold fringe that contrasted against the rest of his dark blond hair. Occasionally she saw that laughter replaced with sadness.

The ladies of the CWA had tried hard to sell him to her at High Tea last week, singing his praises and listing his attributes. There were many, if you believed the grapevine. She smiled at the efforts of their matchmaking attempts. The old dears were keen to see him find a wife, and she could understand why. Even with the smear of grease on his cheek, he was damn near perfect.

But she'd also heard about his parents moving away, his sister's accident and his total devotion to raising his niece. He had no time for dating so she knew her single status was safe. Her own heart was best kept firmly in her job. She couldn't afford to lose either.

He'd thrown on a flannel checked shirt, rolled up the sleeves and forgotten to button up, God bless him. The edges flapped as he walked towards her, giving her the perfect view of washboard abs and sun-kissed skin tainted only by a hard day's dirt.

Her knees threatened to buckle so she leaned against the fender of the four-wheel drive and blamed the heat of the post-midday sun for the weakness.

'Hi, Heather,' greeted Travis.

'Travis.' Heather swallowed. *Oh Lord*. The way he said her name sent tingles down her spine. 'Harry,' she said as the old man hobbled towards her.

'Eileen? Is that you?' Harry asked, squinting against the sun. 'No, you're not Eileen. Who are you?'

Heather sighed. She might as well record her responses and hit replay. Harry forgot every time. 'No, Harry, I'm Heather Penney, remember? I'm with the Department of Health and Welfare. Who's Eileen?'

'Nobody.' Harry sighed. 'For a minute there you looked just like someone I knew a long time ago. Are you here about my sheep then?'

'Have your sheep gone missing again, Harry?'

Finding Harry Murchison's missing sheep was becoming a weekly ritual, as was the discussion with Travis after they'd herded them back into Harry's paddock.

Harry stared off across the creek for a moment then brought his gaze back to hers. The emptiness in the old man's rheumy eyes worried her sometimes.

'Missing sheep? I don't have any missing sheep.

They're down in the back paddock unless those mongrels from the mine site have moved them again.'

Heather stole a glance at Travis who flashed his trademark bone-melting grin. Oh, he knew, the sexy bastard! He knew Harry hadn't lost the sheep, playing along so as not to upset or confuse Harry any more than he already was, protecting him all the way.

'Okay, would you like me to go and check on them just in case they have wandered off?'

'Sure, knock yourself out. I'll put the kettle on.' Harry shuffled towards the front door of the ramshackle homestead. 'Travis, go with the girl. Don't want her getting lost and trampling all over my canola.'

Travis' grin widened and she wished she could wipe it off because it made her feel things she had no right to want. She let it keep until Harry was safely inside the house. 'He knows it's not canola he's growing, right?'

'Daisies, canola — same yellow colour. At least it's not bindii weed. As long as he sees something growing, he still feels like a farmer.'

'He needs to consider his choices, like securing a place in a care facility. His loss of memory and mobility is getting worse.' Travis' eyes lost their sparkle and Heather regretted having to raise the topic. 'It won't be long before Doc Benson assigns me to his case officially. Then I'll have to do what's best for Harry.'

'I know, but without Murchison's Run he has nothing to live for. He doesn't have any family to care for him. Taking him away from here will finish him off. He won't survive in a care facility.'

'I know what you're doing, Travis.' She stepped in closer and lowered her tone in case Harry was listening. 'You can't keep this up.'

His features set to neutral, he turned that hot green gaze to hers. Along his jawline, the shadow of a beard caressed his skin. With almost a foot difference in height, she had the perfect view of his strong tanned throat as it worked around his response. 'Keep what up?'

Her thoughts wandered way off track from Harry's welfare as the heat from his body permeated hers and the smell of his aftershave teased her senses. She drew her mind back into focus.

'Covering for his forgetfulness, taking care of his land and yours. Taking care of him without him knowing it.'

Travis shrugged. 'He's my neighbour. It's what we do out here. We look out for each other.'

'You can't keep the expansion of the gold mine at bay singlehandedly, and you know it. It's only a matter of time before John Bannister figures out you've been covering for him and lodges a court order to have him declared mentally incapable.'

His hands were on her arms in an instant, firm and determined, warm and exciting. 'I won't let them take his land, Heather. I know his mental health is deteriorating, but I won't help it along by taking away the only thing he has to live for. You have no idea how much this land means to him. Do you understand that if we move him away, it will be like ripping his heart out and turning off his life support? He'll die faster in an institution.'

The passion and determination in his voice reached in and twisted her heart. He might have incredibly broad shoulders but he wasn't superhuman. He was simply a man juggling way too many balls, a burden he couldn't possibly shoulder alone for much longer without it affecting his niece's quality of life. And that was her business. Right now, that's where her focus needed to lie.

'They're not institutions. Not anymore. They're care facilities that focus on providing quality of life in the final years.' Sometimes she wished she hadn't had to experience the service they provided first hand. 'Haven't you got enough on your hands raising Casey and managing your own property without taking responsibility for a man who isn't family?'

Temper flashed in his eyes and he dropped his hands. 'Out here, everyone is family. You're passing judgement on things you can't begin to understand.'

'Travis, you can't keep doing this. How long before you wear yourself out? What good will you be to Casey then? You can't care for a child alone when you're too exhausted to take care of yourself.'

The walls slammed up around him as he froze her out. 'You'd love it if I caved, wouldn't you, Heather? Another score on your government reports. Another child ripped from their family and delegated to foster care because the powers that be can't see past the red tape. Another lonely old man torn from his land to be institutionalised so that money-grabbing sons-of-bitches like John Bannister can add to their portfolio.' He slapped his hat on his head. 'You won't take Casey from me. And Harry will be taken care of my way. I'll see you on your official visit as scheduled where you won't find so much as a toilet seat out of place.' He turned and walked away towards the main road, anger etched into every taut muscle.

Tears stung her eyes and she dashed them away. His harshly spoken words cut deeply into her heart. He was wrong. So, so wrong. Any fool could see how much he loved Casey and it would tear her heart out if she did have to move the little girl into foster care. No matter how good a home could be with foster parents, it could never replace the love of your own family. She knew all about never having a family.

'May the cat eat you, and may the devil eat the damn cat.' She muttered the curse under her breath at his departing back and thanked her Irish mother for teaching it to her. She might be a Darwin girl by birth, but the Irish blood still sang in her veins. 'Maybe the long walk to the bus stop will melt all that God damn sexiness from your backside and fry some common sense into your brain.'

She tore her mutinous stare from his back as he stalked away up the gravel road. Turning towards Harry's back paddock, she picked her way through the field of daisies, careful not to squash them as she tried not to dwell on how far out of her depth she was with Travis Bailey.

He wasn't some invincible superhero, for God's sake, but she did respect what he was trying to do for Harry.

At the edge of the daisy field, she stopped and counted the sheep — all five of them — and noted they'd need shearing before too long. Another task that would fall to Travis because Harry probably didn't even remember the sheep needed shearing.

Well, the least she could do was make the old man a cup of tea. No doubt he'd forgotten he'd boiled the kettle, and she could do with a cuppa herself. Heather hoped Harry had chamomile tea in his cupboard since her next visit would be with the man she'd just made angrier than a frill-necked lizard.

Chapter Two

Travis cursed himself for letting Heather get under his skin. Her intentions were good, no doubt about that, but she had no idea how hard it was to keep developers and miners from getting their hands on what was left of the good farming land in the area.

If it wasn't the developers looking to build new housing estates for the mine workers it was the mine owners determined to follow the vein of gold that ran beneath their precious earth, destroying good, fertile farming land for it. He was damned if he'd let it happen before he was ready to abandon the farm he loved. He'd already had to sell the cattle because he couldn't keep up with the chores. It was a stroke of luck that Angus beef had taken off in the south-west and he'd been able to sell them at a good price.

He burned his anger off as he walked the distance to the school bus stop. The main road leading into town was quiet at this time of day and the heat shimmered off the tar. The sun chewed into the flannel material of his shirt. He shrugged it off and tied the arms of the shirt around his waist. By the time he reached the stop, he hoped he'd have walked off his bad mood because he'd hate for Casey to see the knots Heather had him tied up in.

He could still feel the softness of her skin against his hands and wondered if the rest of her felt the same.

She might be an interfering know-it-all, but she sure as hell made her DOHW uniform look like something off a city catwalk. Heather Penney took pale blue shirts and uniform pants to a whole new level of sexy.

Her arms when he'd held them were firm, her skin silky soft and warm in contrast. She was strong enough to flip a man on his arse without missing a breath. He'd seen her do it. She'd have to have had some self-defence training to manage the arseholes she dealt with in her job. Domestic abusers who attacked before they talked weren't fun to handle in a crisis, especially if they were drunk or drugged up.

The thought took some of the sting out of his anger. He wasn't sure he liked the thought of her being in dangerous situations like that. She had a job to do, he got that, but there were kids out there far worse off than

Casey who needed her attention more, and their situations were not nearly as pretty to deal with.

The corrugated roof of the two seater bench bus shelter shimmered in the heat. He slowed his steps and concentrated on breathing to calm his thoughts.

The worst part was Heather was right. He knew he couldn't manage alone much longer. How much time did he have left before Harry's forgetfulness turned hazardous? It wouldn't be long before he forgot a fire burning or left the gas cooker turned on in his kitchen. How did you tell a man who'd been independent all his life that he had to go into an institution?

Slipping into the shade of the bus shelter, he sat down on the wooden bench and stretched his legs out in front of him, studying the worn leather of his work boots.

He'd have to talk to Doc Benson before much longer. Putting it off had felt like a much better route to explore, but with Harry's episodes escalating, he'd have to take action soon.

Pulling his phone out of his back pocket, he checked for a signal before dialling. Mobile phone reception in Western Australia was sketchy at best, out here it was like finding opals among the gold.

He tapped his foot in the red dust as he listened to the phone ringing on the other end of the crackly line. It didn't take long for Mrs Benson to answer.

'Hey, Mrs B. Is the doc in?'

'Travis, honey! Is everything okay? Nothing wrong with little Casey, is there?'

'No, no. She's fine. I just need a little chat about Harry.'

'Oh dear. Hang on a sec, Doc's between patients at the moment. I'll put you through.'

'Thanks, Mrs B,' Travis replied, thankful he didn't need to explain. The whole of Wongan Creek was concerned for Harry's welfare, but all were powerless to do anything, except for Travis who was the closest the old man had to family.

'Travis, my boy.' Doc Benson's voice boomed down the line. 'I heard from Riggs that Harry's having some trouble again?' His tone softened. 'You know it's time to make a decision about his future, right?'

'Yeah, that's why I'm calling.' Travis took off his hat, balanced it on his knee and ran a hand through his hair. 'We need to talk to him, Doc. Any chance you could stop by the house later?'

'Of course, no worries. Harry's place or yours?'

'Harry's, I think. He'll feel less agitated in his own surroundings.'

'Righto, mate. I'll meet you there after my last appointment this afternoon.'

'Cheers, thanks, Doc.' Travis stabbed the button to end the call and shoved the phone back in his pocket, his heart weighing a ton in his chest. At least he had a couple of hours to think things over.

The rumble of the school bus reached his ears and he stood to shrug on his shirt. Casey had lost so much already. Harry was like a grandfather to her and if they had to send him away, it would break her heart. Then it would be just him and Casey, two lonely souls not so different from the old man who'd spent almost all his life alone.

The bus full of local school kids came to a halt in front of him and the doors hissed open. A cool wave of air washed over him from the air conditioning.

'Hey, Travis,' called Marge Everett, one of the few CWA volunteers licenced to drive the school bus. 'I've finished knitting that Wongan Nuggets footy scarf for you. Pity the season's over for another year.'

'There's always next year, Mrs E.' He grinned.

'It's in Casey's backpack. Don't forget to take it out when you get home.'

'Cheers, thanks.'

Casey hopped down off the bus, her feet slapping onto the red dust. She launched herself at him and his arms were ready.

'Uncle Trav! Wait till you see the picture I drew for you.' She squealed as he swept her up, backpack and all, and hugged her tight.

Travis' heart squeezed as she cupped his face and smacked a kiss against his forehead. 'Hey, sweet pea.' He pinched her rosy cheek with one hand while he held her tight with his arm. 'I see your braids survived the day.'

She grinned widely. 'Mrs Everett says you did a great job on them. Look, my tooth's wobbly.' She wiggled a front tooth.

'Wow, wobbly teeth and growing feet. Before we know it you'll be driving.' Reluctantly, he set her on her feet and took her small hand in his.

She turned those big eyes on him, shaped so much like Tracy's, reached down to retrieve her hat from where it had fallen and dropped it back onto her head. 'You're silly. I can't drive yet. Where's the ute?'

'We're walking today, sweet pea. I had to drive Harry's ute back to the farm earlier and walked back.' He squatted down and hunched over a little. 'Hop on, I'll give you a piggyback ride.' He blessed the fact that his and Harry's driveways were only a few kilometres apart.

'Yes!' She did a little fist pump and clambered onto his back, looping her arms around his neck and her legs around his waist. 'I love you, Uncle Trav. Can we go see Harry later? I drew a picture for him too.'

'He'll like that, I'm sure.' Travis hooked his arms under her legs and started walking. 'Doc Benson is coming over to visit Harry too.'

'Is Harry sick?'

'Not sick, just getting older.'

'Oh.' The sadness in her tone made his heart

contract a little more. 'You won't get old like that will you, Uncle Trav? Benji says when people get old, they die and leave us all alone. My mummy wasn't old and she died. You won't die too, will you, Uncle Trav?'

Travis couldn't blame the heat and sweat running down his forehead for the sudden sting in his eyes. 'No, sweetheart, I'll be around for a long time. Long enough to chase away all the boys like Benji when you're a teenager. No boyfriends for you, missy.'

She giggled and pressed her cheek against his back. 'Silly! I'm never getting married. Yuck.'

'Yuck, indeed. You remember that when Benji tries to kiss you on your sixteenth birthday.'

Travis turned his head at the sound of a car approaching and the toot of a horn. He slowed his steps as Heather pulled up next to them.

She rolled down the window. 'Want a lift?'

He eyed her for a moment, still a little angry with her although angrier at himself for having to admit she was right.

'Can we, Uncle Trav? I'm all hot and sweaty and if we do, I can get a drink faster.' Casey bounced on his back excitedly.

Heather wiggled her fingers in a wave. 'Hi, Casey. I've got a fresh bottle of water here if you're thirsty? It's nice and cold from my little cooler bag.'

'That's bribery, Miss Penney,' said Travis, keeping

his tone cool and trying to ignore the pretty flush on Heather's ivory-coloured skin.

'I'd say this was an emergency situation. We'll call it a rescue mission. Come on, Travis. It's hot, and it's a fair hike home for both of you. I know I'm early for our appointment. I promise not to deduct points if you've left the toilet seat up again.' A little smile twitched on her lips.

Her tone offered reconciliation so for Casey's sake, he wouldn't refuse the offer. 'Okay, thanks.'

He squatted down again so Casey could slide off his back, then straightened to open the back door for her. She scooted into the middle and shrugged off her back pack.

'Sit back and buckle up,' said Heather.

He closed the door and walked around the rear of the vehicle to the passenger side to slip into the front seat. Fastening his seatbelt, he kept his eyes on the road and as far to the left as the confines of the car would allow. Out the corner of his eye he saw Heather cast him an amused look, but said nothing as she hit a button on the radio and the soundtrack from Casey's favourite animated movie filled the car. Casey squealed with delight and sang along as they pulled away. As silence stretched between them down the long driveway to his house, Travis wished he was six again.

Heather turned off the driveway to park in the shade of the vacant carport outside Travis' house. She loved the old federation style building with its red brick walls and wraparound veranda set against the backdrop of the hills and canola fields. He'd freshened the green paint on the lattice work and she wondered where the hell he'd found the time with all he had going on in his life.

Under the canopy of a massive old Jacaranda tree, a yellow and green swing set stood silent next to Casey's boxed sand pit. To the left of it, a thriving vegetable patch. Down in the paddock separated from the garden by a white wooden fence, a palomino grazed in the shade of a eucalyptus tree. There was no doubt he'd catered for every need he could think of to keep Casey amused and give her every opportunity available to a kid growing up on a farm.

'Here we are,' she said, stopping the car and turning down the music. 'Was that fun?'

'Yes, thank you, Miss Penney. Benji will be *so* jealous when I tell him at school tomorrow. His mum says he has to wait till Christmas for that CD.' Casey loosened her seatbelt, leaned between the seats and kissed Heather's cheek. 'You're the awesomest.'

'You're pretty awesome yourself,' she said and gave Casey's cute little button nose a tug. The kid was pretty hard to resist with her twinkling eyes and peachy cheeks. Almost as irresistible as her uncle, but Heather wouldn't let her thoughts go down that track.

Travis said nothing as he opened the passenger door and unfolded his long legs from the cabin. What the man did to denim should be illegal, and she shouldn't even be noticing such things. Heather pushed open her own door and got out just as Travis reached the back door to let Casey out. His gaze flicked to hers and held a moment. The sadness in his eyes took her by surprise.

He looked down at Casey. 'Sweet pea, go inside and change out of your school clothes. I'll be along in a minute to make you a sandwich. I just need a word with Miss Penney, okay?'

'Okay. Thanks again, Miss Penney!' She darted off, leaving them alone in awkward silence.

Travis leaned back against the four-wheel drive and folded his arms across his chest. He toed the dirt at his feet with his boot and kept his eyes down. 'I'm sorry, Heather. I was out of line back there.'

Heather sighed and leaned back next to him. 'Apology accepted.'

'I called Doc Benson.'

Her heart sank. She'd only been in town a little over six months. Too short a time to form any long-lasting friendships or know anyone well enough, but she knew the cost of making decisions.

The strong bond between Travis and his neighbour would have made that a tough call to make. She crossed one ankle over the other, unfolded her arms and took off her hat. Twirling it in her hands, she ran her fingers around the trimmed edge, unsure what to say.

'You were right,' he continued. 'I need to help Harry sort out his affairs before it's too late, so we're meeting with the doc tonight.'

'It sucks, Travis, I know.' She knew all too well the emotional and psychological cost of having to put someone into care. 'But there comes a time when you have to realise there is nothing more you can do for people in situations like Harry's.'

Travis blew out a long breath and leaned his head back against the roof of the car, tipping his hat over his eyes. 'He's going to hate me.'

'He won't remember.'

'But I will.'

Yes, he would, and it would haunt him for the rest of his life, just like it haunted her. 'Sometimes doing the right thing feels like the wrong thing to do.'

He lifted his head and tipped his hat back into place on his head. 'That sounds terribly Irish, Miss Penney.'

She smiled, sadness tugging at her heart. 'Growing up in Darwin doesn't make me less Irish. You can take the girl out of Ireland but you can't take Ireland out of the girl. At least, that's what my mum used to say.' He smiled back, albeit a little weakly, and it made her heart flutter. 'If it helps you any, the pain and guilt lessens eventually, and knowing you did the best you were able to will be some consolation.'

'Sounds as if you're speaking from experience.'

His gaze collided with hers again, but this time it was she who looked away. 'I am. I had to put Mum in special care when we lived in Darwin. It was the hardest thing I've ever done. She had aggressive Motor Neurone Disease. Within five years, she had no muscle control and eventually became completely paralysed. I couldn't care for her alone anymore. She needed life support to stay alive.'

The heredity factor meant she may carry that same mutant gene in her blood, and that thought haunted her every day. The preliminary blood tests Doc Benson had taken earlier this month had showed an anomaly that was inconclusive. He'd recommended a specialist in Perth for further testing, the thought of which terrified her. The fear of knowing far outweighed the need to know.

'I'm sorry to hear that.' He leaned closer until their arms touched in a small comforting gesture that lifted the sadness a little.

'I went through all the stages — guilt, regret, blame. Mum was the daughter of Irish migrants. Pregnant, sixteen and kicked out of home, she had to give me up at birth. I never knew what happened to the man who fathered me. Maybe one day I'll find out who he is. She never spoke about him or her family. I don't even know my grandparents' names.'

Travis squeezed her hand but said nothing.

'I spent six years in foster care until she got on her feet and came back for me. Then she spent the rest of her life battling to keep a roof over our heads. She struggled to make ends meet, but she was determined to take care of me. When her condition worsened, I couldn't do the same for her.'

'That sucks. I'm sure you did everything you could.' His arm came around her shoulders and she blinked back her tears. 'Did your grandparents know?'

'No, they went back to Ireland a couple of years after she left home. She had contact with them once after I was born and then never again. Thankfully, she didn't suffer for long in the end, but it's a terrible way to die.'

'Shit.'

'Shit indeed.' And because his arm felt far too comfortable around her shoulders, she straightened and stepped away from him. 'Trust me when I say, it's the best thing you can do for Harry.'

'I know.'

'You've taken on a huge responsibility for someone who isn't a blood relative. Not many people would do that.'

Travis pushed away from the car and straightened. 'We're the closest he has to family. He's a cranky but loveable old bachelor who cared for his parents until they died of old age. By then it was too late for him to begin living himself.' He winked and followed it up with a cheeky grin that had her toes curling against the spike of heat that shot through her belly. 'Although the Wongan Creek grapevine says there's more to the story. There might even be the hint of a not so nice, not so romantic story of unrequited love.'

Heather's eyebrows rose. 'Oh really?'

'Yep. Gossip says his girl, Eileen, upped and did the dirty on him with John Bannister while Harry was away fighting in Vietnam. She was a young Irish nurse doing a little country practice as part of her studies.'

'She cheated on Harry with John Bannister? From Wongan Creek Mining? Why am I not surprised? He has a hand in almost everything that happens around here and it's not always good. Sounds like perfect grounds for a feud and a motive. Sometimes owning a chunk isn't enough. There are those like Bannister who want it all.'

Travis shrugged. 'Ah look, the affair thing is nothing more than grapevine whispers. Neither of the old buggers will admit to anything. But I do know selling is the last thing Harry wants to do, especially to Bannister.'

'But with no relatives, if he dies without a will, the land will end up in the state coffers and they'll sell it off anyway.'

'That's the bitch of a thing. Whether WCM buys the land for property development or mining, my farm is pretty much screwed. Having an estate next door full of houses, no trees and tar roads will be as much of a threat to my land as the mine itself. Suburban sprawl comes with its own hazards — weeds, water contamination, that's barely the start of it.'

Heather patted his arm. 'Development isn't all bad. The town has benefited from the expansion.'

'I know. I'm not against it. I'm just not convinced we need a housing estate in Wongan Creek right away. Not when it's likely to stand empty again when the boom is over.'

'Can't you buy his land?'

'I wish I could, but I don't have the dollars. Rumours are already flying that I'm only taking care of him in the hope of inheriting it.'

'Oh surely not. The people in this town love you, Travis. They only ever have nice things to say about you. And I heard Mrs Everett doesn't knit a footy scarf for just anyone, but she made one for you.' Heather grinned. 'That would pretty much give you VIP status around here.'

He smiled but then his eyes clouded over again and she missed the happy twinkle.

'It's not the townsfolk starting the rumours. It's old man Bannister's infernal one-upmanship and greed fuelling the gossip. It doesn't take long before people start believing the things they hear.'

'I think the people of Wongan Creek are smarter than that.' Heather sighed. 'Look, how about we reschedule Casey's assessment for another day? I think it's fair to say she's in good spirits and well-cared for. I can come back tomorrow to do the official visit.'

'Thanks, I appreciate that.'

Heather touched his arm lightly, his skin warm, the fine layer of hair rough under her palm. 'Good luck for tonight. I hope Doc Benson can come up with a solution for Harry.' She dropped her hand back to her side.

Travis pulled off his hat and raked a hand through his hair, leaving it tousled. God, it was a sexy look on him. One that had her picturing him against a pillow with morning stubble along his jaw. Turning to the car, she rolled her eyes at her wicked thoughts and blamed it on heatstroke.

'I hope so too. Thanks for the ride. Casey will be singing that infernal song for days,' he grumbled, but his smile took the bite out of his words.

'You're welcome. Now you know what to add to your Christmas shopping list.' She pulled open the door and slid into the driver's seat.

'Right, thanks for that,' Travis replied dryly as he stepped up and closed the door.

Heather started the car and drove away before she was tempted to offer to come back later and help with Harry. Her stay in Wongan Creek was temporary. She couldn't let herself get too close to the people of this warm-hearted town. She'd promised herself no relationships, no children for fear of reliving her mother's life.

What good would it do to pass on the Motor Neurone gene anomaly to her children? What if it had skipped a generation only to come out in the next? No, she was happy on her own. That way no one got hurt, no one had responsibility except herself.

Besides, she hadn't come down from the Northern Territory to find love and friendship. She'd come to get away from the sad memories Darwin held, to find her feet and feed her passion for helping others.

This job offer to work in the rural community of Western Australia had come at the perfect time. It would add another layer to her experience. Now her qualifications could take her anywhere in Australia, or all over the world. She'd be able to take away fond memories of this sunburnt corner of the country and the welcoming arms of the locals when it came time to move on.

If there was a time bomb ticking away in her bloodstream, she'd never put anyone through the pain of caring for a loved one with the debilitating disease, especially not a man who already carried the weight of the town on his shoulders.

Chapter Three

Travis smelled trouble, and it came in the form of a white Wongan Creek Mining four-wheel drive mine-spec'd vehicle with the obligatory orange flashing beacon on the roof of the cab. He pulled up next to it and turned off the engine of his own battered ute.

'Casey, go check on the chooks, would you?' he said.

Hopefully the chickens would keep Casey distracted while he dealt with his neighbour's unwanted visitor. Pity Doc Benson hadn't arrived yet. He could do with the backup. And speaking of backup, where was Robbie? Harry's old cattle dog worked better than an alarm system, barking the moment anyone set foot on the property.

Hopefully he was putting his guard dog skills to use

inside the house. How long had the bastards been here? He only hoped Harry's mind was lucid enough not to sign anything they put in front of him or that he'd at least arrived in time to put a stop to whatever tricks they were up to now.

He watched a moment as Casey ran down to the chicken pen at the bottom of Harry's garden that was now little more than a rusty graveyard of abandoned tools. Then he turned and entered the house, following the voices until he reached the kitchen. Harry sat at the table with Robbie emitting low growls and baring teeth at his feet. Across from him, a man shuffled a pile of papers in front him.

'So, as you can see, Mr Murchison, this could be a very profitable transaction for you.'

'I don't care about money, you mongrel. I care about my land. So you can take those papers and shove them right up your arse.'

The man squared his shoulders and clenched his jaw angrily. 'Well ... then we'll have to explore the alternatives —'

'Trouble, Harry?' Travis interrupted. 'That sounded very much like a threat.' He cocked an eyebrow at the man dressed in the standard high-vis yellow and blue WCM uniform, but Harry interrupted before the man could answer. He stood, wobbly on his legs as his arthritic knees took the weight of his body.

'This drongo is trying to get me to sign his stupid

bloody contract. Came in here pretending to be an inspector.'

'Is that so? Impersonation and a threat? I might have to call Sergeant Riggs, then. That might mean some bad press for WCM.'

The man gathered his papers and stood. 'Mr Murchison misunderstood my intent.'

Travis squared up and looked him in the eye. 'He might have, but I didn't. You can go back and tell Bannister that Murchison's Run is not for sale and never will be to him. And if I find you on this property again, I'll have you arrested for trespassing on private land.'

A burly man with broad shoulders, a handlebar moustache and a beer belly, the visitor held out his calling card. 'I only ever enter premises by invitation.'

'I doubt that.' Travis took the card even though he knew well enough who the man was, read it and grinned despite the fear it struck in his heart. 'Big deal, so you're a lawyer the Bannisters can buy to do their dirty work. You're in this house uninvited. Get out. Now.'

'I'll pass your dissatisfaction on to Mr Bannister.'

Travis clenched his fists and bit his tongue, praying for patience before he decked the bloke. As appealing as the thought was of breaking the arrogant man's nose, he didn't want a charge of assault on his record to put his guardianship of Casey in jeopardy.

Luckily, the arrival of Doc Benson's car seemed to make up the arsehole lawyer's mind. He turned and walked towards the front door. Travis followed to make sure he left.

As they reached the veranda, Doc Benson was making his way up the stairs. He narrowed his eyes at the visitor, but said nothing as Travis escorted the man to his vehicle with Harry and Robbie close behind him. The three men stood and watched until the car disappeared down the drive and Robbie barked at the cloud of red dust his wheels raised.

'Looks like we decided to have this discussion at the right time,' said Doc Benson.

'Yep,' said Travis, unclenching his fists and flexing his fingers.

'Who was that bloke?' Harry stared at the disappearing brake lights and scratched his head.

Travis looked at Doc, his heart breaking for Harry's sake. He only hoped they could come up with a solution before John Bannister put his plans into action to take over Harry's land.

'Harry,' said Doc, 'we need to talk.'

'Always ready for a chat, Doc. Been talking to you since the day you were born. Delivered you myself when you decided to make your appearance during harvest. No hospital back then, no doctor, just me and your father. Not a part of your mother I wanted to see.'

Travis smiled at Doc. 'He never gets tired of telling that tale.'

Doc groaned. 'No, he doesn't. Come on, Harry. I think I'm ready for a cup of tea.'

'Billy's on the boil out back. Always is for you.' Harry turned and hobbled inside.

'Every time he says that, I'm scared he really has made a fire in the middle of his kitchen to boil the billy.' Travis shoved his hands in the back pockets of his jeans.

Doc sighed. 'Me too. I think I might have a solution to the problem, at least until we can convince Harry to go into care in Perth. It's a pity we don't have aged care facilities here.'

'I don't like the way the Bannisters keep upping the pressure on him.'

'No, me neither, which is why I think my plan will work, but it will take time to sort out the legalities. I hope Bannister's money doesn't buy that time from under us.'

'Well, let's hear it.'

'It's complicated.'

Travis shrugged. 'What in life isn't?'

'True that. Let's go in and have a chat to Harry about it, shall we?'

'Righto. I'll just check on Casey quickly and I'll be there.'

Doc smiled and patted his shoulder. 'You're a top bloke, Travis. You need a good wife to stop you becoming just like Harry — an old and lonely man.'

Travis laughed. 'Not until Casey's all grown up. I

think I'll have my hands full until then.' His smile subsided. 'Besides, I owe it to Tracy to give Casey my full attention. I can't afford any distractions.'

'What happened wasn't your fault. When will you stop punishing yourself, son?'

'Never.'

The pain might have subsided but the guilt remained. He'd lost his family that day, in some way or another, and now he was set to lose his best friend and neighbour. Life sucked.

Sundown crept across the sky as Heather turned her four-wheel drive into Travis' driveway. She hadn't planned on visiting after she'd finished work, but she was worried about Harry, and if she allowed herself to be honest, worried about Travis too. So the glass of wine she'd promised herself at the end of a long day would have to wait a little longer.

Heather braked to a stop and the tyres crunched on the gravel. Her heart skipped a beat or two when she spotted Travis on the veranda.

Relaxed with his bare feet up on the rail and seated on a worn out old sofa with Casey snuggled up beside him, they were reading together. Heads bent close, he smiled as Casey pointed to the page then turned her angelic face to his. He high-fived her little hand and pressed a kiss to her shiny strawberry-blonde head.

Travis lifted a hand to wave, dropped his feet from the rail and stood as Casey clambered off the sofa. She slipped her hand into his and looked up at him with excitement beaming on her face. What a beautiful pair they made, Heather thought. Travis was a good father to the little girl who'd lost her mum in such tragic circumstances.

The townsfolk thought he was nothing short of a superhero. Sometimes they praised him a little too much and she had to draw the line on the matchmaking they had in mind for her and Travis. A relationship was definitely not something she had on her agenda no matter how kissable he looked right now with a slow smile spreading his lips.

Casey let go of Travis' hand and skipped down the stairs to greet her. 'Miss Penney! I learned a new word! It's a big one.'

'Really? You're a clever girl. Can you say it for me?'

'Yes! It's exis ... exhil ... oh darn! I could say it a minute ago.' She tugged on Heather's hand. 'Have you come for dinner? Uncle Travis is cooking steak on the barbecue.'

'Oh no, darling, I only popped in to ask your uncle something. I won't be staying long.'

The little girl's smile faded and she looked up at

Travis. 'It's okay if Miss Penney stays, isn't it, Uncle Trav?'

Travis hooked his thumbs into the front pockets of his jeans and Heather's eyes followed the movement. God damn it, the man was built for loving. Long rangy legs, muscled thighs stretching the denim around them, the waistband clinging to the rise of his hips and in the gap between the hem of his T-shirt and his jeans, a glimpse of smooth, taut, tanned skin her fingers itched to touch.

Only in her dreams would she allow that though. Travis Bailey had enough on his plate. She had to be happy on her own.

He pushed away from the post and strolled down the stairs. He moved like liquid gold — hot, smooth and easy. Without his hat hiding his eyes, she was treated to the full impact of his gaze. It sent shivers coursing down her spine and a healthy shot of want to parts she didn't want it to touch.

'Hello, Heather. Not sure to what we owe the pleasure of your visit, but you're welcome to stay.'

She tried, and failed, to push a 'no' past her lips. What harm could it do? It wasn't like she had plans past a glass of wine and a microwave meal anyhow. Plus Casey was there and it was unlikely anything would happen between them. The last thing she wanted was conflict of interest on the case file, the barrier against forming a friendship with this little family. Travis was just being neighbourly. The most they had to worry about was the gossip it might start in town.

'Thank you, I'd like that.'

He delivered a knee-buckling smile to match Casey's excited whoop. 'Come on then. We were just finishing Casey's reading lesson before lighting the fire out the back.' He led the way up the veranda stairs, giving her a fine view of his denim-clad backside. A very fine view.

If she treated him like eye candy, he couldn't steal her heart, because Travis Bailey had all the makings of everything she wanted in a life partner except, she reminded herself, she wasn't in the market for one.

When her mother died, she'd packed away all the good, happy memories in Darwin and run away to escape the sadness, the emptiness. If she didn't look for happiness here, there would be nothing to leave behind when it came time to move on and no sadness to run from.

'Miss Penney?' Casey's voice broke her thoughts.

'Yes, darling?'

'Will you help me make the salad to go with the steak? Uncle Travis says I need to eat all my greens to grow big and strong like him.'

'Your uncle is a very wise man. Yes, I'll give you a hand. What are we putting in the salad bowl?'

'Lettuce, tomatoes, kale — that's a super food, you

know. Makes you super strong and healthy. Uncle Trav says so and look how big and strong he is.'

Yes, indeed, she thought as she watched him disappear through the front door.

Casey tugged at her hand and Heather followed her into the house. She took a moment to appreciate the air of peace and tranquillity in the cool entrance hall. On her routine visits she usually didn't stop to notice anything more than the neat orderliness of Travis' home. It was so much more pleasant to visit in an unofficial capacity, she thought.

Polished jarrah floorboards ran the length of the hallway to the rear of the house and the bedroom wing. Off to her right the sunny kitchen beckoned with its cheerful bay window filled with potted herbs. Casey's handiwork, Travis had told her on her first visit to his home. This was the room she loved the most. Warm, homely and inviting, it ran the full length of the right side of the house with a door leading out to the backyard and another out onto the front veranda, built for large family gatherings.

On the left, the lounge room had French doors leading out onto the side of the house where the veranda faced another view of the majestic slope of Whispering Hills. How lucky he was to have a three hundred and sixty degree view of rolling countryside and open space.

Near the leadlight front door, above a table against

the wall, hung a gallery of family photos. She slowed her steps to study them under the soft lighting from the antique chandelier suspended from the decorative ceiling rose.

'That's my mummy,' said Casey, pointing up to a photo of a woman who shared the same green eyes as Travis. 'Mummy and Uncle Travis were twins.'

'I know, sweetheart. That's pretty cool, isn't it? Twins always have a special bond.' Heather looked at the photo a little more closely. That would have made his loss an even harder one. It must have been a nightmare for him. She couldn't imagine what it was like to lose a sibling, let alone a twin.

All she'd had was the other foster kids until her mum had come for her and taken her home. No one formed long-lasting bonds in foster care and her mum had never married or even been in a relationship to produce siblings. She'd never considered how alone they'd been before, until now when she saw their situation mirrored in Travis and Casey's.

'What are the two of you up to?' Travis asked, turning to come back down the hallway when he realised they weren't following him.

'I'm showing Miss Penney the photos. That's okay, isn't it, Uncle Trav?' Casey's voice wobbled. 'That's not naughty, is it?'

'Of course it's okay, sweet pea.' He lifted her up and

balanced her in his arms so she was face-level height with the photos. 'We have lots of happy memories to share.'

He cast a look Heather's way. A few unhappy ones too, she thought, seeing the fleeting sadness in his eyes.

'That's my nan and pop,' Casey continued. 'They travel a lot so we don't get to see them often.'

'Grey nomads,' added Travis. 'Never in one spot for long. They're travelling around Australia in a camper van.'

Heather wondered at the hitch in his voice, the underlying pain she heard there. What had happened that had made his family leave him to raise his sister's child alone and run his farm as well as the neighbour's? She frowned. How could they leave their grandchild behind?

'Don't judge them, Heather. I don't. It's their way of dealing with what happened to Tracy. They took it hard. We all did, and then we had to find a way to work through it. Mine was to stay here, theirs was to travel until the memories fade. Trust me, it was for the best.'

'I understand,' she said, even though she didn't. She held his gaze a moment, felt his sadness and loss, tinged with a shade of guilt. All she could be was the ear to listen when he was ready to tell her the whole story.

She wanted to ask about Casey's father, but now was not the time. All her file notes only mentioned Casey's mum. Not even the little girl's birth registration named the father. Heather knew what it was like to have 'undeclared' stamped into that empty spot.

'My mummy was very brave, wasn't she, Uncle Trav?'

'Yes, she was, sweet pea.' For a moment silence stretched between them as Casey hugged his neck tightly and he hugged her back. 'Come on now, why don't you introduce Miss Penney to Fantasia before it gets too dark?'

'Ooh yes! Do you like horses, Miss Penney?' Casey looked up at her with hope in her eyes.

'Well, I don't really know. I've never met one before,' Heather teased.

Casey giggled. 'You'll like Fantasia. She was Mummy's horse. She's very gentle and even I can ride her.'

'Until she gets the wind up her backside and then she's off. Lucky she knows only to do that when I ride her. Off you go, and don't stay down there too long, okay?' Travis set Casey to her feet and on her way with a little tap on her shoulder. 'Stop on your way through the kitchen and grab an apple.'

'Okay. You coming, Miss Penney?'

'Sure am,' Heather said, stepping around Travis. Her stomach pitched as her arm brushed his. He was warm and inviting, and it had been so long since she'd felt strong arms around her. So long since she'd felt loved and wanted. As perfect as Travis might be as a lover, she couldn't let him be the man for her.

Ignoring the flare of heat in his eyes as she glanced at him, she took off after Casey.

Chapter Four

Travis cranked up the gas on the barbecue to burn the residue fat from the cast iron grill and watched Casey and Heather play with Fantasia. God damn it, Heather was getting under his skin in a good way that was bad. Whatever her reason was for the visit, he couldn't help being pleased to see her.

Looking scorching in a pair of skinny leg jeans, bush boots and a chambray shirt rolled up at the sleeves, he could picture her riding Fantasia through Harry's daisy field. Bloody hell, he could picture her naked in the daisy field, on her back, with that long red hair spread out around her. And that was not a good thing to be picturing when playing with fire.

He turned down the gas to regulate the flame before

it set the barbecue alight, and wished he could do the same with the flame burning inside him.

His senses had been on red alert since Heather had accepted the position with the Department of Health and Welfare and come to the town six months ago to take over from the taciturn and inflexible, no rule-breaking Mrs Wallace.

He'd taken one look at the five-foot-nothing redhead and fallen a little in ... no, not love. He wouldn't call it that because love meant engagement rings and weddings and forever. He wasn't a forever man. He hadn't earned the right to be. So he'd call it good old-fashioned lust that a night of sheet wrinkling would cure.

The lilt of her voice had invaded his dreams, along with that sweet face and big smile that made her cheeks lift and her nose wrinkle. And those eyes the colour of well-aged whiskey had his heart pounding every time she looked his way.

Across the fence that separated the garden from the paddock, Fantasia nudged Heather's shoulder, blew out through her teeth and tossed her head. He smiled. It looked like she had the horse's approval too. Until now, he'd kept the old girl down in the back paddock during Heather's visits in case the palomino got it into her head to nip. Tonight's surprise visit hadn't given him time to do that and he prayed Fantasia would behave like the lady she usually was.

Heather bent her head to Casey's and laughed at

something his niece said. His heart missed a beat. It was a move Tracy had made often with a similar touch of motherly tenderness. Heather had that same sweet softness about her, that caring nature that drew people in for comfort.

Oh God, was that why Casey had taken such a shining to her? Because Heather reminded her of Tracy? Was Casey seeing a mother figure in her? Which meant ...

Travis picked up the flat stainless steel spatula to scrape the loosened residue from the grill on the barbecue. Jesus, he hoped the ladies at the CWA and all the others in town weren't seeing the same thing.

He wasn't looking for a wife, or a mother for Casey. They were doing just fine by themselves, but he could almost hear his sister's voice saying, 'She's the one, Trav.'

'No, she's not,' he mumbled, as if his sister was listening from somewhere high above the clouds. 'We're fine on our own,' he added, in case she hadn't heard his thoughts.

He wondered who he was trying to convince as Heather and Casey made their way back up from the paddock. If Wongan Creek Mining were looking for their precious metal, it was right here on his land, and he wasn't talking about underground.

The last of the sun's rays picked out the lighter streaks that threaded Heather's red hair. She'd let it loose from the restricting, official ponytail she wore on the job. He followed the skeins of gold to where that glorious mane caressed her collarbones.

Oh for Christ's sake, he was waxing lyrical like one of the bloody poets at the annual writers' festival. At this rate, he'd have his own entry next year.

Talk about conflict of interest. Case worker or not and despite the threat she might be to his family, that sway of Heather's hips, the angle of her shoulders and the perkiness of her breasts had him by the short and curlies. Which made now the right time for him to get into the fridge to grab a beer and the steaks before he embarrassed himself. The best he could do was focus on proving to her he was the best uncle and guardian Casey could ever wish for.

'You girls better get into gear with that salad,' he called over his shoulder as he headed inside. 'I'm ready to cook.'

And ready to heat up a whole lot more than the steaks. He hoped Heather had something up her sleeve for discussion that would piss him off enough to forget about her attributes and single status.

Heather and Casey came up from the paddock into the kitchen and girl chatter filled his kitchen as they gathered the tools from the cupboards and drawers to make their salad. He leaned into the refrigerator to grab hold of the neck of a beer bottle from the six pack. It was kinda nice, almost like the old days when Mum and

Tracy would go at it over doing the dishes. They'd always had so much to say to each other, while he and Dad ... well, they'd never really seen eye to eye, so conversations had been stilted and focused on farm business.

Irritation and more than a little regret shimmied across his memories. Not much he could do about that now with them hardly ever coming home, not even for Christmas — especially not then. Not when, with each passing year, they saw a little more of Casey's father in her features when all they wanted to see was their daughter and erase the ugliness of the past.

He shrugged off the grump that had settled on his shoulders and forced a smile onto his face. 'Want a drink, Heather?' he called without removing his head from the fridge.

'I don't suppose you have any wine?'

'Nope, sorry, closest I can get to that is apple juice,' he teased, his spirits lifting at the sound of that lilt. 'I have beer, or some fabulous local stuff I picked up at the markets last week.'

'Moonshine? I hope it's legal. That stuff can lead to a lethal hangover.'

He knew she was teasing but her words hit close to home. He probably shouldn't be drinking beer in front of Casey, not even when he rationed himself to one. He couldn't afford any black marks against his name to jeopardise his guardianship or the upcoming adoption application. If that meant giving up beer for Casey, he would. Without hesitation. 'Best we stick with the juice then.'

He put the bottle back into the six pack and swapped it for fresh, locally pressed apple juice. Holding two in one hand, he grabbed a third bottle for Casey then nudged the door closed with his foot.

Putting the bottles down on the kitchen counter, he twisted the lids off and tossed them in the trash. He handed a bottle to Casey where she stood at the table sorting the salad ingredients. She giggled and his grin widened.

'Uncle Trav! You know we always have apple juice out of Mummy's tea service.'

Travis ruffled Casey's curls. 'How could I forget?' He reached into the middle shelf of the old pine dresser and took down the tiniest set of teacups and a mini teapot. He proceeded to pour the juice into the pot and handed it to Casey. 'There you go, Miss Casey. Please pour the tea.'

Casey grinned and concentrated on pouring the juice into the cups. Over her head, Heather smiled at him and his heart melted a little more.

'Thank you, darling.' She sat at the table and took the teeny cup and saucer Casey handed her, only spilling a little from the overfull cup.

He looked down at his hands that made the porcelain look even smaller as he struggled to hold it by the minuscule ear. 'Cheers,' he said, taking a sip which for him was the whole contents of the teacup.

'Cheers.' Heather smiled at him as he held out his cup for a refill.

He took another mouthful and, from the corner of his eye, watched Heather do the same.

Hot damn.

He lowered the tiny cup an inch from his lips to watch her drink. Her eyelashes fluttered down to meet the upper edge of her cheekbones as her lips pursed on the rim of the doll-size teacup. She tilted her head back and drank, a swallow his gaze followed way past where it should.

Holy fucking bat shit.

Her beautiful, long-fingered hand cupped around the porcelain like a lover's would and it was hard not to imagine them curling around him. But it was the creamy skin of her throat he was hooked on, that he wanted to press his lips against.

'Uncle Trav?'

He tore his gaze from Heather. 'Yes, sweet pea?'

'The barbecue's on fire,' said Casey, pointing out the door to where bright orange flames licked their way past the grill.

That's not all that was on fire, he thought, as he grabbed a jug of water from the kitchen bench and dashed out to dip his hand in the liquid and douse the flames with a sprinkle from his fingers. Heather followed, carrying the tray holding the steaks.

'You forgot these,' she said as he turned the knobs on the barbecue to the off position to give the flames time to settle. 'You know ... most people would use a fire extinguisher.'

'Cheers,' he answered, taking the tray from her with a grin. 'Too messy with a fire extinguisher. I'd never get that powder off the grill and we'd never get the steaks cooked. How do you like yours done?'

'By anyone other than me.'

And then she smiled and it hit him square in the groin, so he turned the flame back on and slapped the steaks on the grill. Getting all hot and bothered over Heather was only asking for trouble. He'd have to get it together or he'd need a long, cold shower before bed time.

'I meant rare, medium or well-done,' he said.

'I know what you meant, Travis.' She put a hand on his arm and he tried hard not to flinch under her touch as it grazed and heated his skin. 'Are you okay? You're more skittish than a cat at the vet.'

He flipped the steaks on the grill and she pulled her hand away. He missed it and he shouldn't. God help him, he wanted those hands all over him like he'd never wanted it before. No girl had ever fired him up the way Heather did. Maybe it was the result of the no sex rule he'd set for himself since he'd become the responsible guardian to a little girl and to an old man with a fading mind.

'It's all good.' There, the Aussie male cop-out. Hopefully it would get her attention off his discomfort. 'How's the salad? These will only take a minute or two.'

If he was lucky, she'd put some distance between them and go and check on Casey's attempts at putting the finishing touches on it. Because, God help him, he really wouldn't mind kissing her right now and if she hung around much longer, he might just give in and do it.

'It's Harry, isn't it?'

Damn it, he'd let the edginess show. He sighed. 'A little Harry, a touch of annoyance and a whole lot of irritation. That's life.' He tried to smile, knowing it didn't reach his eyes. He hoped it at least doused the burn in them a little. 'Nothing a steak won't fix.'

And a kiss or two from those sweet, rosy lips. What would they taste like? He studied them a moment until she shifted under his gaze.

When she spoke, her voice held a husky note. 'I'll go inside and check on that salad now.'

Who knew rabbit food could sound so damn sexy?

Heather eyed Travis across the table as discreetly as she

could. Whatever had crawled up his bum before dinner time had dissipated with food as he'd promised.

Oh, she hadn't missed that searing hot look he'd sent her across the barbecue tools — or his eyes on her when she'd sipped her apple juice from the tiny rose-patterned doll's teacup so out of character in his big, working hands — but since nothing good could come of it, she'd ignored it. Ignored the look and the shot of hot, liquid desire that poured through her like a fine whiskey on a cold, wet and blustery winter's night.

Casey chatted between them, oblivious to the apprehension that still hung in the air. No one could doubt for a moment that Travis adored his niece and she loved him right back. It was times like these she missed her mum terribly. Missed that connection and affection with someone you were close to.

Lining up his knife and fork on his empty plate, Travis wiped his lips on a paper napkin. Heather tried not to follow the movement but it seemed her mind had a will of its own. She looked away quickly before he could catch her staring at his mouth.

Harry, she reminded herself. She was here to inquire about Harry and as nice as this little tête-á-tête was, she couldn't ignore the business at hand.

'Okay, sweet pea, time for you to go shower and get ready for bed.' Travis took Casey's plate and placed it on top of his empty one.

'Aw, Uncle Trav ...'

'Don't pout those lips at me, young lady,' he teased, giving her cheek a squeeze. 'School tomorrow. It's Friday, so I get to come into town to pick you up so we can go shoe shopping. I might bring Harry along for the ride. What do you think?'

'Awesome! Can we go to Mama Bella's for a milkshake?'

'Of course we can. What will it be this week?' he asked as he stood to clear the plates away.

'I don't know. What flavour do you like, Miss Penney?'

Right now? Apple juice from a teacup, steak and salad mixed with a little cowboy. There was something sexy about a man who cleared the dinner table with such ease. 'Erm, chocolate ... yes, chocolate with a touch of caramel.'

Travis arched an eyebrow at her. 'Double thick?'

'Oh goodness, yes. With a cherry on the top.'

He smiled, slow and sexy, in a way that heated her core temperature to a thousand degrees. 'I like mine with an extra dash of ice cream, and maybe cream and chocolate sauce.'

Heather swallowed the sound that rose from somewhere deep inside her. Holy Mother Mary's kittens, he even made a milkshake sound like a trip to heaven. It was the wink at the end of his statement that almost had her undone.

It would be so easy to fall in love with that boyish

charm, to bask in the warmth of his smile, and laugh with him at his quick wit, but this girl had no right to fall for a country boy with a ready-made family. Not when she couldn't guarantee forever.

She scraped her chair back and stood. 'I'll give you a hand with the dishes, and then I should make my way home. Dinner was lovely, thank you. I really only stopped by to see how Harry's doing after today.'

In an instant the cheerful glint in his eyes disappeared. 'I'll just get Casey sorted. Make yourself comfortable on the veranda and I'll bring us out a coffee in a minute.'

'I'll clean up in here while you finish up. It's the least I can do. Sleep tight, Casey.'

The little girl rushed over and threw her arms around Heather's waist, hugging her as hard as her arms could. 'Thank you for the sing-along in your car today, Miss Penney. It was totally awesome.'

'You're welcome, sweetheart.' Heather hugged her back, trying desperately to squash the surge of affection that rose in her heart. 'Off you go now. Your uncle is waiting.'

She met Travis' gaze across the room, found it filled with sadness that tugged at her soul. What was he thinking that brought him such pain?

Casey released her hold on Heather's waist and skipped across the room to slip her hand into her uncle's big, strong one. She turned with a little wave. 'Night,

Miss Penney. I hope you'll come have dinner with us again soon.'

'I'd like that.' More than she professionally should.

Heather watched as they disappeared down the hallway then turned to the kitchen sink. Methodically, she scraped the residue of their meal from the plates into the trash, rinsed them under the warm running water then stacked them in the dishwasher, grateful she didn't have to wash everything by hand. A domestic goddess she most definitely was not.

A quick search in the cupboard under the sink turned up the dishwasher detergent which she added to the dispenser, closed the door and set the program to turn the machine on. Then she filled the electric kettle and set it to boil. Not sure what else she could do or how she could keep her mind off how incredibly gorgeous he'd looked sipping apple juice from a toy teacup, she made her way out to the front veranda and settled on the old sofa.

The sky was a deep shade of midnight now the sun had set, and the stars were twinkling overhead. Heather loved the sound of the bush at night. With a sigh, she curled her legs up under her, rested her head on the back of the sofa and closed her eyes.

Out in the paddocks, the crickets were chirping and the occasional croak of frogs erupted from the creek. Somewhere, an owl hooted and in the nearby gumtree, a family of possums scurried about in search of a meal.

She'd almost dozed off when she heard Travis' footfalls mix with the sounds of the night. She kept her eyes closed a moment. She felt the worn sofa dip under his weight. His warmth infiltrated her space as he leaned back and she inhaled the warm, spicy smell of Travis and aromatic coffee.

'Gone to sleep on me?'

As if her heart wasn't beating erratically enough at his nearness, the sound of his deep baritone made it beat a little faster. She really had to find a way to control that. With a sigh, she opened her eyes.

'No, just listening to the night.'

'Great, isn't it? I love the stormy nights when lightning flashes across the sky and lights up the land. We don't get many of those storms here in Western Australia, but when they do come, it's quite a show. Coffee?' He held out a steaming mug.

Heather uncurled her legs and straightened to take it. 'Cheers, thanks. Casey settled?'

His smile was so full of love and affection, it made her toes curl.

'Almost. I think she's still plotting how she's going to stick it to Benji as to how she got to hear the soundtrack for *The Prince and the Peasant* before he did.'

'Looks like I might have to take Benji for a ride in the car too. Wouldn't want to ruin a good friendship,' she teased.

'I tell you what, wait another ten years and I'll be cursing him for trying to woo Casey. That kid has a few smooth moves under his belt already.'

'She's a cute kid. I think you'll have your hands full when she gets to dating age.'

'Tell me about it. I'm already stocking up on ammo for the shotgun,' he teased.

'And targets for practice too, I bet. I might have to write that up in my report as something to watch. It could earn you a stern talking to.' Heather sipped her coffee. At least the banter would chase that sadness from his eyes, she thought.

He leaned back with his hands wrapped around the coffee mug, stretched out his long legs and settled into his relaxed position with his feet up on the rail. 'Miss Penney, you can scold me for being naughty any time.'

And because any comeback she could make would only lead the conversation somewhere it couldn't go, she said, 'That's the first time in a while I've had apple juice out of a teacup. Pretty cool thing to do for a manly bloke like you.'

Travis grinned. 'It makes the kidlet happy. It was a ritual she and her mum used to go through at least once a day. I'm just carrying on the tradition.'

Heather smiled back and ignored the flutter in her stomach at the upward slant of his mouth. Somewhere in the conversation he'd got lost in a memory. His eyes softened then saddened, and his lips pulled back into a grimace.

'So how did you go with Harry today?' she asked softly, hating that the question might make him even sadder.

He sighed. 'Stubborn old bugger is insisting he stay on the farm, but we knew that would always be the challenge. When I got there today, Bannister's lawyer was sitting in the kitchen like he already owned the place. He had the paperwork for an offer on Harry's land, tapping his pen, ready to sign.'

'Oh no!'

'Yep. Luckily, Harry was in one of his more lucid moments but he'd been duped enough to let the man through the front door. Thought he was an inspector of some kind.'

'Ah, Travis, that's no good.' She touched his arm gently. Under her fingers his skin was warm, the muscles hard as they twitched under her palm. She pulled her hand back to embrace her coffee mug instead. Touching Travis only set fire to a need she didn't want. 'What did Doc Benson say?'

'We've worked out a plan and Harry's agreed to it. He knows he's not as mobile as he used to be, even if he doesn't realise his memory is a problem. Harry will give me Enduring Power of Guardianship which means I can make decisions for his care and treatment but not his property and financial decisions.'

'That makes perfect sense in his situation. That way there's no conflict of interest over the property and it might lay some of those rumours to rest.' Heather nodded.

'Ah, there'll always be rumours unfortunately.' He lay his head back against the sofa and turned his green gaze on her. 'Doc Benson will take on power of attorney since he's the only other person Harry trusts, with the exception of Sergeant Riggs.'

'You'll want to get that all sorted soon if Bannister's lawyers are knocking at the door.'

His eyes were so sad that Heather wanted to trace his face with her fingers, reassure him everything would work out fine, that Harry would be okay, but they both knew the struggle that lay ahead.

'Yeah, another reason we're going into town tomorrow. Doc Benson will have to write a report on Harry's state of mind and then to avoid any issues with conflict of interest, we have to appoint an administrator. That way there's no loopholes for Bannister to wiggle through.' He drained the coffee from his mug and balanced it on the arm of the sofa. 'All that's left then is to convince Harry he can't stay in the house alone anymore.'

Heather knew what a struggle that was going to be. Her mum hadn't wanted to go into care either, even when she knew she had no choice. Heather reached over to squeeze the hand that rested on his flat stomach. He turned his hand palm up and entwined his fingers with hers.

'Thanks for the support.'

'I'll help where I can, Travis. You only need to ask.'

He smiled and her heart tripped. The warmth of his hand on hers, the intimate touch of his thumb drawing a circle on her wrist made her want to touch her lips to his, taste the flavour of coffee and man. 'I'd best be getting home. It's a half hour drive into town and the roos are out.'

She tugged at her hand and he let it go, taking his time to free up his hold. He sat up and heaved himself off the sofa, holding out a hand to take her coffee mug. He placed it on the arm of the chair next to his own. 'Call me when you get home, okay? Just so I know you've made it safely.'

Heather nodded. 'Okay.'

She pushed off the sofa, fishing in her pocket for her car keys. With Travis' hand warm in the curve of her back, she made her way down the stairs to her car. He opened the door and she slid inside.

'Thanks for dinner.'

He stood, elbows resting on the top of the door frame. 'Any time. Take care now, Heather. Drive carefully.'

She held that beautiful green gaze for a moment, long enough for it to make her body tighten. Travis

Bailey was temptation on legs and those eyes the colour of emeralds could make a girl melt into a puddle of goo.

She tugged on the door handle and he obliged by lifting his arms and closing the door. Rolling down the window, she said, 'Goodnight,' and started the engine.

He lifted a hand in a wave and smiled that sexy smile of his. Heather put the car in gear and drove away before she was tempted to forget her vow not to get involved with this very hunky man from Wongan Creek.

Chapter Five

After dropping Casey at the bus stop the next morning and waiting for her to get on board, Travis took a drive up to Wongan Creek Mining in the hope of persuading John Bannister to back off and keep away from Harry. He much preferred face-to-face confrontation. People couldn't hide behind lies that way.

He dragged a hand across his face. His night had alternated between dreams of holding Heather, and being chased by a mountain of legal paperwork wrapped up in red ribbon. He was only just beginning to understand the enormity of the task ahead to keep Harry's mental integrity safe. Then there would be the months of legal red tape during which he'd have to keep Bannister off the old man's back.

He cursed the day they'd found that additional vein

of gold in Wongan Creek. Now they were looking at twenty-five years plus of mining operations that meant the farm land would be left to go to seed while people chased gold and money. In this town you were either a farmer or a miner, and the increased operations had changed some men into the latter.

Stark white four-wheel drives now replaced the old farm vehicles that once lined the road to the mine. The flashing lights and reflective yellow striping were a constant reminder of how much life had changed.

He frowned at the sight of the skeletons of trees that had fallen victim to dieback disease when the mine had first opened, spread when the land was cleared to prepare the site for excavation. The environmentalists had stepped in to put procedures in place to stop it, but not before it destroyed acres of precious vegetation.

To satisfy the protesters, mine management had put a re-vegetation program in place, but it would take years to restore what they'd lost. Travis couldn't believe a man of the land like John Bannister would sell his soul to the devil for gold, but he had.

Sure, the industry had breathed new life into the town, although that was not always a good thing either. More people brought more problems, especially when it came to alcohol, and the once quiet country pub had become a den of trouble.

The white corrugated steel building of the security checkpoint loomed ahead, an ugly scar on the once thriving bushland. Outside, contractors in high visibility yellow work shirts queued for a pass to sign in and enter the site.

Travis followed the example of the other visitors and reversed his ute into a vacant parking spot. Slipping on his hat and sunglasses, he joined the queue to the booth.

Twenty minutes later, with the sun burning down on his back and his irritation growing, he made it to the counter.

'Name?' barked the big guy dressed in a black security uniform, sweating heavily.

'Travis Bailey.'

The big guy ran a finger up and down the sheet on his clipboard. 'You're not on the list.'

'I'm not a contractor. I'm here to see John Bannister.'

The guy swapped clipboards and checked. 'Still not on the list.'

'I don't have an appointment.'

'Then you can't come on site. Next!'

'Mate, all I want is a quick word with John Bannister in his office.' Travis bit down on his frustration. 'When did they change the rules about administration activities needing appointments?'

'When they appointed a safety committee. Have you done a site induction?'

'No, I'm not here to work. I'm here for a chat.'

'Got a hard hat, hi-vis vest, gloves and steel cap boots?'

Okay, now the guy was starting to piss him off. 'No, but I'm sure you have some spare.'

The men who'd joined the queue behind him began to grumble and shove.

'Not unless you're a contractor. No appointment. No induction. You can't come on site. Make a phone call. Next!'

The giant of a man behind Travis elbowed him aside. Damn it. He whipped off his hat and raked an impatient hand through his hair. He didn't want to talk to John Bannister over the phone, but if he couldn't get on site to see the man, he'd have to come up with another plan.

Pulling open the door of his ute, he tossed his hat onto the seat and looked around. Temporary buildings and bulldozed red dust roads stretched around the landscape for miles. A boom gate separated the main road from the mine access road.

Beyond that, the skeletal structure of a conveyor loomed against the distant skyline. Below it, big arse yellow dump trucks and diggers would be working their way up and down the winding platforms of the open pit mine.

If he was in the mood, Travis would take the time to admire the skill and engineering of the mining operations, but right now he wished he could blow the whole damn thing to hell.

He remembered the days as a kid when he could ride his horse through bushland on the other side of that boom gate long before the expansion of the mine.

It had once been a small family operation, before Bannister sold out the lion's share to Wongan Creek Mining when the vein of gold proved bigger than expected. Now he couldn't get past the gate to have a friendly chat with the man who leased the land back to the company. Whichever way you looked at it, Bannister was the winner.

Sliding in behind the wheel of the ute, he slammed the door shut and gunned the engine. As he pulled away, he hoped to hell they could cut through the legal shit before Harry lost his mind completely and the mine's boundaries encroached on their land. Some days he felt he was fighting a losing battle — like he was alone in taking on the world.

If the rumours were true and Bannister expanded operations again, the whole town of Wongan Creek would become a slave to the big gaping hole in the ground they called a gold mine.

Irritation clawed at his gut and made him restless. He checked the time on the digital display of his radio. He had a couple of hours to kill before picking up Harry and driving into town to get the ball rolling on the paperwork that would change the old man's life.

A good, hard ride down by the creek on Fantasia would settle his nerves for sure. The old girl hadn't been out for a while, so she'd enjoy the wind up her tail and a splash in the creek. It would be a good opportunity to check the fencing and firebreaks. With bush fires still a threat until the weather cooled down, he couldn't risk his or Harry's property.

A smile on his face and some of his humour restored, Travis headed down the road to the T-junction and turned right onto the road that would take him home. The ride might help clear his thoughts of a certain woman who had taken up residence in a larger corner of his mind than he liked.

Pulling into his driveway, he rolled the ute to a stop outside the house, pocketed the keys from the ignition and made his way down to the paddock where Fantasia grazed peacefully in the shade of a gumtree. He whistled and she tossed her head. Tracy's palomino was the only other girl he needed in his life right now, besides Casey.

He smiled as Fantasia walked up to the wooden fence and lowered her head for a pat. She nudged at his shirt pocket, looking for a treat.

'Fancy a ride, old girl?' He stroked the length of her nose and she shivered with pleasure. 'I'll take that as a yes.'

He covered the short distance to the barn and back in quick, long strides to collect the bridle and saddle. Fantasia danced, skittish with excitement, as he adjusted and checked straps then did a quick inspection of her shoes for stones and burrs before unlatching the gate that closed the paddock off from the open bushland on the property.

He shrugged out of his button down shirt and hung it over the fence. It wouldn't do to get it all sweaty and smelling of horse when he still had to go into town with Harry. He tossed his hat onto the fencepost.

Today he wanted to feel the fingers of the breeze in his hair, the rush of the wind on his face and the cool air on his skin. Maybe it would blow the cobwebs from his mind and he would see a solution to the growing problem of Harry.

'Steady now, girl.' With his foot in the stirrup and his hand on the front of the saddle, he swung his leg across Fantasia's rump and settled into the seat. Reins in hand, he touched his heels to her side and walked her through the gate. Easing her into a trot, he let her warm up even though she trembled with excitement at the prospect of a run. Then he let her have her head.

Heather pulled the four-wheel drive wagon over to the shoulder of the road and got out to watch the symphony of horse and rider play out on the firebreak along the fence line of Travis' property. Fantasia's hooves kicked up red dust as she galloped with Travis low in the saddle, his hands loose on the reins. They moved like dancers in the wind, at one with each other as they flew down the stretch.

Her heart stalled at the beauty of horse and man in synchronisation. Shirtless, Travis' torso glistened under the sun with a sheen of sweat. The muscles in his arms and chest bunched with power as he used his body to control his seat. The strength in his thighs drew the denim taught across his legs as he raised his rear in the saddle and put some weight into the stirrups.

Fantasia's blonde mane flared in the wind along her outstretched neck, her ears back as she concentrated on her gallop. The ground vibrated under the rumble of hooves, matching the thunder of Heather's heartbeat.

As they flew by, she caught a fleeting glimpse of the concentration on Travis' face before being treated to a view of the rippling control in his back. Her breath caught at the raw beauty of his body in motion. *Sweet Holy Mother Mary*. Her hands itched to feel the strength of those muscles beneath her palms.

She watched as they slowed to a trot then a walk, and waited as Travis turned the horse around and headed towards her. Fantasia tossed her head, nostrils flaring as her breathing deepened and adjusted to the slower pace. Her coat gleamed with sweat, darkening it to the colour of a good Irish whiskey, the perfect backdrop for her rider's golden tan.

Travis reined in to stop and adjusted his seat as

Fantasia danced under him. 'G'day. To what do I owe this pleasure?'

Heather adjusted her hat to give her hands something to do, and wished she'd worn her reflective sunglasses. She'd hate for him to see the hunger in her eyes.

'Travis.'

He smiled and her heart did cartwheels.

'Missing me already?' he teased.

'As if,' she returned, hoping she sounded indifferent and that he couldn't hear the pounding of her pulse rate. 'I'm on my way up to the mine. I'm delivering my first presentation on balancing family matters for shift workers.'

'Wow, that's a tough gig. Hope you've filled out all the paperwork to cut through the red tape. It's damn hard to get past that gate.'

Heather shaded her eyes against the sun with her hand. 'Sounds like you've tried.'

'Yeah, thought I could catch Bannister in his office and have a little chat about them harassing Harry but security wouldn't let me past the gate without safety gear and an induction.'

'I had to spend a whole day in training to do a half hour presentation. Mine rules. Not much you can do.'

'I'd like to tell them what to do with their rules. Maybe I should put a few of my own in place for when they want to enter Harry's property,' he grumbled.

'Well aren't you a grumpy bum today?' Heather grinned. 'I'd love to stay and chat since you're in such a great mood for it, but I have to be on my way. I don't want to be late and hold up their production schedule.'

Travis laughed. 'I was a lot grumpier earlier. Lucky you got to see me after I worked the edge off. Bloody Bannister.' He frowned. 'So we won't see you in town then? I was hoping you could join us for that milkshake.'

'I'm tempted. If I finish up in time, I might pop in.'

He leaned down towards her. 'I'll save you a seat.'

'Travis ...' Common sense argued against accepting his invitation, but the lure of chocolate, caramel and his company teased her senses. 'We'll see.'

'Great. Hope you can make it.' He stared at her a moment, his eyes full of mischief and a touch of heat Heather ignored. 'I'd better get Fantasia home.' He squinted at the sun. 'I need to hose her down and take a shower myself before I pick Harry up.'

'Yeah.'

Anything more comprehensible than that one word died at the vision in her head of him in the shower. He straightened in the saddle and she found herself staring at his chest, his abdomen, the trail that led to the button of his jeans. His chuckle had her gaze swinging up to his.

'Miss Penney, are you checking me out?'

Heat filled her cheeks and there was no getting away

with blaming it on the sun. 'Put your shirt on, wise guy. You're courting sunburn.'

He shrugged, leaned down a little and twisted his body towards her, his eyes pinning hers like a butterfly on a cork board. 'You don't have to be embarrassed, you know. I don't mind you watching.'

Lord help her, if she looked away now it would be the equivalent of admitting she'd been having a damn good ogle, and Heather couldn't let him have that satisfaction. She tilted her chin and stared him in the eye, ignoring his cheeky grin.

'Go ride your horse. I've got work to do.' A smile stretched her lips despite her resolve to keep a straight face. Serious was hard to do when those green eyes smiled back and dimples appeared in his cheeks. The man was far too sexy for his own skin.

'You make it very hard for a man to obey when you tell him to get lost and smile at the same time.' He chuckled again, a deep, sensual sound that played up and down her spine with fiery fingertips. 'Catch you later,' he said with a mischievous wink then he turned Fantasia's head in the direction of the homestead, tapped his heels on the horse's flanks and set off at a trot.

'I'm not embarrassed! I'm amused by your very large ego,' she called after him.

With a glance over his shoulder and a wicked grin, he deliberately lifted his rear in the saddle, bent forward over the horse's neck and set her to a gallop. Heather sighed as she watched the contours of that jeans-clad backside move with the beat of the horse's hooves.

'I've seen a better rear on Miss Turner's donkey!' she called after him, cupping her hands around her mouth to amplify her taunt.

So maybe she was a little interested. Who wouldn't be? She cursed the failure in her resolve not to get too close to the locals and got back into the four-wheel drive.

Travis Bailey would be a lover no girl in her right mind could ever forget, and there was no doubt he'd been flirting. But she wasn't a girl who could afford to play the game, not when the outcome of that game could only result in hurt and loss for the players.

Chapter Six

'What kind of bloody music is this?' Harry stabbed a finger on the tuner button on the ute's radio and set it searching for channels. 'Sounds like someone swallowed the devil and he's screaming to get out.'

'That's why they call it screaming. Modern rock music, Harry. If you changed your radio from Old Fogey's Top Ten Hits, you'd recognise it.' Travis grinned and reset the radio to a more mellow station.

'I'll show you "Old Fogey", you cheeky shit.' He grimaced. 'This sounds like funeral music. Are you trying to put me in a bad mood?' He pressed the button again and released it when cheerful Big Band tones filled the cab of Travis' ute. 'That's better. They don't make music like this anymore.'

Amused, Travis cast a look at his neighbour. 'That's

because they're all dead. Seriously, 1940s swing? I pictured you as more of a Slim Dusty kinda guy.'

'And I pictured you as less of a wally. Stop taking the piss and concentrate on the road. You should have let me drive.'

'You don't have a licence anymore, remember?'

Harry sighed and looked out the window. 'In my day, we didn't need a licence and kids as young as ten were driving the farm utes everywhere.'

Travis listened as the old man rambled through the memories of his younger days. Harry was fairly lucid today, thank God. A good thing considering what lay ahead. He hoped it lasted so the old bloke could enjoy his independence a little longer because soon Travis would be making the decisions about his future.

He hoped to hell he made the right ones. It was tough enough making decisions for a minor like Casey, but making life-changing calls for a man old enough to be your grandfather was bloody hard.

The sign welcoming them to Wongan Creek loomed as the speed limit slowed to eighty kilometres per hour then to sixty kilometres on the fringe of town. Main Street stretched ahead with its newly painted island in the middle of the road to keep visitors from straying too close to each other when passing — an addition since a ute and a car collided in the early hours one morning.

Before the mining boom, there'd been no need for a white line to remind drivers where the centre of the road was, but now the population had grown from eight hundred residents to over two thousand, the council had called for more traffic control.

At any given time, that number rose with the influx of tourists, motorcycle riders and guys ending or starting their shift at WCM. The once sleepy town had come to life leaving the residents to clean up the scars of revelry in the form of litter and broken hedges just in time for it to start all over again. There was little they could do about the blackened tyre tracks on the road outside the pub.

'Mongrels have been doing burnouts again,' muttered Harry. 'Someone should take a whip to their backsides.'

'Come on, don't tell me you didn't do the odd stupid thing when you were young.'

'Yeah, but I didn't do it in the middle of Main Street.'

'Main Street wasn't more than a dusty track back then. You couldn't do burnouts with a horse and cart.' Travis indicated to turn off into the service station.

'Smart arse,' growled Harry, doing his best to smother a smile. 'Why are we stopping here?'

'I've got to see Mick about getting my tractor fixed.'

Harry's shoulders sagged. 'You've got a bucket load on your plate, mate, and here you are babysitting me.'

'Now don't you start with that rubbish again.'

After Tracy's death and his parents' decision to take

off around Australia, Travis had relied heavily on his neighbour's knowledge and help. In the early days, he'd struggled to raise a child and do the chores around the farm. Every time he turned around, Harry was there, feeding the chickens with Casey or slapping a few sausages on the barbecue to feed them.

Casey had the next best thing to a grandfather in Harry. He took time to read and toss a ball, show her how to fasten the straps on a saddle and set up a herb garden for her to muck around in. There was nothing Travis wouldn't do to repay him.

'You're the only family we have, Harry. You're stuck with us.'

'You should be making your own family.'

'I'd rather keep practicing, thank you.' Travis grinned. 'It's much more fun.'

Harry snorted. 'Like you even have time for fun or anything else. Before you know it, you'll be a miserable old sod just like me, always regretting the one who got away.'

Turning off the ignition, Travis opened the door and tried to think when last he'd been on a date, let alone had a girl in his bed or anywhere else. That would likely account for his reaction to Heather. She stirred his blood more than anyone had for a long time, but his focus had to be Harry and Casey's welfare.

'All this talk of fun won't get the tractor fixed. Come on, old man, Mick's been hanging out for a visit from you. I did warn him you'd be a bit grumpy about it.'

'Not the visit to Mick making me grumpy.'

'Ah, so it's old age then?' Travis teased.

'Your turn will come, lad. You'll see. Gives me the shits that this old body doesn't work the way it used to.'

Harry climbed out of the car, his movements stiff and awkward, and slammed the door behind him. He paused a moment to look around, as if drinking in the view and etching it into his memory.

Travis' heart ached for his friend. He knew it wouldn't be long before Harry didn't recognise much at all, let alone the town he'd grown up in and the people he'd known for over seventy years.

With a gentle hand on Harry's shoulder, Travis said nothing as he steered him towards the doorway of Mick's old garage that had once been a drafty railway shed. All he could do for Harry was make sure the old man made the best of the time and memory he had left.

Half an hour later, with an order placed for a new engine, Travis and Harry left the ute parked at Mick's and walked the couple of blocks to Doc Benson's surgery. With every step, Harry's humour evaporated further, but Travis ignored the bite in his tone.

The wait for Doc Benson to finish with his last patient only made the old codger grouchier. So when the door opened and John Bannister strode from the consulting room, Harry was ready to spit spiders.

'Shoulda known it was you holding things up, Bannister. You think you own this bloody town.'

'Harry,' Travis growled, putting a restraining hand on Harry's arm as the old man reared up off his seat and almost lost his balance.

Harry shook him off and advanced on Bannister, poking a crooked finger into the man's chest. 'Keep your bloody thieving mongrels off my land.'

Bannister, to his credit, kept his hands firmly at his side and let Harry poke away. 'It was an honest offer, Murchison.'

'Honest offer, my arse! You've never had an honest bone in your body. Take, take, that's all you bloody Bannisters know.'

'I've never taken anything from you, Harry. At least nothing that wouldn't come willingly.'

John Bannister's crafty smirk had Harry's ears turning red. Face purple with rage, he took an unexpected swing at the man's jaw, his knuckles connecting with a whack. Mrs Benson gasped in horror and called out to Doc.

Travis leapt into action, stepping between the men and stopping Harry from taking a second shot. 'Harry, enough!' He placed firm hands on the old man's shoulders and walked him back until his knees hit the chair and he collapsed into it.

Bannister wiped the blood from his mouth. 'You're a fool, Harry. You had nothing to offer a woman like

Eileen anyway. She had high hopes, expensive dreams, wanted things you'd never be able to afford to give her. I did you a favour taking her off your hands.'

Harry's hands shook between his knees where he had them clasped tightly. 'Fuck you, Bannister.'

'Oh she did that all right. Well and truly. A wild one, she was. Took a real man to tame her.'

'John, that's enough now.' Doc Benson's quiet tones filtered through the tense atmosphere as he appeared in the doorway of his consulting room. 'Leave it be.'

Bannister turned away to settle his bill. As he opened the door to leave, he threw out, 'See you in court, Murchison.'

Travis watched the door close with dread in his heart. Harry didn't stand a chance with the justice system firmly in Bannister's pocket.

'Now what did you do that for? Come into the consulting room, Harry. Let me look at those knuckles.' Doc Benson helped Harry up off the chair.

The old man stumbled and Travis took his other arm to stabilise him. Between them, they walked him into the stark white room.

'Shoulda clocked the bastard years ago,' muttered Harry.

'Those things just get you into trouble, you know that. Sit down,' ordered Doc Benson.

He eased Harry into a chair and Travis took the seat next to him. Doc picked up a cotton swab from the bench behind his desk, dropped antiseptic onto it and pressed it to the weakened skin of Harry's knuckles.

'Worth it. Damned satisfying,' grumbled Harry.

Doc Benson stood to toss the cotton swab into the trash, washed his hands in the sink and dabbed them dry on paper towel. 'Eileen's been gone a long time, my friend. Even Bannister couldn't hold on to her.'

'He's still a mongrel for taking her from me.'

'Let it go. He'll lay charges for today.'

Harry's shoulders sagged, his age etched into his face. 'Don't care as long as he doesn't get his filthy paws on my land when I'm gone.'

'I've written the letter regarding your decline in mental health. Travis will be granted power of enduring guardianship to take care of your medical and lifestyle needs. I'll have power of attorney to take care of your financial affairs. Do you understand the implications of that, Harry?'

'You're telling me I'm forgetful. I'm not stupid.'

Travis grinned. 'Any more of that attitude and we'll put you in a nursing home,' he teased.

Harry snorted. 'You'll bury me first, you bastard.'

'Harry, you know that a nursing home is a very likely event as things get worse, don't you? I need you to be clear on that.' Doc Benson sat down in his chair and pulled a manila folder filled with paperwork towards him.

'Clear as bloody daylight.'

'For now, until all the paperwork has gone through the legal system, you can stay up at the house but Travis will be keeping a close eye on you. I'm also registering you for home care with the Department of Health and Welfare so Heather Penney can add you to her visitation schedule.'

'I'm not a child. I don't need a babysitter.'

Doc Benson ignored him. 'Any signs that you're not capable of looking after yourself anymore, and Travis will make the call.'

Harry sighed, sadness weighing down his shoulders. He eyed the swelling around his knuckles for a moment. 'You'll look after me, won't you, son? For as long as you can? I can't bear to leave the land, to never see the sun rise over the creek, or go looking for those mongrel sheep. Everything I have is on Murchison's Run. It's the only home I've ever known.'

Travis stood out of the chair and went down on his haunches in front of him. He placed his hands on Harry's knobbly, arthritic knees. 'I swear I will do everything in my power to keep you on your land for as long as I possibly can, Harry.'

Harry gripped Travis' shoulder with his uninjured hand. 'On ya, son.'

Doc Benson called his wife into the consulting room to witness the signing of the documents. The pen trembled as Harry turned to the desk and pressed the nib to the paper that would take away his independence, his signature resembling chicken scratch compared to the flowing cursive it had once been. And then it was over. Travis hated the slump in Harry's shoulders, the emptiness in his eyes. A man didn't deserve to be stripped of his dignity this way.

Harry hung his head for a moment, his hands clasped tightly between his knees. Then he slapped his palms on his thighs and stood. 'Let's get out of here, son. I need a drink.'

Heather tossed her hard hat onto the seat and shrugged off her orange safety vest, her temper only barely restrained. There always had to be one heckler in the crowd. She looked around the mine carpark, irritated and more than ready to leave the dusty site operations behind. If it wasn't for the fact that she cared for the welfare of the mine workers, she wouldn't have agreed to give the talk here at the operations centre. This was Bannister territory and Zac Bannister thought he was the big dog in the pack.

John Bannister's grandson was an idiot of note — big, tough and with a reputation for being a troublemaker. He'd proved himself worthy of the title many a Friday night down at the pub. This wasn't the first time he'd tried to belittle her in front of a crowd. She'd hoped he wouldn't be on the day shift, wouldn't show up for her presentation. She should have known better. He still held a grudge for the many times she'd turned down his lewd invitations, the final altercation when he'd grabbed her from behind and his big ugly paws had been all over places she didn't want them.

She'd stomped on the arch of his thong-clad foot, elbowed him in the stomach and pushed him to the ground on his backside, a self-defence move that made a fool out of him in front of his mates and earned her an enemy for life.

'Hey, bitch!' he called after her now.

Temper morphed into disquiet. Heather ignored his taunt and swallowed down the panic that squeezed the air from her lungs. She got into her car and locked all the doors in case he got it into his head to open one. He stopped in front of the hood and placed his gorilla paws on the big steel bull bar that protected the front of the four-wheel drive.

Zac Bannister wasn't a tall man. He was short and stocky with a fast-developing beer belly where defined abs should be. His long, shaggy beard and greasy hair lent him a thuggish look, and the company he kept when he was off site suggested links to a rebel motorcycle gang. Until now, she hadn't been scared of the big ape, just wary. Today his behaviour was a lot meaner.

She wound the window down a crack. 'Move, Bannister, or so help me God, I'll drive you over.' Heather hoped she sounded strong and confident.

'You wouldn't have the guts to do that.'

She started the engine, one foot shaking on the brake pedal, the other ready to accelerate. 'I'll count to three. One ...'

She prepared to change gear from neutral to reverse. His grip on the front was loose, so if she drove backward his hands would slip easily and maybe with a bit of karma intervention he'd land on his ugly mug in the dirt.

'You think you're so much smarter and better than anyone else with your pussy-whipping talks. One day, I'll show you what a real man can do.'

'Two.' She revved the engine, fear forming a sweat on her forehead, his threat conjuring awful pictures in her mind. What would he do if there weren't a few hundred people on site who might walk out any minute and witness his bullying behaviour?

'I'll teach you a lesson, you stuck up bitch. You won't walk for weeks.'

'Three,' shouted Heather, panic making her voice pitchy. 'Last call to get away from my car.'

With a feral growl, he let go of the bull bar and launched himself around the hood to the driver's door, his hand ready to rip the door handle off.

'Zac!' Old man Bannister's warning rang out across the carpark. 'Get away from there, you bloody drongo.' With a hand on his grandson's collar, he yanked him away from the door. 'Sorry about that, Heather. I'll deal with it from here.'

Heather nodded, her heart pounding. She wasn't sure where John had come from but she was glad he'd appeared in time. Oh God, had she pushed too far? The look in Zac's eyes as he'd glared at her through the window went beyond anger. It touched on madness that promised unspeakable revenge, and for the first time had her terrified of what he might truly be capable of. Hands shaking, she put the four-wheel drive into gear and drove off site as fast as the thirty kilometre per hour speed limit would allow.

Twenty minutes later, the confrontation with Zac still whirling in her mind and unease in the pit of her stomach, Heather pulled into the parking lot in front of Mama Bella's. She hadn't even noticed the rolling landscape she loved so much or taken the time to admire the majestic Whispering Hills that rose up across the creek. As she'd driven out, her focus had been solely on reaching the safety zone of the town, as far away from Zac Bannister as possible.

With its pretty yellow painted walls, blue planter boxes filled with geraniums and a red and white welcome sign above the door, the homeliness of Bella's café would provide the warmth and comfort she needed. A cup of chamomile tea would be just the thing to settle her nerves.

This time Zac Bannister had scared her. In his eyes

she'd seen murderous intent where before they'd only held the stormy look of a bully and troublemaker. Now she'd think twice about going down to the pub alone on a Friday night, or would cross the street if she ran into him town.

She pushed open the door to the café and stepped into the lunchtime rush of Mama Bella's. Taking a quick look around, she noticed almost every booth was occupied, but with edginess still snapping at her heels, she didn't take time to study the faces of the occupants. Were Travis and Harry here yet? Had they made it in for the milkshake he'd promised? The thought that they might be eased some of the knots in her belly. It would help take her mind off things, give her something else to think about.

'Heather, come on in, love.' Bella Hicks waved to her from behind the shop's teak counter laden with pastries and slices under glass domes. 'Oh my goodness, child! You're as white as a sheet. Are you okay?'

Heather placed her hands on the counter top and saw they were still shaking. She tightened her grip on her car keys and purse to try and stop the reaction. 'I'm okay, thanks.'

With a weak smile, she scanned the collection of herbal tea caddies lined up between the ornamental teapots, cups and saucers on the shelves behind the counter.

'Sweetheart, you don't look okay. You look like

you've seen a ghost.' Bella wiped her hands on her floral apron and scanned Heather's face. 'Tell me to mind my own business if you like, but a girl's hands don't shake like yours are doing for no reason.'

Heather sighed. The small town rumour mill would no doubt be running hot anyway once it got wind of what had happened up at the mine. There were plenty of people leaving the operations building bordering the carpark after the meeting. They would have been coming out just in time to see John Bannister giving Zac a dressing down. No doubt speculation would be running high over a beer or three at the pub later.

'I had a run in with Zac Bannister after the meeting today. It shook me up a little.'

Bella tut-tutted and shook her head, making wayward strands of grey hair escape from her bun. 'That boy, I tell you. He's always been a little troublemaker. A big bully, that's all he is. You be careful though, love. His temper is getting worse. John will have to do something about that boy soon or all hell will break loose in this town.'

'Lucky Mr Bannister was there. He gave Zac a talking to. It's okay.' Not wanting to discuss it anymore, Heather focused on the plastic-sleeved menu. 'Can I have a pot of chamomile and peppermint tea please, Bella? And a ham and cheese croissant. Thanks.'

'That's barely enough to keep an ant alive, dear. I

tell you what; I'll throw in a piece of my Irish Cream slice for you. You'll need the sugar after such a shock.'

'Shock? What shock?' Warmth enveloped her back and the smell of Travis' spicy aftershave teased her senses as his voice sent a thrill down her spine. 'What happened, Heather?'

His hand came to rest on her shoulder. She was so tempted to lean back into him, to feel his strength, to absorb his warmth and let it ease the chill from her fingertips.

'That bloody Bannister boy had a go at her up at the mine,' Bella filled in for her.

Turning her towards him, he tipped her chin up with his forefinger. 'You okay? What did the dickhead do this time?'

Heather read the concern mixed with annoyance in his eyes. 'It's nothing, really. John Bannister dealt with it.'

'Heather, the last time you had a run in with Zac, you put him flat on his arse in front of his mates. And as much as I enjoyed watching you do that at the pub that night, guys like him hold grudges. So don't tell me it's nothing.'

Bella leaned forward over the counter. 'Travis, the girl was shaking like the ground after a blasting up at the mine on a Tuesday. Take her to a booth and I'll come out with her tea and take your order.'

With a nod to Bella, he lowered his grip to Heather's elbow. 'Come on. You and Harry are quite the pair.'

'How so?' Heather fell into step beside him as they located Harry in a booth in the far corner of the shop.

'Harry had a run in with John Bannister at Doc Benson's. Looks like they're causing trouble all over town today.'

'Bloody mongrels,' grumbled Harry from the corner near the window. 'I got him a good shot though.'

Travis grinned. 'You sure caught him off guard all right.' He let Heather slip into the booth and took a seat next to her. 'Harry clocked him one on the mouth. Split his lip. Not that I'm encouraging your behaviour, Harry,' Travis warned, shaking his forefinger at the old man.

'Oh, Harry!' For a moment, Heather forgot her own run in with a Bannister. 'Are you okay?'

'Yeah, mate, except for these.' He showed her the torn skin on his knuckles. 'Those bastards think they run this bloody town.'

Bella arrived with Heather's tea. She slid the teapot onto the table and turned the cup up on its saucer. 'Here we go, love. Get that into you. Your croissant will be along soon. What can I get you and Harry, Travis?'

They placed their order and Bella bustled away. Travis turned to Heather.

'So, what happened with Zac?'

Heather shrugged and held onto her saucer as Travis poured her tea. 'He came after me when I left the meeting. I got into the car and locked the doors, but he tried to stop me leaving by standing in front of it.'

'Shoulda driven the little bastard over,' grumbled Harry.

'What did he do?' Travis put the teapot down with a warning glance at his neighbour.

'Called me names, threatened me. He tried to wrench the door open, but his grandfather saw him and dragged him away.'

'The little shit. I hope you're going to report it to Riggs.' Travis gave Heather's arm a squeeze.

She let herself lean into his shoulder a little, just for a moment. Her stomach churned at the thought of what might have happened if Zac had got the door open. There'd be nothing gentle about him at all, unlike Travis' warm and comforting touch.

The more she thought about it, the more fear ate its way into her mind. Reporting it to the cops would only make Zac's anger worse, and his need for revenge greater. Even if they issued an AVO, it would be nothing more than a paper shield that would do nothing at all to protect her.

She shook her head. 'No, it's okay. John Bannister promised he'd deal with it.'

'That bloody mongrel's no better at keeping his word than a two-bit scammer,' said Harry. 'Wouldn't trust that bloke further than I can throw him.'

'Which is not very far, and you're not helping here,

Harry.' Travis let his arm drop around her shoulders. 'If he ever threatens you again, you tell me, okay?'

Heather nodded. 'Thanks.'

With a weak smile, she looked up into his face. His beautiful green eyes filled with concern that made her heart stutter and miss a beat, the comfort of his arm around her reassuring.

Where before she felt cold and afraid, now she felt warm and safe. She burrowed closer, looked down at her cup and sipped her tea, not minding his arm around her at all.

Bella arrived with the rest of their order. 'Here we go. I've given you each a slice of tart on the house. Travis, I've told Janet you're here. When school's out and her class has left, she'll collect Casey and bring her over so you don't have to walk over to pick her up.'

'Thanks, Bella.' Travis grinned. 'Doesn't sound like she needed convincing.'

Bella smiled back. 'That girl loves kids. She did the right thing becoming a teacher. She'll make a good mum too.'

Travis squirmed beside her and Heather looked up. His cheeks were slightly pink.

'Yeah, she'll make someone a good wife one day.'

Bella laughed. 'Just not you, right?'

'Right.'

'Hmmm.' Bella looked at the arm around Heather's

shoulder. 'Right. Well, enjoy your meal. Good to see more colour in your cheeks now, Heather.' With a wink, she turned back to clear off a recently vacated table.

'Oh my God, does she think ...?' Heather shifted away and Travis' arm dropped into the space between them.

Travis grinned. 'I don't know but if that stops her matchmaking me with her daughter, I'll play along. Not that Janet isn't a lovely girl. She's just not my type.'

Harry snorted. 'Do you even remember what your type is, boy? How long has it been since you got laid?'

'Bloody oath, Harry, what have I said about filtering what comes out of your mouth?'

Heather felt laughter bubble up over her fear. She caught Harry's eye and his wink. 'You're a stirrer, Harry.'

'You'd better believe it. Where's my beer?'

Travis pushed a chocolate milkshake in front of him. 'This is as close as you're going to get, you old bugger.'

'Got a head on it, I guess. You like a good head, lass?'

Travis almost choked as he sipped on his milkshake. Heather patted his back.

'As much as the next girl, Harry. Now behave. You're embarrassing Travis.'

Harry barked out a laugh. 'You go all right for a girl.'

Under the table, Travis gripped her hand and squeezed. Heather smiled up at him, not objecting at all when he didn't let go.

Chapter Seven

Travis shifted on the bench in the booth. With Heather's hand clutched in his, he figured she was safe. For now. That didn't mean he wouldn't be keeping a close eye on Zac Bannister. The man was trash, an embarrassment to the Bannister name and a danger to the people of Wongan Creek.

No matter what John Bannister thought, Travis doubted the old man had control of the situation. Zac's behaviour was escalating again and the last time he'd been so out of control, someone had died. Unfortunately Travis still didn't have the means to prove it had been at the hands of Bannister's unstable grandson.

Heather squeezed his fingers and smiled at him. Some of the edge lifted from his mood. This whole holding hands thing must mean some of Heather's control was rubbing off on him. He felt less like beating

Zac Bannister to a pulp with every passing moment. At least for now.

He liked the warmth of her small, soft hand in his. He wanted to feel her touch on his thigh again, like he had the night on the veranda. Hell, he'd like to feel her hands on a few other places too.

Dangerous territory considering her position at the department and the repercussions it could cause if they fell into a relationship. Any romantic link between them could jeopardise his guardianship of Casey if the department thought Heather might be biased in their case.

He couldn't help but feel a connection with this beautiful, strong, brave woman who could take on arseholes like Zac Bannister and ignore Harry's politically incorrect innuendos. No doubt about it, she was one of a kind, and he had the horrible suspicion he was falling in love, whether he wanted to or not.

Thankfully the tinkle of the bell above the shop door distracted him from his thoughts. Casey pushed through, leaving Janet to catch the door as it swung closed.

'Uncle Trav, Uncle Trav!' she called out, skipping down the aisle between the booths.

Travis grinned, let go of Heather's hand and stood up out of the booth, arms wide open to catch Casey as she picked up her pace. She slammed into him, throwing her arms up around his waist as she pressed her cheek to his side.

Travis' heart squeezed with love for his precious niece as he hugged her tightly. She wriggled out from under his arms, slid into the seat next to Harry and gave him a smacking kiss on the cheek before turning to greet Heather. 'Hey, Miss Penney.'

Travis turned back to Janet. 'Thanks for bringing her over.'

'You're welcome.'

Janet's flirtatious smile said he was welcome to a lot more, but it didn't stir him the way Heather's did. Travis rubbed the back of his neck, feeling awkward. He sneaked a glance back at Heather and found her studying them with interest.

'Um ... yeah, thanks.'

'Hey, you know how there's the bush dance after the rodeo next week?'

Janet laid a hand on Travis' arm to get his attention and he tried not to flinch under it.

'Ah ...'

'Would you like to partner up with me?'

Shit, he should have known that was coming because in the past, he had. Not that he'd ever been in a relationship with Janet, but he had been her plus one on a few occasions. Normally he'd accept, but with Heather on his mind, it didn't feel right.

'No, he wouldn't,' barked Harry. 'He's taking Heather.'

'Harry!' Heather patted the old man's hand on the table. 'Mind your own business.'

Travis rolled his eyes and put his hands on his hips. 'Well, I hadn't got around to asking her yet, so thanks for nothing, Harry. But, yes, I'm sorry, Janet. I won't be able to partner you this time.'

Janet looked between Heather and Travis then winked. 'I get it. No harm done. Enjoy your lunch.' With a little wave to Heather, she mouthed, 'you lucky girl' and moved across the shop to chat to her mum.

Travis felt the tips of his ears burning as he sat back down into the booth. 'Jeez, Harry.'

'What?'

'Well ... like ... jeez.'

Harry snorted. 'You're too slow, boy. No wonder you haven't had a sh—'

'So, Casey,' Heather broke in, cutting Harry off. 'How was school today?'

'Pretty cool. Benji and I found this huge gecko climbing up the wall outside the toilet block. We had to call the teacher cos the other kids wouldn't go inside cos they were scared. But Benji and I weren't scared.'

'Oh? What did they do with it?'

'Well, they called the ranger and I think they took it away cos it wasn't there at recess.'

As Casey chatted away, Travis felt Heather slip a hand on his thigh under the table and give it a gentle pat. God damn it, she'd meant it as reassurance, but his hormones had read the whole thing wrong. He shifted on the seat and fidgeted until the pressure in his jeans eased, but he kept a hand firmly over hers in case she moved it away.

The temptation was too much. With Travis' denim-wrapped thigh so close to hers and embarrassment turning his ears red, she had to give him a signal that it was okay.

The moment her palm felt the heat of his body under it though, her thoughts turned to another direction entirely. She was sure that if she let her hand travel north a little, she'd feel a definite reaction. When he squirmed in the seat, she knew she was right.

Casey chatted on about her day at school and Harry retreated into his lost world again, staring blankly out the window into the street. Heather's heart ached for him. There were so many things he'd forget, so many memories he'd lose, and so many faces he would no longer recognise.

Sitting here close to Travis with Harry and Casey across from them, it would be easy to fool herself into thinking they could be a family. One she realised she wanted badly. It was far too late to warn herself against falling in love with little Casey and Harry, she was already there. And Travis, God help her, she was falling deeper for him every day.

With each layer she uncovered, she wanted more until she had him stripped bare, and not just his soul. No, she wanted to take off that shirt, feel the muscles ripple beneath her hands, touch the skin that stretched across his body, all tanned and taut.

She listened to the rumble of his voice as he talked to Casey, deep and sexy with rich velvet tones she'd like to hear whispering words of love in her ear as they moved like dancers in a darkened room with nothing but skin between them.

Her hand twitched under the warmth of his as if her fingers agreed and wanted to begin the journey of exploration.

The movement brought his gaze to hers. He smiled, slow and sweet with a touch of mischief that told her he knew exactly what she was thinking before turning his palm up and threading his fingers through hers. The pad of his thumb grazed her wrist where her pulse pounded, and all plans to stay away from him on a personal level melted away like ice cream on a forty degree day.

'Well, isn't this just cosy.'

Zac Bannister's bulk shadowed their table. Heather's heart stuttered and stopped, all thoughts of Travis fleeing from her mind as fear gripped it instead. She eased her hand from Travis' and clung to her empty tea cup with both hands.

Travis stretched his legs under the table and took a lazy sip of his milkshake. 'Bannister.'

Big apish hands slapped down on the table. Casey edged closer to Harry, her eyes wide with fright before she hid her face against the sleeve of his blue flannel checked shirt. Her tiny hands fisted into the faded material as Harry patted her head gently.

'It's okay, kid,' he soothed.

'You're scaring my little girl, Bannister. Take a hike.'

There was control in Travis' voice that Heather admired and wished she could summon.

'Your little girl? You see, I have a theory about that.'

'No one gives a toss about your theories. Rack off.' Travis eased out of the booth, all hard muscle and broad shoulders, dangerously calm and controlled.

'I reckon Miss High and Mighty Penney here would like to know. I bet her boss would like to know who the kid's real daddy is. Now that would throw a spanner in the works, wouldn't it?'

Heather watched as Travis straightened to his full height, squared his shoulders and towered over the ape-like Zac, his neck corded with control. 'Take your filthy mind somewhere else.'

'She was a good lay, your sister. Opened her legs for anyone. Kid could be anybody's, but you know that, don't you?'

Casey whimpered, her fear of the man tangible.

Heather reached out for her hand across the table. 'It's okay, honey.'

'The truth will come out eventually,' taunted Zac, stepping into Travis' space, his beer belly the only thing stopping him getting too close. 'You can't escape it, Bailey. That slut's reputation will follow you no matter where you turn.'

Travis' fists clenched and unclenched at his sides and Heather knew he was itching to put the man flat on his back. Her heart pounded in her chest. 'Travis,' she said, willing him to back away.

'Tracy lived a tart and died a tart.'

Travis' eyes narrowed. 'Be careful what you say, Bannister. I'd hate to make you eat your words. Now back off. This is a family restaurant and I don't want to get blood on the floor.'

'Take a swing, Bailey. I dare you.' Zac leaned in, his width and weight making up for what he lacked in height.

'The only person taking a swing here is me!' Bella cruised between the booths like a battleship on the warpath. 'The first one to throw a punch gets this rolling pin across their arse.' She waved it in the air then crossed her arms across her ample breasts. 'Get out, Zac. You've caused enough trouble today and I won't have you smashing up my shop.'

Zac backed away. 'See you around, Bailey.' He turned and walked away with the swagger of a bully who thought he'd gotten away with terrorising his prey.

Travis relaxed his shoulders and put his hands on his hips as he watched Zac push his way out of the shop and into the street.

'That boy is a few hidings short,' said Bella. 'You be careful, Travis. I'm not sure what it is he thinks he knows, but you'd better be sure of the truth. There's trouble coming. I see it.'

Travis sighed. 'I know, Bella.' He looked at Casey then at Heather. 'You girls okay?'

Heather nodded as Casey sniffed back tears.

'He's so big and scary, Uncle Trav.' Casey's lip quivered. 'He said nasty words about my mum.'

Travis scooped her up out of the booth and cuddled her close. 'Your mum was a champ, Casey. Sometimes people say mean things because they don't know the truth and they want to hurt others with lies.'

'But I don't have a real daddy. And that makes me a ... a ... illegit ... a ...bast ...' Her bottom lip quivered and her big green eyes filled with tears. 'Those naughty words.'

'Oh, sweet pea, who told you that?'

'The kids at school. They said that man told their daddies so at the pub. And they also said those words he said about my mum.'

Travis sighed as Casey lowered her head to his shoulder and snuggled her forehead into his neck. 'Baby girl, you're not any of those things. They're horrible words and the kids shouldn't be repeating them. Nor should their daddies be saying those words in front of them. You have me and Harry, Nanna and Pop when they're home. We all love you more than a daddy ever could.'

'And Miss Penney. We've got her too now,' she murmured on a hiccup.

Heather's heart flip-flopped as Travis looked across at her, easing a little of the sadness she held there for Casey. No child should be so afraid, so hurt by words.

'Yes, we have Miss Penney too.'

She wondered at the fleeting doubt that made his brow narrow in a frown and his eyes cloud over. What secrets did he hold? What truth lay behind the mystery of his sister's death and his niece's lineage? And what threat was Zac Bannister in the middle of it all?

'Heather,' said Travis quietly over Casey's head. 'We need to talk.'

'Ah bugger,' said Harry, who until now had remained silent and watchful. 'Now the shit'll hit the fan.'

Loaded down with shopping bags, Travis let Casey lead the way into the house, happily sporting her new pair of shoes. No fancy Mary Jane's for Casey. No, she preferred her pull on brown leather boots.

She clumped down the hallway revelling in the squeak and thud of the rubber soles against the polished wood floors, the earlier scare at Mama Bella's all but forgotten. Travis wished he could shake it as easily.

It had taken a lot of cuddling, soothing and a scoop or two of Bella's magic rainbow ice cream to settle her back down. Something about the confrontation today niggled in the back of his mind, but he was too exhausted to process it. He only hoped Casey wouldn't have nightmares tonight.

Those nightmares caught him by surprise every time. He'd wake up to her crying and then he'd find her under the bed in his parents' room with her teddy cuddled close and her thumb in her mouth. That meant half an hour of coaxing, singing and cuddles before she was calm enough to come out from under the bed. He was still trying to figure out what set them off because Casey could never remember what the dreams were about.

Heather had promised to stop by later when Casey went to bed. Travis didn't want the little girl overhearing the discussion to come. God, it was one he'd avoided since Tracy died. Even before that. The truth no one in their family had ever wanted to face even though it was bound to bite them on the arse sooner or later. That moment had arrived. The band aid would be ripped off the wounds and all the ugliness would resurface. All he could hope for was that he could keep Casey protected from the worst of it.

He packed the cold stuff into the fridge and rearranged the pantry shelf to fit in the canned goods and remainder of the groceries. Regret, fear, sadness— all of them churned in his belly. Dread jumped into the pool at the sound of a four-wheel drive engine coming up the corrugated road leading up to the house. Too early to be Heather.

He made his way back down the hallway and out the front door onto the veranda. Sure enough, old man Bannister pulled to a stop, turned off the engine and got out. He shrugged out of an orange high visibility safety vest stamped with the Wongan Creek logo before making his way towards Travis.

'I'm sorry, I can't allow you on the property without the proper gear.'

John Bannister stopped and eyed him warily. 'What?'

Travis waved a hand at his navy cotton drill pants with the silver hi-vis stripe and the bright yellow shirt. 'Where's your jeans, gloves and akubra. Have you done the cow pat induction?'

'What are you on about, boy?'

'Seems fair you should be appropriately dressed to come and see me on my farm. Apparently, you've forgotten the dress code.' Travis pushed away from the veranda post. 'I tried to come and see you today. I wasn't allowed on site because I didn't have the right gear and hadn't done an induction. All I wanted was to say g'day. If I'd been able to reach you we could have avoided at least two of the incidents that took place today.' He strode down the stairs.

John grimaced then put a hand to his lip. Travis had a small moment of satisfaction knowing it must still hurt like hell from Harry's fist.

'Security told me someone was asking for me. Rules are rules. Heard my boy's been causing trouble.' He held out a hand to shake.

Travis took it, despite the urge to ignore the greeting. 'He needs a lesson in manners.'

'For what it's worth, I'm sorry. Bella bailed me up and ripped me a new one. I've had a word with him.'

'I don't think having a word with him will cut it anymore. He's gone beyond that. I heard what happened up at the mine today.'

'Yeah, had a word about that too.'

Travis stared at the old man in front of him aware for the first time that just like Harry he seemed older and frailer. He'd seemed so much taller and broader before. His hair appeared whiter, his leathery skin more wrinkled and his eyes rheumy and tired. Not so long ago, he'd had a straight back and strong arms. That's what happened to a man of the land who traded his seat on a horse for one behind a desk, Travis thought. There was a time when John Bannister had been the wood chopping champion of the south-east. These days he was a champion arsehole, a slave to gold and profit margins.

'Keep him out of my way, John, because if he threatens my family or Heather again, I'll make sure he doesn't come out of it with just a few words.'

'Righto. Fair call. It won't come to that. But that's not what I'm here for. I came to talk some sense into you about Harry's place, and yours too.'

'Our land is not for sale. And keep your legal boys away from Harry.'

'Come on, Travis. Be sensible, boy. You're literally sitting on a gold mine here. Harry could retire to one of those fancy lifestyle villages down south and you could shake the dust off your boots and get a life.'

'I like my life fine as it is, thank you. The gold will still be there when I'm done farming. And I reckon you need to respect Harry's wishes and let him live out his last years in peace. Haven't you destroyed enough of this town by selling off prime cattle grazing and replacing it with a great gaping hole in the ground?'

'It brought jobs.'

'It killed cattle and plant life. It spread dieback disease and created an environmental nightmare in the making.'

'It's under control now.'

'Is it, John? The environmental issues, maybe.'

Anger vibrated through Travis' body. 'But how do you explain what happened to Heather today, the fights at the pub or the harassment the girls in town are experiencing. Zac's mates ride in at every opportunity they get so they can make trouble with the locals and trash the town. And don't get me started on you destroying good farming land to build houses that will stand empty in twenty-odd years' time because the boom is over. What then, when we're another ghost town on the map?'

'That's the cost of progress.'

'There's progress, then there's greed, mate. I'm not sure you know the difference anymore. Not when your name is on those real estate boards as the developer. You own shares in the mine, they lease your land from you to mine it, and now you're a property developer too?'

Was there anything the Bannister name hadn't touched? But it wasn't that he resented the Bannister family's success. It was that they trampled all over everyone in their rush to get there that made him mad. The people they hurt, the lives they destroyed in the process and the shit they got away with because they could afford expensive lawyers.

John ignored the dig. 'Mate, I know Harry's getting worse. His mind has gone. In a few months, he won't remember he has a farm.'

'That's not the point.'

'Good God, boy, are you that stupid? Get him to sell

out now. Or are you holding out to inherit? Is that why you're hanging on his coat tails? Can't afford to buy it, so you'll steal it instead?'

Travis' patience and tolerance hit ground zero. 'And now I know for sure where that rumour sprouted from. Get off my land,' he growled. 'You've overstayed your welcome.'

John stared him down. 'I thought I could talk some sense into you, but now I see I'll have to lay charges on Harry for assault after all.'

'That sounds a lot like blackmail to me.'

Contempt for the man rose up through Travis' gut as he tried desperately to hang on to control, to remind himself that even if the bloke was an arsehole, John Bannister was an old man and his mother had taught him to respect his elders.

He felt a tug at the leg of his jeans and looked down to see Casey standing next to him, looking up at him through eyes filled with fear.

'Uncle Trav?'

'Hey, sweet pea.' He ruffled her hair. 'Why don't you go down and see how Fantasia is doing while I say goodbye to Mr Bannister?'

'Okay,' she said, but didn't seem to want to let go.

'It's okay, I promise. I can see you from here, sweet pea. I'll be watching out for you,' he said gently, smoothing her curls back from her face.

She let go and walked away slowly with a wary

glance at John Bannister. The old man watched her thoughtfully for a moment before turning back to Travis, his eyes narrowed.

Travis could almost hear the man's mind ticking over and he knew John would be looking at Casey and thinking of her resemblance to Tracy. He prayed the old man didn't see the resemblance to his own family and what Travis already suspected.

'Cute kid. Looks just like her mother at that age. Must be hard on a bloke like you, raising someone else's child, knowing that at any time the real father could stake his claim. You never did find out who her father was, did you? Might be worthwhile asking around. Seems a bit unfair that her real father might be missing out on watching his little girl grow up.'

'Mind your own business, Bannister.'

'I am,' said John. He turned, got into his car and drove away.

Travis watched the dust cloud kicked up by the tyres dissipate, and remembered exactly what it was he was protecting.

Chapter Eight

Heather parked the car outside Travis' house and admired the warm glow of light on the veranda and through the open curtains on the windows. His home had such a warm, loving feel to it. As if many Baileys had lived and loved there, leaving their stamp of approval on it for future generations.

Travis sat in his favourite spot, bare feet up on the railing, leaning back on the couch with a beer in his hand. No apple juice tonight. Cuddled in his lap and secured by his free arm lay Casey, fast asleep with her head on his chest.

She smiled at the picture they made and tried not to think of how lucky the little girl was to be in that position. She imagined it would be a very nice chest to be curled into like that.

Opening the door, she got out, closed it and pressed

the button on the remote control to secure it, even though she knew that out here it wasn't necessary to lock doors.

She felt Travis' eyes on her and was pleased she'd taken the time to shower and change. The swirl of the cotton skirt around her legs and the hug of the matching shirt with a sweetheart neck made her feel fabulously feminine after the required drill pants and yellow shirt she needed to wear to the WCM meetings.

She'd added a spritz of her favourite perfume for luck, even though she knew this wasn't a date but rather a meeting at the request of a case client.

Walking up the stairs, she watched as he sipped from the bottle. His lids fluttered shut as he drank. Long golden eyelashes that would make a girl weep with envy, cast shadows on his cheeks. And when he opened those eyes, they were empty of the light that normally shone there, replaced by sadness that went bone deep and apprehension that spoke of a fear so great it made her spine tingle.

'Hi,' she said quietly, not wanting to disturb Casey.

'Hey.'

He lowered the bottle to rest on his knee and she saw it was still almost full even though the condensation from the chill had long since dried up. A man who let his beer go warm had something serious on his mind.

His gaze followed hers to the bottle. 'You're not

going to have a go at me for having a beer, are you?' His words were quiet, his tone flat and tired.

Heather shivered. 'No. Why would I do that?'

'The last social worker we had frowned upon foster parents and guardians having a drink.'

She sighed. 'Are you planning on getting drunk and starting a fight? Hurting anyone?'

'No.'

'Are you an alcoholic? Do you have to down a drink every morning to get through the day?'

He shook his head. 'Nope. I allow myself a six pack every couple of weeks and only have one after Casey is taken care of. Never more than one.'

'That sounds very grown up and responsible.' Heather smiled. 'It would be hypocritical of me to take you to task over one beer when I enjoy the odd glass of wine myself.'

She leaned over and tucked a curl behind Casey's ear. The little girl mumbled and snuggled closer to her uncle. His arm tightened around her and Heather knew it was a movement born out of instinct.

'She's beautiful,' she said.

Travis looked down at the sleeping child. 'She is. I'd do anything for this kid.'

Heather moved to sit beside him. 'I know that. Is that what's bothering you, Travis? That we're going to take her away from you? I'm doing my best to make sure that doesn't happen.'

'I know, thank you. You might change your mind after tonight though. You might not have a choice.'

Heather frowned, a heavy feeling settling in her stomach. She wanted to reach out and touch him, thread her fingers through his and reassure him everything would be fine, but the set of his shoulders and the closed expression he wore stopped her. She was here on professional business.

'Whatever it is, Travis, we'll work through it to find a solution that's beneficial for Casey.'

He nodded and shifted forward, taking Casey's weight as he stood. 'I'll put her to bed then we'll talk. Can I bring you back a drink?'

'Cheers, that'll do the trick nicely.'

She watched as he walked away, the denim loving the sway of his hips, his back stiff and straight as he edged through the front door with his precious package in his arms.

Patiently she waited, a sense of *deja vu* settling over her as she listened to the night sounds beyond the veranda once again and pondered on what Zac Bannister had said to Travis that had sparked this sudden need for an official chat.

Her run in with the little bastard today had done enough damage to her own peace of mind. There was nothing nice about him, no redeeming qualities at all. He was mean and a bully, probably always had been.

She dreaded the next session she had to attend on

site, terrified he'd try that stunt again. The best she could do was hope John Bannister's chat with him had worked. Even so, he was the least of her worries today.

After lunch and a trip to the shops to pick out boots for Casey at the little girl's request, she'd arrived home to a letter in the mailbox. The specialist at the MND research centre in Perth had acknowledged her referral and invited her to make an appointment for the DNA testing.

Avoiding the monster in her mind seemed like a good idea because it opened up a whole new can of what-ifs she wasn't ready to face. Being torn between wanting and not wanting to know was a crap place to be.

Travis appeared in the doorway, flicked off the veranda light and turned on the ultra-violet bug light. 'Stops the mozzies from making a meal of us. Zaps them before they zap us.' He padded out onto the veranda and handed her a bottle of beer. 'Cheers.'

She took it and sipped, allowing the smooth taste to caress her tongue for a moment before she swallowed. 'Cheers.'

The sofa dipped under his weight and he leaned back with a sigh. He picked at the label with restless fingers. She let him, even though her own fingers itched to stop the motion.

'You don't have brothers and sisters, do you, Heather?' His voice rumbled through the dark, the only glow now coming from the weird purple light in the caged contraption that sparked every time a bug landed in it.

'No, I'm an only child. Mum never married and I don't remember her even having a date before she fell ill.'

'It makes me sad to think Casey will grow up the same.'

'Maybe one day she'll have cousins to keep her company.'

He shrugged. 'Maybe if the right girl comes along, who knows.' He looked at her, their shoulders touching. 'Do you want children?'

There was that million dollar question that ripped her heart out every time. She pushed down the pain that tore at her chest. 'Yes, I'd love to have children, but—' Could she confide in Travis? Tell him her fears, about the life sentence over her head? No, tonight was about Travis. She had to keep it professional. Her personal life had no place in his. 'Time will tell.'

Time and the DNA testing she couldn't pluck up the courage to take. If she carried the MND gene, she could never risk passing it on to her children. No, then it would be better to not have children at all. The miserable neurological disease had to end with her.

Next to her, Travis nodded. 'I loved my sister. My mum used to say we might as well have been born Siamese twins. We were inseparable. As babies, we were almost identical. The only way anyone could tell us apart was because Tracy didn't have the white fringe. Even then, they'd still get confused.' He smiled wistfully. 'Then we reached our teens and we couldn't fool anyone anymore.'

'I bet you two got up to plenty of mischief,' Heather teased, trying to ease his sombre mood.

'Oh, we did.' Travis laughed and took a swallow of his beer. He pulled a face and set it aside. 'Ugh, hadn't realised it got so warm.'

'Here, share mine. I shouldn't drink too much anyway. Not if I'm driving.' She held out the bottle and after a moment's hesitation he took it.

'Cheers.' He sipped and handed it back.

As she took it, his fingers brushed hers and sweet tremors tingled through her blood. He eased down on the sofa and stretched his legs out in front of him, linking his hands over his flat stomach. Heather tried hard not to follow the movement or let her eyes linger on the areas where his jeans were almost white with wear, especially around the zipper.

She dragged her thoughts away from the danger zone. 'Tell me about her.'

'Tracy was full of life. She loved the outdoors. She swam like a fish and climbed like a billy goat which is why the way she died still makes no sense at all.'

Heather tucked her legs under her and leaned closer to catch his words. He'd spoken them quietly, almost to himself.

'How so?'

He turned his head to look at her, their faces close. 'The coroner determined it was an accident. That she'd slipped, hit her head and fallen into the river. We'd had a lot of rain that year and the river was swollen. There was also speculation based on Tracy's behaviour leading up to her drowning that it might have been an attempt at suicide.'

Suicide? Oh God, what an awful thing for his family to face. Heather's heart ached for Travis, for Casey. 'You don't think that's what happened?'

He shook his head. 'Tracy and I had this weird kind of telepathic link. The one always knew when the other one was in trouble. If Tracy got hurt, I'd know it because I'd feel the same pain she did. That day I was competing in the open saddle bronc in Newman. I was waiting at the release gate when I felt a pain in my head. It felt like someone hit me in the back of the head with a rock. The pain was sharp and stabbing.'

Heather shuddered. She couldn't begin to imagine the horror Travis had been through, but she knew the pain of watching a loved one die.

'And then I felt nothing for a moment. Nothing. Absolute silence in my head like I'd never known before. That's when I knew something bad had happened to Tracy.'

He reached for her hand and she let him hold it, as much for her own comfort as his. It was cold against her skin, so she leaned down to put the beer on the floor then sat back and rubbed some warmth into his fingers.

'I felt myself sinking, surrounded by water, my head pounding, my eyes stinging.' His fingers tightened around hers. 'Then the pressure on my lungs and I couldn't breathe. I could feel my arms reaching upwards, my legs trying to kick but something held me down. A pressure on the top of my head. I struggled, but I could feel myself getting tired, heavy. And then I was floating into darkness.'

Sweet Mother Mary. Heather felt sick just thinking about it. This was a pain that would haunt Travis forever.

He sighed and leaned his head to hers. Heather dropped her head to his shoulder and let the pressure of his head on hers comfort her whirling thoughts.

'Tracy could bench press eighty kilos, ten kilos more than me. She spent hours in the gym in the shed, the only place she went outside of the house. She was strong. She should have been able to rise above the weight that held her down. Fight her way out of the current. The river was swollen but it wasn't running fast due to a blockage by a tree downstream. None of it made sense.'

Heather could feel his frustration in the stiffness of his body, the clutch of his hand between hers.

'I heard her voice calling me, terrified, exhausted ... then nothing. Jesus, Heather, it was like someone took my soul and ripped it out of my body. I've never known such pain.'

Heather lifted her head and watched him raise his free hand to his face, swipe it across and then press his fingers against his closed lids. She drew his hand down and snagged his gaze.

'I'm sorry.'

He shook his head, his eyes glistening. 'Then she was gone. I woke up flat on my back in the dust surrounded by people. I had no idea how I got there, no memory of passing out.'

He shifted away from her and stood, walking over and leaning his hands on the veranda rail. Heather stayed where she was, watching him stare out into the inky black horizon.

'The circuit paramedics thought I might have passed out as the gate opened. It was a hot day, so they thought it might have been dehydration. I don't remember being bucked or hitting the ground. All I remember is the pain Tracy felt. I should never have gone to Newman. I've lived the last couple of years wishing I hadn't made that decision. If I had, Tracy might still be alive. It doesn't make sense why she went down to the creek alone that day. Not when she hardly left the house anymore. And she definitely never left Casey alone in the house.'

Heather stood and moved to the rail, her arm touching his. 'It's not your fault, Travis. It was an accident.'

'That's what doesn't make sense. When I got back and after the police had finished their investigation, I went down there. The rock she allegedly fell from was flat, nothing sharp that would cause the stabbing pain I'd felt. She used to polish her boots with black polish. If she'd slipped, the polish would have left a streak. And there was nothing that could have held her down in the water. No trees nearby to get tangled in the roots. Nothing. And definitely no note to suggest she'd contemplated suicide.'

'Was she suicidal?' Heather's blood ran cold and she shivered against the goosebumps on her skin.

'She was troubled, yes. Suicidal? No. Casey was her world. She would never have taken her own life and left Casey behind.'

'You think she was murdered? But who on earth would have a motive?'

Travis nodded. 'I wish I had proof, but I don't. I only have suspicions. The police wrapped up the case too quickly, missed vital clues like the footprints of bigger boots in the mud, the broken branches and a piece of Tracy's shirt caught on a sharp piece of wood where the branch had snapped off. The coroner turned out the results of the autopsy in record time. I think it was a cover up.'

'Oh, Travis.' Heather stood closer and put a hand on his back. 'But why? Why would anyone want to murder her?'

He shrugged. 'To keep her quiet, maybe? Tracy knew too much about what went on over at the Bannister place when Zac threw his parties. There were rumours of drugs and dirty deals, but no one believed it. Not with his grandfather covering his butt at every turn. And this is a small town. Folk can be a little naive about those things, especially my parents.'

'What did Riggs do? Surely he couldn't ignore the possibilities of her death. He's been the town cop forever.'

Travis ran his hands through his hair and let out a long sigh. 'Riggs was away on long service leave. We had another officer in charge at the time. One who was suspiciously friendly with Zac's biker mates and very keen to file the report as a drowning accident.'

'A crooked cop? So besides the parties and drugs, why would Zac want to keep her quiet?'

His hands slapped against the wood as his fingers gripped the railing, knuckles white against the enamel finish. 'When Tracy came home from a party over at the Bannister's one night, she was in a bad state. She was drunk and dosed up on drugs. She was a health freak so that in itself was totally out of character for her. We suspected her drink had been spiked. Even back then Zac was hanging out with some debatable characters. I had a bad feeling about it and wanted to go to the party too, but she said I couldn't be attached to her hip forever. I was never a fan of the Bannisters. I didn't trust

Zac one bit. He's always been a troublemaker. But she said her friends were all going and his parents and grandparents would be there to supervise, so Mum let her go.'

'She lied?'

'Yes. We found out later that his parents were away in Perth and John was playing an all-night poker challenge at the pub. The whole night, I had this feeling of being hunted, trapped, tortured. I wanted to go over there and bring her home, but Dad told me to stay put and to stop being over-protective. When she came home, her clothes were messed up and her legs were bloody.' He closed his eyes against the memory. 'We suspected she'd been ... hurt ... but she wouldn't talk about it, refused to go to a doctor or report it to the police. She locked herself away in her room, withdrew from us, from the farm she loved so much. A few months later we found out she was pregnant with Casey.'

'Sweet Jesus, Travis.' The horror of it all left her cold. She saw many cases of abuse in families, but for Travis to have lived with it made her heart ache.

'She refused to name the father, but deep down, I knew who it was — who it could be — and how it came about, but Tracy still refused to admit to what happened.' He turned to her, cupped her face in his big hands. 'Promise me, Heather, that you'll never let the Bannisters take Casey from me.'

Fear, cold and hard, churned Heather's stomach as she frantically searched Travis' eyes, seeing the pain and the pleading in them. She'd seen what Zac Bannister was capable of and it wasn't something a little girl should be exposed to.

If Travis' suspicions were right and he proved to be Casey's father, the children's court could very likely rule in Zac's favour as the only surviving parent. She couldn't promise Travis they wouldn't succeed.

She raised her hands to cover his and pressed them to her cheeks, but she closed her eyes against the vulnerability in his gaze. 'Why have you waited this long to tell someone?'

Travis sighed. 'I tried to get the police to reopen the case, but they said there was insufficient evidence. John Bannister labelled me the troublemaker for trying. Zac knows what he did. He's capable of terrible things. I'd hoped Casey would have more of the Bailey genes so they wouldn't recognise it, but the older she gets the more she looks a little like a Bannister. I can't let him win a custody battle. John Bannister suspects who Casey's father is and he'll have no hesitation in making it look like Tracy's fault. Her reputation suffered enough abuse at the hands of a Bannister. He'll use Casey as a bargaining tool when his fight for Harry's land and mine heats up. He'll take everything I love from me. Casey, Harry, our land. Gold fever is a bitch, sweetheart.'

She felt his fear, his pain, but she was his case

worker and she had a duty to do. 'You know I have to report this, don't you? It will reopen wounds, drag Tracy's reputation through the mud again, raise gossip and speculation. The victims often get the blame in cases where drugs and alcohol are involved. And Tracy isn't here to defend herself.'

He nodded. 'It needs to be done. I want them to know the truth before they hear Bannister's lies, so I at least have a chance at keeping Casey.'

Heather reached up and stroked the rough edge of his jaw where a day's growth of stubble had formed. She wanted to comfort him, to reassure him they could win a custody battle against the most influential people in Wongan Creek, but it felt like an empty promise so she committed to what she could. 'I'll do everything I can to make sure Casey stays with you.'

'I know you will. Thank you.' His thumbs stroked across her cheekbones, long fingers cradling the base of her skull. 'Thank you,' he repeated as his gaze held hers.

Heather felt the depth of that look all the way to her toes as it changed from gratitude to something else, something deeper and hotter than it should. His eyes dropped to her lips and then he closed the gap.

Warm and full, holding only a hint of the flavour of his beer, his mouth brushed hers gently in the sweetest of kisses that had her wanting more. But even as she rose on her tiptoes to take it, he was retreating. He dropped his hands to his side and stepped back.

'You should go. I'd hate for you to be out too late.'

Disappointment flooded her, but she knew he was right. As much as she wanted to take that kiss further, they had too much to lose, too much to fight for. Maybe when this was all over ... maybe then she could admit she was more than a little in love with Travis Bailey.

Chapter Nine

'For God's sake, Harry, give me that wrench. What do you think you're doing?'

'Fixin' your tractor, you grumpy little sod.' Harry pushed back his cap with a tap of the wrench on the peak and hitched up his jeans.

'What for? Shouldn't you be rounding up your sheep instead?'

'Are you taking the piss, boy? You know my bloody sheep are in the paddock where they belong. I might be forgetful sometimes but I sure as hell know what's going on in my own back paddock.'

Travis sighed. He'd seen the sheep down by the creek again which meant they were nowhere near Harry's paddock, and he'd have to round them up later himself. 'The tractor can wait another day, Harry. I'll get to it tomorrow.'

'You won't have time.'

'What do you mean I won't have time?'

'Bella called earlier. She said you hadn't signed up for the annual rodeo yet. So you're going into town to fill out the paperwork. God knows, in my day you didn't have to do all that shit. You got up on the bloody horse and rode the damn thing, insurance and accidents be damned.' Harry turned back to the tractor and attached the wrench to a nut.

'Jesus, Harry! You know I don't ride anymore. Not even for fun. I'd be no bloody good to you or Casey if I came off the bronc or got trampled by a steer.'

Travis ripped off his hat and tossed it onto the tractor seat. He was tired and grumpy from lack of sleep. He'd waited up for Heather's call to let him know she'd arrived home safely last night and then they'd talked for another half hour after.

His attraction to her was wrong on so many levels yet it felt so damn right. And now he'd tasted her lips he just wanted more which had kept him awake right up until he'd heard Mrs Everett's bloody rooster crowing from across the creek.

Then he'd felt guilty for thinking of Heather's luscious curves when he should have been thinking of Casey's future and the renewed threat the Bannisters posed to his family.

'A man's got to get back up on the bronco sometime. You'll bloody ride that rodeo, boy. Going to Newman that day didn't kill Tracy. Deep down, you know it. It's time you got back on the bike so to speak. Do you think I'll forgive you if you allow that fat arse Bannister boy the opportunity to win? Not a chance, matey.'

'I don't have time, Harry. Besides, I don't think Zac will make it up onto a horse this year.'

'You've got all the time in the world, son. Bella said to make time. She's got something for you to do.'

Travis wanted to bang his forehead against the tractor hood in frustration. 'Oh God. Not the kissing booth again.'

Harry smirked. 'Nope, you know all that political correctness twaddle put paid to that one. Bella doesn't want anyone getting sued for harassment.'

Travis' brow shot up. 'Twaddle? You learned to put that filter on your mouth?'

'Fuck no, but that's what Bella calls it and I don't fancy a rolling pin to the head if I call it shit instead.'

'Right.' Travis let the word stretch out as he wondered what the hell Bella had in store for him this year.

Last year he'd had to kiss the ladies of the CWA three times each, and not on their powdery cheeks either. Not that he minded, not at all, he loved them all to bits, but it was the flurry of knitted jumpers and home-baked pies that appeared on his doorstep after the fair that had him worried, because each of them had an eligible daughter to marry off.

The irony of the situation was that the perfect girl was right here, right now and he couldn't do a damn thing about it because she was the one who held Casey's future in her hands. Pretty hands they were too. Soft and gentle, the kind a man wanted all over him. But it wasn't just her hands that were beautiful, it was her soul.

For the first time ever, he'd found someone he could really talk to, someone who wasn't connected by blood and an invisible telepathy who understood him, his fight for Casey and the preservation of his precious farm land. And that girl was so far out of reach she might as well be back in Darwin.

'You still with me, son? Gone off into bloody LaLa land here. You thinking of that pretty little redhead again?'

'No.'

Harry chuckled. 'Liar. If I was your age, I'd be doing more than thinking.'

Travis grinned and tapped the peak of Harry's cap down over his eyes. 'Well lucky you're not my age anymore then. Get back to work, you old bastard.'

'Make up your mind, son. Do you want me to fix the tractor or not?'

Heather untangled her legs from the twisted sheets. She hadn't slept a wink. At least that's what it felt like.

Every time she closed her eyes she felt Travis' lips on hers and the sharp stab of disappointment that she hadn't had the opportunity to taste more.

Then there was the whole mess with Zac Bannister and little Casey. Adorable, sweet little Casey who'd stolen a piece of her heart, the bit that didn't already belong to her uncle and crazy old Harry. So much for not getting involved with the locals.

Swinging her legs to the floor, her eyes fell on the letter from the specialist, the stark white paper bearing the MND research centre logo a sharp reminder of her gene pool. She pulled it out from under the lamp and let her eyes blur out the content.

How was it she had the guts to stand up to bullies like Bannister in her job, yet the thought of taking a simple battery of tests that would determine her future had her wanting to curl up in a corner and pretend diseases like Motor Neurone didn't exist.

She tucked the letter back under the lamp and stood. A shower would clear her mind and prepare her for the conversation to come with her supervisor. She'd never felt this much conflict in a case before. But then her heart had never been this invested. Rule number one of social work was not to let your heart rule your head. In Travis' case, it was proving difficult. All she could do was pray that the department saw it the same way she did.

She considered delaying the submission of the report, but if Travis was right and the Bannisters were about to play their cards, a delay could cost him all he'd worked hard for.

The court would order DNA testing before proceeding, but too often they ruled in favour of the wrong party. Her heart ached at the thought. But it did buy them time because court orders and DNA blood test results all took time, especially in a small town. Hopefully that meant Travis could sort out one battle before starting another.

Going through the motions of showering and getting dressed, her mind churned. What if it all went wrong and the Bannisters got custody? Travis would surely hate her for unleashing those monsters on his niece. How was it possible for her to remain neutral when there was so much speculation around Tracy's death and Zac's behaviour already proved the violence he was capable of?

Which was why she was heading into her office at the Town Hall on a Saturday when she could be sleeping in. Perhaps if she put it all down on paper it would help separate emotions from facts and she could present an unbiased report. The short walk down Main Street would give her time to work through it all.

Locking her front door behind her, she set off down the gum tree-lined street, turned into Jacaranda Road then, a few blocks later, onto Main. The walk was peaceful and shady past the old cottages. Heather loved the rich history of the town. Originally cattle country, it grew into a saw mill then a railway town before giving way to gold in the eighties.

She could imagine the saw mill workers coming home, hot and itchy with sawdust clinging to their clothes, and the railway workers grimy and sweaty after a day laying tracks to extend the line to Narrogin, a mere one hundred kilometres away. Each little home would have a story to tell, if only walls could talk.

She opened the door leading into the hall and found it bustling with the ladies from the CWA and volunteers scattered around, either on ladders putting up bunting or stacking seats and moving tables.

'Heather!' Bella called out from across the hall, waving.

Well, that pretty much put an end to her plans for writing up the report today. With all the action going on, the ladies would be popping their heads in her door every five minutes to offer tea or ask advice. She made her way over and Bella seized her in a voluminous hug.

'Hi, Bella, ladies,' she greeted as they swarmed around her.

'Are you okay after that little incident with the Bannister boy yesterday, dear?' Bella released her from the bear hug.

'Yes, I'm fine, thank you.'

'Ah, I heard about that from Mavis Upton,' murmured Mrs Everett.

'That boy needs his ears boxed,' agreed Mrs Benson.

'More than just his ears from what I hear,' added Miss Turner. 'I could take my cane to his backside like I did to his father's many moons ago.'

'Oh, Virginia! You know they banished corporal punishment years ago. You can't do those things anymore.' Mrs Everett popped her hand over her mouth.

'More's the pity if you ask me!' Virginia Turner turned to Heather. 'You just let me know if he gives you any trouble, love.'

Heather smiled. 'Of course, Miss Turner.'

Everyone in town knew not to mess with the should-be-retired school principal who'd probably started the first school in Wongan Creek. A woman of indeterminable age, she could still stop a scuffle in the street with the tap of her cane.

Heather decided it was best to change the subject before she took off in search of Zac to follow through on her threat. 'So, what's happening here today, ladies?'

'We're getting ready for the annual rodeo weekend markets.'

'Oh? A rodeo? But surely your market stalls should be on the oval where the action is?'

'Well you see, dear ...' Miss Turner adjusted her multi-focal eye glasses. 'We had a little incident a few years back when a micky broke free and trampled all the stalls. It was chaos, I tell you.'

'A micky?'

'A wild, young bull,' said Bella.

'People running everywhere!' added Mrs Everett, nodding enthusiastically. 'Lucky no one got hurt though.'

'Except for the bull. And he made an excellent steak. You could cut it with a fork.' Miss Turner winked at Heather. 'So now we have the market stalls here at the Town Hall where it's cool and safe.'

'Ah, makes sense,' said Heather. 'Well, I've got a report to write, so if you'll excuse me?'

'On a Saturday?' Bella's indignation was clear by the positioning of her hands on her ample hips. 'You need some time off, girl. Surely it can wait until Monday?'

'Erm, well ...'

She wanted to protest that it couldn't, but that would raise a flurry of questions from the ladies who would no doubt want to know what was so important that she couldn't leave it for another day.

She was saved from replying as a collective sigh echoed through the hall and heads turned towards the door. Her heart did a little misstep of its own and her cheeks blossomed with heat as Travis entered the chaos inside.

Looking devilishly handsome in a V-necked khaki T-shirt and faded blue jeans touched with a smear of grease on the thighs, he owned the room without even trying.

Heather searched his body language for signs of the tortured soul he'd been the night before, but he'd buried the hurt back under his mega-watt smile.

She watched as he made his way through the volunteers, stopping to shake hands with the men or pull the ladies in for a quick hug and a peck on the cheek. From the snippets of conversation and murmured words, everyone appeared unusually excited to see him.

'Oh thank God he's here,' muttered Bella. She leaned her head to Heather's. 'We desperately need him to ride in the rodeo events or the bloody Bannisters will monopolise the competition.'

'Does he ride every year?'

'He hasn't for a while now, dear, but he should. We ask him every year in the hope he'll ride again. Poetry in motion on horseback, that boy.'

Oh, glory be, didn't she know it? She'd seen that poetry in action.

'He got thrown in Newman a couple of years ago. Nothing broken, but it shook him up a little. Then he was back looking after Casey on his own, and he hasn't ridden since. We're hoping he changes his mind this year, but he's terrified that if he gets hurt, he won't be able to look after Casey and Harry properly, you see.'

'Well, that's a fair call, isn't it?' Except he hadn't

been thrown, he'd fallen. Heather wondered how much Bella really knew about that day in Newman and the events that had unfolded here in Wongan Creek at the same time.

Bella sighed and nodded. 'But such a shame to waste that talent.'

Talent indeed. She watched the sway of his hips, the stride of those denim-clad legs and the play of muscles in his thighs with every step he took. She'd seen those thighs clenched against the saddle in full gallop and wondered what they'd look like naked.

Heather frowned at her thoughts as she watched him move closer and tried to quell the swirl of excitement in her own belly as his gaze connected with hers. His eyes softened and she found herself smiling tentatively at him, the burn in her cheeks escalating.

Mrs Everett nudged her gently. 'Oh my!'

'Oh no, Mrs Everett, it's nothing like that at all!' Heather jumped in quickly before speculation turned to gossip.

'You keep telling yourself that, love,' said Bella with a knowing smile. 'Ah, Travis, you got my message then?'

'Not even Alzheimer's could keep Harry from remembering a missive from you, Bella.' He kissed her cheek, mock-groaned as she squeezed him into a tight hug and exhaled an exaggerated breath when she let go.

'You've been practicing for the log throwing, haven't you?'

'You betcha! And the dummy spit.' Bella patted his cheek.

'I thought Miss Turner would have that one covered.' Travis grinned as the retired principal tugged his ear.

'You're still as cheeky as ever, young man. When are you going to settle down with a good woman and give young Casey little cousins to play with?'

'Ah, Miss Turner, I'm waiting for you to marry me.' The twinkle in his eye was downright cheeky as he turned his attention to Heather and it whipped her already quivering insides to jelly. 'G'day, Heather.'

'Travis,' she breathed over the pounding of her heart as he pressed his lips to her cheek. She closed her eyes to the whisper of his kiss, the touch of his hand to her waist, and listened to the noise in the room fade as his mouth lingered a little longer, his fingers pressed gently into her side.

Slowly he withdrew and her eyes fluttered open to meet his. Heather swallowed the rising emotion, refused to name it, and saw it reflected in his gaze. If they were alone, he might have kissed her lips and she might have kissed him back.

'Oh my,' whispered Mrs Everett again.

Bella cleared her throat. 'Well ... so ...'

The world spun back into focus and the chattering of

the volunteers filled the hall once more. Heather stepped back and let Travis' hand fall from her waist. 'Erm ... if you'll excuse me?'

'Of course, love.' Bella nodded, a smile stretching her generous mouth.

Heather willed her knees not to give out as she made her way to her office with the feel of Travis' eyes on her back. Closing the door behind her, she leaned back against it, her head resting against the hundred-year-old wood.

Oh. Wow. She slid down to the floor and rested her head against her fists. Oh boy, was she ever in trouble. She'd gone and fallen in love, all the reasons her conscience gave her not to, ignored.

Before nightfall, the rumour mill would be buzzing with recollections of that moment outside from various viewpoints, and no doubt, each version would be embellished at will with no end to the storyteller's imagination.

Then the story would reach the department head's ears and she'd be pulled from the case due to conflict of interest, no matter how much she chose to deny it.

The Bannisters would have a field day with the ammunition against them and Travis would hate her forever if he lost Casey because of it.

Oh God. The pleasurable churn in her stomach turned sour and the magical feel of his lips against her skin faded. What a mess. All because she'd got her knickers in a twist over a man. A very sexy, very sweet, gorgeous, kind-hearted, built-for-loving man.

It was a peck on the cheek, that's all. Please God let that be all the ladies had seen. Sadly, rumour mills never worked the way you wanted them to, and the ladies with their beautiful romantic hearts were likely already planning a wedding.

Heather eased her way back up onto her feet from her squat position and walked to her desk. Pulling out the chair, she sat and rubbed at the headache forming behind her brow.

If only she'd ignored the lure of the ladies, their need to stop and say hi, she'd be halfway through the bloody report and wouldn't be sitting here all hot and bothered by a stupid damn peck on the cheek.

She turned to pull open the top drawer of her filing cabinet and picked out the manila folder containing the Bailey file. Spreading it open on the desk, she held up the copy of Casey's birth certificate, her eyes drawn to the line where the name of her father was listed as 'undeclared'.

Poor Tracy. The horrors the girl must have lived through if what Travis was saying was true. Not that she doubted it. Any hope that Zac Bannister wouldn't eventually come forward to claim Casey as his could be forgotten. The man was horrible enough to force the issue and with the backing of Bannister money and his shady biker mates, he could easily make it stick, even if it wasn't a possibility he was her father.

A simple blood test and all Travis' nightmares would come true. And by behaving like a lovesick cow, mooning all over him, she might just as well have given them the stick to beat him with. *Sweet Mother Mary*.

A knock sounded against the heavy door and her heart skipped a beat. 'Come in,' she called.

Travis eased the door open, squeezed inside and closed it quietly behind him. 'Hey.'

'Hey.' She feigned interest in the folder but all she could smell was his woodsy cologne, hear the intake and expulsion of his breathing and God help her, she thought she could even hear the thundering of his heart.

His palms flattened on the top of her desk and he leaned closer. 'That our file?'

Heather nodded, words fleeing as she felt the heat from his body roll over her.

'You're writing the report.'

His words were a statement that needed no confirmation and her heart grew heavy. How could she do this to Travis, even with his permission? How could she submit a report that would almost certainly always swing in the favour of the natural parents? She was no longer an unbiased party.

Tears stung her lids at the thought of Casey being ripped from his arms, from the only home she knew, from the memories of her mum, and thrown into a strange, loveless environment with a possibly murderous, dangerous man. One they couldn't pin a crime on. Frustrated and angry at the system, she swiped a tear from her cheek.

'Hey!' He tipped her chin up with his finger. 'What's up?'

She shook her head and cursed her soft heart for the tears that always surfaced when she was angry.

Before she could stop him, he was around the desk hauling her out of her chair and up against his chest. She meant to push him away, but instead her hands fisted around his T-shirt as his strong arm hugged her closer. The warmth of his palm cupped her head and he pressed a kiss to her hair.

'Oh, baby, you're only doing your job. You have to. It will kill me slowly, but the truth needs to be out there and I'll do everything in my power to make sure Zac Bannister doesn't get custody. I have a whole town on my side.'

The pain in Heather's chest grew as she listened to the steady thump of his heartbeat against her ear. 'But what if they do take her away from you?'

Travis released her and cupped her face between his hands, forcing her to look up at him. 'I'll have to build a case strong enough for them not to. It's time for me to get justice for Tracy. I'm not sure how, but I'm determined to prove he murdered her and why. The only way I can make it happen is for the world to know he had a motive.'

'Travis, what if he turns on you? Then Casey has no one.'

'I won't let that happen. Save your tears. Don't waste them on me.' He ran his thumbs over her cheeks, catching the teardrops on his skin.

He smelled like earth and spice, heat and sin, and when his green gaze held hers, all she could feel was him, all that mattered was that he was there, holding her. And that made her so terribly selfish when there was so much at stake.

His warmth drew her in as his eyes seared her soul. She flattened her palms against his chest, feeling his heartbeat stutter under her hands. She heard the slight hitch of his breath before his head descended and his lips touched hers.

And in that brief sweep of his mouth, she felt every emotion trapped inside his heart and the complex workings of his mind. Frustration, pain, turmoil, attraction—all these and more vied for her attention as she reached for him.

Those beautiful big hands, callused from physical work, moved from her face, trailed down her shoulders and arms before his fingers spread out along her back and pressed her against him.

There was nothing to do but melt against him, her hands travelling up over his shoulders, reaching around his neck to lace her fingers through his thick, blond hair and bring him closer still.

He breathed her name against her mouth and Heather opened her lips to swallow his words, the taste of him heating her blood, sending delicious shivers through her.

His hands followed the trail down her spine as his tongue engaged hers in a dance that had her fingers curling around the hair that brushed his collar.

Zac, Casey, the office they stood in, all faded into the mist that cloaked her mind until all she could do was feel, smell and taste Travis.

One hand in her hair, the other on her bottom, Travis lifted her against the ridge of his jeans. Through the thin material of her skirt, she felt him hard and long against her. With a whimper, she pressed against him, the sweet ache at the junction of her thighs seeking his heat.

Travis moaned and increased the pressure of his kiss as if he couldn't get far enough inside her mouth. She returned each stroke of his tongue feverishly as his hand found its way under her skirt to caress the sensitive skin on the underside of her thigh.

She shivered against him, reaching down between them to feel him, to run her palm up the length she now so badly wanted to feel inside her. His breath hissed out to mingle with hers, the taste of mint and coffee on his tongue.

Loosening the button on his jeans, her fingers played

with the tab on his zipper, inching it down as their mouths danced and his hands roamed her body, touching, kneading, sending sparks through her bloodstream. Then her palm made contact with the ridge concealed by his boxer briefs, close but not close enough. She let it slide the length of him, her own body crying out to feel the hardness.

Travis leaned her back against the desk, pressing into her, his hand removing hers and the barrier between them. As she arched her back, he came with her to follow the line of her neck with his lips and kissed a path to the valley between her breasts.

Wanton and needy, all logical thought fleeing, she squirmed deliciously under the brush of his touch. Then his mouth was on hers again, stealing her breath and her soul. Her hands couldn't work fast enough as she reached for the hem of his T-shirt.

Under her dress, his fingers skimmed the soft skin of her belly making the muscles clench with pleasure before travelling south where she wanted him most.

'Sweet Jesus, Heather, stop me now,' he said, lifting his head to look at her.

In his green eyes, alight with need, she saw the questions reflected there. Nothing in the world could make her say the words that would end this journey of sensations. She covered his hand with hers and guided it lower.

'Don't stop,' Heather whispered. 'Just this once, please.'

He lowered his head to her breasts and cushioned it there between them, his hand still moving under hers, seeking the heat between her legs. Shuddering against her, he found his target and his fingers began a slow dance.

Sensations like she'd never felt before swamped her as she writhed under him. He covered her mouth with his to muffle the noises coming from her lips. Behind her closed eyes, the world exploded. Her hands fisted in his hair as she devoured his talented mouth with hers. Her muscles clenched around his fingers as spasms of pleasure rattled her body until all that was left were the aftershocks.

Boneless, she floated back to the present. Gently, he lifted her from the desk and settled in the chair with her on his lap, his own unsatisfied need still apparent. Heather writhed against him.

'For God sake, sit still,' he groaned into her hair. 'I don't have protection on me.'

'Oh, Travis, I'm so sorry.'

'For what, sweetheart?'

'For this. Oh my God, what have I done?' Reality came crashing in chasing away the pleasure. 'I've compromised our professional relationship, your custody case. I've broken every rule in the book.' She buried her face in his neck, his scent filling her nose.

Regret rolled over her in waves, making her stomach churn. 'If they find out, they'll pull me from your case.'

'You didn't do it alone. I was there all the way with you. This is between you and me, no one needs to know.'

'It can't happen again.' Panic and guilt warred with self-disgust inside her. She should have said no. She should have stopped it before it started. His silence was all the agreement she needed. 'You should go. The ladies will be wondering why you're in here so long.'

Heather inched out of his lap and straightened the skirt of her dress, embarrassment making heat flare in her cheeks. She dragged her gaze away as he stood and fastened his jeans, clasped the desk behind her to stop herself from reaching for him again.

He tugged down the hem of his T-shirt over his zip, stepped closer and dropped a quick kiss to her lips. 'Whatever happens, Heather, I have no regrets about what happened here today and when this nightmare is over, we'll finish this.' He dragged a thumb over her swollen lips then turned away towards the door.

Heather watched him move, the stiffness in his back as he walked and the taut pull of his jeans across his backside as he leaned across to open the door. Her body missed him already.

The door swung open and three ladies almost fell over at his feet. Oh Holy Mother Mary's cats, had they heard what she and Travis had been doing? Her embarrassment level rose three-fold even as dread took hold of her stomach.

Travis nodded to the ladies, held his forefinger to his lips as though to shush them and winked. Then he was gone, leaving her with her hands to her flaming cheeks and speculation running high among the ladies.

Miss Turner, Mrs Everett and Bella watched her curiously, their eyes taking in Heather's messed up hair, wrinkled dress and burning face. 'Oh my!' said Mrs Everett, a sigh escaping her lips.

Chapter Ten

Travis cursed himself for the need to taste Heather's lips again and the hormones that had made him take the plunge. He made it halfway to his ute before he realised he hadn't got around to signing up for the wood chopping. He'd refused the rodeo and negotiated an alternative event. No way was he ready to get up on a bronc again, not even for the ladies of the CWA.

Damn it, now he'd have to go back and face the knowing glances of Bella, Mrs Everett and Miss Turner. He couldn't say for certain that they'd all had their ears to the door when he'd opened it, but he knew he could rely on Bella to keep them quiet and not spread any gossip about it if they had. Surely they wouldn't have heard much more than silence through the thick jarrah wood of the door anyhow.

He hadn't lied when he'd told Heather he didn't regret what had happened between them in the office, but what he did regret was the trouble it could cause for both of them.

The moment his lips touched Heather's cheek, he'd known he was in trouble. Deep trouble. She was his case worker, damn it. And now that he'd confessed to Heather about what happened to Tracy, she knew all the sordid details.

It could work in his favour or it might not, and he wasn't one to gamble with Casey's future. Sooner or later the truth would come out, because every day Casey grew older and lost her baby face, the more she got a Bannister look about her.

He slapped his hat onto his head and cursed the day Zac Bannister was born. Turning on his heel, he headed back to the Town Hall. He pushed through the door and aimed for the line at the events registration table.

'Fuck sakes,' he muttered as his nemesis pushed his way to the front of the queue.

'Where's that bloody Bailey?' Zac roared. 'Too chicken shit to register? All froth and no beer, ay?'

Travis gritted his teeth and ignored the itch in his fists.

'Yep, saw him bail earlier. Ran like a girl with her pants down. Reckon he knows when he's beaten.' He signed the register with a flourish, the reflective strips on his dirty yellow work shirt flashing under the fluorescent lights. Imitating a rooster, he turned and crowed his way back up the line. 'Oh, there he is! Showed up after all, did ya?'

'Arsehole,' muttered Travis, hatred for the man burning in his gut. He looked forward to the day karma bit him squarely in the arse.

'What was that, chicken shit?' Zac stopped next to him.

'You heard me.' Travis took his hat off and turned it through his hands.

Bannister looked around, pleased to see they had an audience as people turned their heads to see what the fuss was about. He took a step back and placed pudgy hands on his hips. 'Smart words coming from a man whose sister banged like a dunny door in a hurricane.'

In the queue behind him, truckie Pat Doolan muttered aloud what Travis was thinking.

'Fuckwit.'

Travis bit his lip and prayed for patience, but the insult to Tracy ripped open wounds that had barely had time to heal.

'I'm going to pretend you never said that. Move on, Bannister. You've done what you came to do.'

'Or what, you drongo? What if I don't move on?' He stepped into Travis' space.

Travis felt his temper rising and tried hard to clamp it down. He couldn't afford to rise to Bannister's taunts, so he aimed for dismissal. He stepped forward as the queue moved, putting space between them.

'You think you're better than anyone else in Wongan Creek. Bloody Baileys are no better than cashed up bogans whose women squeal like bush pigs when their legs are open.'

Anger, blood red and hot, bubbled up like a volcano inside him. Travis straightened his shoulders and stiffened his spine, his fingers clenching into fists at his side. The little bastard wouldn't get away with that. Not when Tracy had screamed at the hands of this filthy mongrel. His own throat had ached for days after her death. All he needed was the evidence to prove it.

Sensing his anger, the people in the queue around him moved away, except for big Pat Doolan.

'Shut your mug, you fool,' the truckie warned Zac.

Travis had never had much time for Pat Doolan. He was as shady as the Bannisters were. But right now, he agreed with the man. Apparently Zac was too dumb to take the hint.

'Have you ever made a woman scream, Bailey?'

He leaned in and Travis caught a whiff of whiskey on his breath as Zac explained in detail a repulsive version of how to pleasure a woman. There was nothing nice or romantic about it at all. If what he'd described was what he'd done to Tracy that night, the man deserved the death penalty. Travis' blood pressure rose along with his disgust.

'That's what I'd like to do to the little social worker because you wouldn't have a clue how to give it to a woman like her.'

White hot fury gripped him and common sense fled in its wake. Travis' fists curled around the disgusting little man's shirt and hauled him up on his toes.

'If you lay a hand on another woman in this town, I swear to God I'll rip your dick off and shove it up your arse. Now get out of my face before I forget my manners,' he snarled.

He shoved Zac away and watched him stagger back. Around him, silence filled the room as people watched, held their breath and waited for the first punch to be thrown. Travis turned to walk away instead.

With a roar, Zac launched forward and wrapped his arms around Travis' waist. The momentum sent them crashing to the hard jarrah floor, the thud echoing around the hall.

Travis barely had time to notice Heather's office door open before they rolled and Zac's meaty fist connected with his jaw. His head snapped back against the floor with a thump. Pain exploded in his brain, leaving him light-headed.

He saw the next fist coming as it plunged towards his left eye. He tried to block it with his forearm but his reflexes were too slow with his head spinning like a top. Zac's knuckles smashed into the side of his face and it became a fight for survival.

Travis heard Heather's shout, ignored it as he raised his knee and shoved it into Zac's chest with a roar of his own. Zac staggered back, winded but not deterred because he came back for more.

This time Travis was prepared. He held up his feet encased in steel-capped boots stopping the big ape short as they connected with his groin.

Travis felt the shudder of the impact all the way through his leg muscles. They'd be damn sore later but it was worth it to see the bastard crash to the floor cradling his nuts.

He staggered to his feet, tempted to go over and stomp on his balls for good measure, to make sure the dickhead didn't use them for a very long time, but Heather barred his way.

'That's enough, Travis Bailey.'

His chest heaved as he tried to catch his breath, his eyes never leaving the man now rocking on the floor in agony.

'Someone get Doc Benson in here,' Heather called as Travis swayed on his feet.

He wiped the side of his face on his arm. It came away sticky with blood.

Heather's tiny hand pressed firmly into his stomach. 'Sit down, idiot.'

He sank to his haunches and then dropped on his backside, the room whirling around him. Elbows on his bent knees, he cradled his head against his fists, wincing as his knuckles grazed the tender spot on the side of his face.

'What the hell was that about? Look at you! Jesus, Travis, what were you thinking?'

He wanted to answer her, but his jaw ached too much. He shook his head and regretted that too as pain speared his scalp. With a moan, he leaned back and lay down on the hard wooden floor.

'I'd rather have you kiss me better than go through it all again.'

'You're dreaming. What were you doing picking a fight with that bully? This isn't the schoolyard.'

Travis covered his eyes with his forearm, hoping to ease the headache pounding between his eyes. 'He started it.'

'Well you didn't have to go and finish it, did you?'

'You're very sexy when you're angry,' he said, peeping out from under his arm.

Heather clamped her mouth shut, her eyes glittering angrily, suspiciously wet.

'I did warn you not to waste your tears on me.' He winced as she slapped the arm he held against his head. 'Ouch.'

'May the cat eat you, and may the devil eat the cat, you ... shit!'

'I'm pretty sure you've used that one on me before,' he muttered as he heard the click of her heels retreating across the floor. 'Except for the shit bit, that's new.'

A couple of hours, three stitches at the corner of his eye and two painkillers later, he sat beside Heather in her four-wheel drive groaning as she found every pothole in the road to go through.

'Jesus, Heather, go easy.'

He moaned as she swung into the turn of his driveway and rattled over the drain grate. His ribs ached from the thumping they'd taken when Zac had tackled him to the floor.

She mumbled something he wasn't sure was English and most likely another of her Irish descendants' curses. He hung onto the armrest on the door and prayed for the end of their journey.

'Mrs Everett will drop Casey and Harry off. Just as well they had a play date over at Benji's while you were brawling like a hooligan.'

'Harry won't be happy if he hears you calling it a play date.' She glared at him and he wisely closed his mouth, saying nothing until they pulled up at his front door. 'Wasn't a play date. It was canasta with Benji's grandad.'

But then again when two old men were well on their way to their second childhood, he guessed it could be called a play date.

He winced as Heather slammed the door. Okay, so she was mad at him. That was cool. But with Bannister's taunts ringing in his ears, he wouldn't let her make him feel guilty for fighting back.

If he hadn't, Zac would have had no qualms about smashing his face in, and he had his girls to protect. *Oh shit, no.* Girl, only one girl could be considered his and that was Casey. And even that was touch and go.

'Do you need help getting out?'

The girl he couldn't think of as his looked up at him with those eyes like hot chocolate sauce, and even if they were still at boiling point, they were damn sexy pools he wanted to dive into.

'I'll be okay.' He slid down off the seat onto the dusty drive, the contact jarring the stiffening muscles in his legs. 'Thanks for bringing me home.'

'Doc Benson didn't want you driving. I didn't have an alternative.'

'I'm sorry.'

'You will be.' Heather sighed. 'Go on … go inside. Standing out in this heat won't do that thick head of yours any good. Doc Benson says I'm to stay with you. The painkillers will make you sleepy soon. We have to check you every few hours for signs of concussion. I told the doc your head's too hard for that.'

'I'm feeling the love, thanks.' He tried to grin but his jaw ached with the effort. 'Jesus, did he break my jaw?'

'No, but you've got some nice bruises there.' Her tone softened, the brush of her hand on his jaw gentle against the tender flesh. 'Somehow I think Zac's suffering more than you are.'

'I bloody well hope so,' said Travis. 'I hope he never

gets to use his balls again. And just for the record, if he doesn't, I will have succeeded in protecting every woman within a hundred kilometre radius of Wongan Creek from his idea of romance. He's a mean bastard, Heather. Promise me you'll stay far away and never be alone anywhere near him.'

Heather took his arm and placed it around her shoulders, sending delicious tingles travelling up all the way to his heart then hooked her arm around his waist.

'That's one promise I'll give you. Come on, let's get you inside. I need a cup of tea.'

No way in hell would he argue with a woman who fit so perfectly against him, even if she was only offering support for his injured body. A guy could get used to this kind of pampering.

At the top of the stairs, he leaned his pounding head on the wall next to the front door.

'Keys?' Heather held out her hand.

'Front pocket on the right.'

'Last I knew there was nothing wrong with your hands.' She eyed him squarely.

'I'm using them to stop my head from falling off my shoulders.' He demonstrated by cupping his face.

Heather chuckled, a wicked light in her eyes. 'Fine then. I'm going in,' she warned.

And oh God, did she take her own sweet, punishing time about it. The flat of her palm grazed his abdomen as long fingers for such small hands reached into his pocket at a painfully slow pace.

Her fingers played around in search of the key, coming close to a stiffening muscle that had nothing to do with his recent rumble in the Town Hall, but ached no less for it. He sucked in a breath that hurt his ribs and let it loose on a groan.

'You're killing me.'

Finally, she fished the keys from his pocket with a grin and dangled them in front of him. He closed his sore eye which was already swelling shut and watched her insert the key into the lock. He caught the exact moment she twigged she'd been conned.

'You sneaky bastard!'

'We don't lock our doors here in Wongan Creek, but that was a helluva lot of fun.' Although he thought the joke might be on him as he pushed away from the wall with yet another ache to contend with.

She glanced at the zipper on his jeans. 'I can tell. Pity you're all banged up already then, isn't it?' She swanned into the house, leaving him to follow her deliciously rounded arse and wishing he hadn't gone back to sign up for the wood chopping.

Shit!

Chapter Eleven

Heather sipped her tea and watched Travis sleep. Long golden lashes caressed the skin above his cheekbones, marred only by the purple bruise forming around his eye socket and the angry red cut stitched closed by Doc Benson.

She sighed. Her heart had almost stopped when she'd opened the office door to see what the noise was. And then to see Zac Bannister deliver those blows ... God, she'd thought he'd kill Travis.

Her fingers tightened around the mug. After that kiss in the office, she'd totally lost her heart to this complex, funny, kind and lovable man prepared to sacrifice his own life for the people he cared for.

No way could she let the Bannisters ever have custody of Casey, not when her uncle was the best father a girl could wish for. But to do that meant distancing herself emotionally from them both, and she wasn't at all sure how she could manage that.

Travis stirred in his sleep, his hand moving over his ribs where yet another bruise blossomed. She let her eyes travel the length of his chest to his abdomen. Hard muscles and sinew, sculptured by physical work made for an impressive man-scape. Her hands itched to touch him again.

She was still mad at him though, for getting into the fight in the first place, for letting that nasty piece of work rile him up to a point where it involved fists. If the Bannisters laid charges, it would go on his file at the Department of Health and Welfare who didn't look kindly upon violence of any sort in a guardian.

The ladies had assured her it wasn't Travis who'd started the fight and she believed them, but he'd fought back and was clearly the victor. The only bit about that, which gave her a great deal of satisfaction, was that Zac Bannister's pain would surely be more severe than Travis'. Perhaps it would teach him a lesson. Then again, he was the sort who never learned.

Heather smoothed the shock of white fringe away from his forehead and let her hand and fingers slide gently down his cheek to the roughness of his unshaven jaw. Her insides tightened with want as he turned his head and pressed into her touch.

Oh Saints, how awesome it would be to wake up to that face on the pillow next to hers. To see that sexy grin in the early light at dawn and trail her fingers across that firm, warm body.

When he'd held her earlier, she'd had a taste of what it would be like to make love with Travis Bailey, a dream she could visualise, but dared not make come true.

How sweet it would be to steal a kiss from those full lips as he slept. His mouth was hard and firm, his kiss full of passion and heart, his tongue skilled in the art of dance. And lordy, the feel of his body against hers, the length of him promising unbridled passion and fulfilment.

Oh good heavens, Heather Penney, listen to yourself! Lusting after a man you can't have.

She drew her hand away from his face and wrapped her fingers around her mug instead. Her focus had to lie with the welfare of an almost six-year-old. Even though it was clear that Travis was the one who deserved to keep her, the department and parties involved didn't always agree.

Heather checked the slim gold watch on her wrist, a little piece of her mum she carried with her. It was almost time for Mrs Everett to bring Casey and Harry home, and Travis would need to take more painkillers soon.

She abandoned the idea of kissing him awake. That would only lead to trouble. Unfolding her legs from under her, she stood and waited for the pins and needles to subside before walking to the kitchen and rinsing out her mug.

She grabbed a packet of frozen peas from the freezer, moved back to the sofa in the lounge room, and because she was still a little mad at him, placed the ice cold packet on his left eye.

'Fu ... far out!' His body jerked against the cushions of the sofa and he glared at her from out of his good eye. 'There'll be payback for that one, baby.'

'Toughen up, big guy. How's your head?'

'When it defrosts, I'll tell you. Oh God, how can that feel so good yet so painful at the same time?' He placed a hand on the packet of peas to hold it in place.

'It's almost time for Casey to come home. Should I ask Harry to stay the night with you?'

His cheeky grin was lopsided due to the swelling in his jaw. 'I'd rather you stay the night.'

Heather ignored the shaft of lust that speared through her at the thought. 'Can't. I have plans to watch reruns of *Heartbeat* on telly.'

Travis chuckled then groaned. 'That'll be the first time I've been stood up for PC Mike Bradley.' He pushed himself up, leaning on his elbow on the sofa cushion, one hand still holding tightly onto the impromptu cold press. 'Seriously though, Harry wouldn't remember he's meant to be looking after me. What if he gets up, doesn't recognise his surroundings and wanders off during the night?'

Heather sighed. He had a point. Harry wouldn't remember to wake him up every couple of hours to check for signs of concussion either.

'If you're worried about being alone with me ...'

'I'm not!' Heather answered, too quickly.

Travis raised the eyebrow that didn't hurt at her. 'You're not, hey? Okay then. In case you are though, we'll be well chaperoned by Casey. I bet my farm she won't leave my side tonight.' A hint of sadness crept into his voice. 'If I get so much as a cut on my finger, she thinks I'll die and leave her. She's gonna hate this.'

'Should've thought about that before you got into a scuffle then.'

He removed the packet of peas from his eye to reveal the swollen mess. 'You know I had no chance of avoiding the confrontation. He came at me. There are witnesses who'll confirm it. Even his mate, Pat Doolan saw that.'

Heather took the peas from his hand and pressed it back to his eye. 'I know, but let me be mad at you for a bit longer. It makes me feel better. Lie down.'

'Feel better about what?' Travis covered her hand with his and lay back down, his head against the armrest on the sofa.

'About what happened before the fight.' She shivered at the warmth of his touch and pulled her hand from under his.

'I'm not going to lie to you. I like you more than I should.'

'For Casey's sake we have to let it go.'

Travis lowered the packet of peas and looked at her, one green eye bright, the other red and puffy. Her heart did a little dance because even injured, he was still a handsome devil who stirred things in her she'd never felt for anyone else before.

With her mum so ill, there'd never been much time to date, but on the odd occasion she had, she'd felt an attraction to her partners. Just never this deep, heart-wrenching, gut-twisting, aching need to be with someone. And this was the first time she'd felt comfortable with a man who enjoyed silence as much as he did conversation, who loved so deeply and cared so much for the people around him. Perhaps in another time, another world ...

'Come here.'

The sexiness of his request washed over her, reached in, and tied her stomach into knots of desire to do as he asked, but her mind screamed resistance.

'No.' The words came out on a whisper without much conviction, so she tried again, 'No!'

He tugged gently until she toppled onto his chest and their legs tangled on the sofa. Travis adjusted her weight to perfectly align with the length of his body, wincing as her weight tested the bruising on his ribcage.

His hard, firm body pressed against hers, his warmth

seeping through her skin and melting the resistance in the muscles she held tight. His big palm pressed her head against his chest and she could hear the soft thump of his heart, feel the rise and fall of his breathing as the tension eased out of her.

Giving in to his warmth, she let her fingers rest on the skin at the curve of his ribcage. Then his arms were around her hugging her to him and she knew there was no place she'd rather be. Ahead of them lay a battle, behind them a struggle. For now she wanted to pretend neither of those existed.

Underneath her, his body warmed and grew harder, starting a delicious tingle where she lay in the cradle of his hips. Heather inhaled his scent — a mix of man and the arnica cream Doc Benson had slathered on his ribs. She wrinkled her nose.

'You've got to let me go, Travis. Casey could walk in any moment.'

'I have an ear out for the bus. Mrs Everett won't drive anything else. Let me hold you a while? I might not get another chance now.'

Heather lifted her head to look at him, and because he felt so good against her, she said, 'Okay.'

He grinned that bruised, lopsided smile then lifted her face to his to press a soft, tender kiss to her lips. 'Ouch,' he whispered. 'That bastard will pay for my sore lip.'

'Might be a good thing.' Heather laughed then sobered. 'Travis?'

'Heather,' he teased.

'If things were different ...' She closed her eyes against the soothing stroke of his hand on her hair and followed the movement of his body with hers as he released a deep sigh.

'I know.'

The rattle of the bus coming up the drive reached Heather's ears. 'Let me go now,' she said gently, not wanting to leave the warmth of his arms but knowing she had to. With one last squeeze, he let go and groaned a little as she eased off him. 'You might need that frozen pack somewhere else now,' she teased.

He glared at her out of one eye as he slapped the peas back on his eye and tossed a cushion across his groin, his fingers clutching the woven material of the cover. 'One day we'll finish this.'

With every bone and hormone in her body, Heather hoped so as she waited for the bus to stop and then Casey came hurtling in through the front door.

'Uncle Trav!' She stopped short at the sight of Travis sprawled out on the sofa. 'What happened? Are you okay?'

Travis winced as he sat up and swung his legs to the floor. He kept hold of his ice pack while he held out an arm to hug his niece closer. Her fingers peeled back the edge of the packet.

'Ouch. Why's your eye all red and purple? Did you get bitten by a spider? Ooh, I hope it's not a red back or a white tail, cos they can make you very sick.'

Travis tossed the rapidly defrosting packet of peas onto the sofa. 'No, sweet pea. Now, you know we always promised to tell each other the truth, so I'll tell you I had an argument with Zac today and things got a bit out of hand.' He pointed to his eye. 'And this is the result.'

'He got you good.' Her lip pouted as she touched his cheek with her tiny hand. Heather's heart melted a little more.

'He sure did, but you know how I told you to always walk away from bullies?'

'Yeah?'

'I still want you to do that. The trick is to never turn your back on them as you're leaving because sometimes they take you by surprise.'

'Okay. I'm sorry he hurt you, Uncle Trav. He's just a mean bully.'

Travis pulled her into a hug. 'Yes, he is.'

'Is it my fault you got hurt, Uncle Trav?'

'No, sweet pea. What makes you think that?'

Casey's fingers traced the skin under the bruise growing near Travis' eye. 'Did I do something naughty that made the man angry with you?'

Travis frowned and flicked a look at Heather.

Heather's senses went on high alert but she couldn't

think of a reason why Casey might think Travis getting hurt was her fault. Perhaps she related what had happened to their confrontation with Zac in Bella's café.

Travis ruffled Casey's curls and hugged her tighter. 'Not at all, sweet pea. You haven't done anything wrong. He's just a mean bully like you said. He's the naughty one, not you. Now go get cleaned up and we'll start on dinner soon.'

She kissed him loudly on his uninjured cheek. 'Okay. I'll take good care of you, Uncle Trav, and I'll try extra hard to be good.' She turned to Heather. 'Hi, Miss Penney.' And then surprised her by throwing her arms around her waist and hugging her tightly. 'Thank you for taking care of Uncle Trav.'

'You're welcome.' Heather hugged her back. 'You may call me Heather, you know.'

Casey let go and grinned. 'Thank you, Heather. My mummy always used to say that it was polite to call people Mister or Mrs or Miss until they said you could call them by their name.'

Heather pressed a kiss to the little girl's forehead. 'Your mummy was a very smart lady.'

'I know,' said Casey. 'Are you staying for dinner?'

'I might have to stay the night to keep an eye on your uncle. We have to make sure he doesn't get sick from the bump on his head.'

Casey's eyes widened. 'Oh! Like con ... concu ...

confu ... oh, what's the word again?' She stamped her boot on the hard jarrah floorboards.

'Concussion? Yes, darling. So we have to wake him up a couple of times through the night to make sure his headache doesn't get worse, okay?'

Casey nodded her head. 'Okay. I'll go clean up and get some sheets for the bed in the spare room. It used to be my mummy's room. I like to sit in there and talk to her sometimes because then I can pretend she's still with me.'

Heather's heart squeezed with sadness. 'Oh, sweetheart ...'

Casey smiled up at her, her cherubic face pink and grubby from her play date with Benji. 'It's okay. It doesn't make me sad anymore. It makes me happy cos I can tell her everything about my day.'

'Well, that's a very nice thing to do for your mum. I'm sure she loves listening to your stories.' Heather knelt to give the little girl a hug. 'Now off you go and clean up then we'll look at making dinner.'

'Oh you don't have to do that,' said Marge Everett, coming into the room with a bag in each hand. 'I've got a nice casserole right here with a salad. Young Travis, you get the protein shake because you won't be able to chew with that jaw. You're lucky it's not broken!'

Travis groaned. 'Can't we mash up the casserole instead?'

Marge gave him a stern look. 'You'll drink the

protein shake like a good boy and there'll be no complaints. We have to get you back on your feet and a good healthy shake will do that. It contains organic veggies straight from my garden, I'll have you know.'

Travis winced as Heather smothered a giggle behind her hand. 'I'll be sure to watch him finish it,' she said, ignoring the warning look he shot her that promised payback later.

Harry wandered over, hands behind his back and studied Travis' face intently. He let out a low whistle. 'He got you good, didn't he, mate? Bloody drongo.'

'I got him a far better shot,' mumbled Travis.

Harry raised an eyebrow. 'Right in the gonads, I heard. Good lad.'

'Harry!' scolded Heather.

'What? Bloody good thing he did, I reckon. That little sod might leave the women alone for a while. I'd like to stay and chat but I've got to go herd the cattle before it gets dark.'

Travis pressed the rapidly defrosting packet of peas to his forehead to ease a new ache. 'Harry?'

'What?'

'You don't have any cattle.'

'Oh. Well, the sheep then.' Harry flexed his fingers and frowned.

'We herded all five of them into my bottom paddock ready for shearing this morning before you got to work on fixing the tractor.'

'Ah ... right.' Confusion blurred Harry's rheumy eyes further.

Heather looked at Travis, worry etched into his brow. He turned his gaze to hers and in it she saw concern mixed with his pain. She turned to Harry. 'Why don't you stay here tonight? We have to keep an eye on Travis and I could use some help.'

'Nah, can't do that, matey. Dog's all alone on the farm then. She still needs to be fed.'

Marge Everett stepped forward. 'Why don't I drop Harry off and keep him company for a while, hey?'

'Be a bit like the old days, hey, Marge? Before you married Errol? We could ... ya know ...' He winked at Marge playfully.

'Now don't go getting any ideas, you old codger. I'm only doing this so young Travis can get a good night's sleep and not have to worry about you.'

Harry sighed. 'A man can hope.'

Travis groaned and lay back down on the couch. 'No amount of painkillers in the world will get that image out of my head.'

'Mrs Everett, it would be a great help if you could drop Harry home, thank you.' Heather put a hand on Harry's shoulder. 'I'll stop by on my way through tomorrow morning for a cup of tea.'

'Righto, mate. Come on, Marge, we've got a date with the kettle.'

Heather walked them to the door and waved them

off before returning to the lounge to find Travis had moved from the couch. She found him with his head stuck in the fridge, holding a cold beer bottle to his jaw.

'You're not thinking of drinking that, are you?'

'Nah, it's just colder than the packet of peas right now. Although the beer mixed with the painkillers might help get the image of Harry and Marge together out of my head.'

Heather laughed. 'Here, sit down and let me find something else to cool it down.'

'There should be one of those instant ice packs in the first aid kit under the sink.'

Heather opened the cupboard door and bent to retrieve it. As she straightened up, she caught the burning look in his eyes and felt the answering dip in her belly.

'You've got to stop looking at me like that. It's no good for either of us.'

He sat relaxed in the chair, back curved, strong thighs apart stretching at the denim of his jeans. His lap looked more inviting than it should. The temptation to straddle him where he sat, to kiss that mouth, caress the warm skin of his face and body— it was all too appealing. His eyes narrowed on her face, hot and searching, as if he knew she was tempted and daring her to do it.

'Stop that now, Travis Bailey, or I'll have to blindfold you.'

He choked back a laugh. 'Really? That sounds terribly kinky, Miss Penney.' The suggestiveness in his tone had her shivering with heat.

'All right, enough now. Go on back to the sofa while I pour your protein shake and put the casserole in the oven for me and Casey.'

'Way to kill a man's passion,' he grumbled, pushing himself out of the chair with one hand on the kitchen table. 'Protein shake.' He snorted.

As he passed her, his arm brushed against her. He stopped, pulled her into his arms and kissed her softly on the lips, wincing a little at the contact.

Plastered against his chest with those beautiful arms anchoring her there, Heather's head spun from the feel of his mouth on hers. She wanted so much more but then he set her away and dropped his arms from around her.

'Thanks for looking after me. A man could get used it, you know.' With one last searing look, the hurt curbed only by the swelling of one eye, he moved around her and went quietly on bare feet.

Heather clamped a hand on her chest to still the erratic beat and prayed she could withstand the call of attraction before it broke her heart.

Chapter Twelve

Heather stretched on the soft mattress, aware of the silence around her except for the early morning call of the parrots and the cries of black crows in the trees. The unfamiliar bed was comfortable and she'd slept well in between checking up on Travis.

She'd thought about sleeping in the chair next to his bed, but the temptation to crawl into the bed next to him was too great. He'd been right about Casey though. She hadn't left his side all night.

Heather sat and swung her legs to the floor. At least she'd been able to keep an eye on them both. The last time she'd checked in, Casey had been tucked up in her sleeping bag on a mattress on the floor, her teddy squashed in against her and her thumb in her mouth.

Moving to the bathroom across the hall, Heather

located a tube of toothpaste to finger-brush her teeth. God, she was dying for a cup of tea. She tugged on the skirt of her dress to straighten it and smoothed out the wrinkles as best she could. There was little she could do for her tangled mass of curls.

Quietly, she pushed open the door to Travis' bedroom from where she'd left it ajar in case he called out during the night. He slept soundly on his back with Casey curled into the crook of his arm on top of the covers. Heather's heart softened. Somewhere before dawn the little girl must have crept in beside him. Her love and concern for her uncle couldn't have been clearer. If they were ever parted, it would hurt Casey deeply. She had to make sure that never happened.

In sleep, they looked so alike, the Bailey genes Travis and his twin had shared obvious in the little girl's features. Except for the nose. The shape looked awfully like Zac Bannister's, just smaller. And that struck the fear of God into her.

Travis stirred, his right eye flickering open while the other stayed swollen closed. 'Hey.'

'Hey, yourself. How's the head?' she whispered, not wanting to wake Casey just yet.

He pressed a hand to his face. 'Head's fine, face hurts.'

'Poor baby,' Heather teased. 'I'll get you fresh water and painkillers.'

'What time is it?'

'After half six.'

'Shit. I should be fixing the bloody tractor. If I don't harvest the canola by the end of next week, it'll be too late.'

He eased his arm out from under Casey's head and threw back the covers. She whimpered in her sleep and turned over to cuddle down under them. Travis sat up and tucked her in.

'You heard Doc Benson yesterday. Until he gives you the all clear, you're not to do a thing.'

He stood, dwarfing her with his height and width. Gentle hands wrapped around her upper arms. 'You want to stop me, sweetheart?' he asked, his voice a low throb in the room. 'A man's land waits for no one unfortunately. Although, if my ribs didn't hurt so damn much I could happily be kept from it in other ways.'

Those magic hands ran the length of her arms and up again, leaving a trail of happy goosebumps in their wake and a vision of ways to distract him from his work.

Heather tried hard to concentrate on his words, but his bare chest was level with her face and all she could see was him.

After his shower the night before, he'd pulled on a pair of cotton sleep shorts that hung tantalisingly low on his hips and revealed a dusky trail from below his navel to under the elastic waistband. Standing this close, she was left in no doubt of what that trail led to. Temptation she had to resist.

Raising her hand, she let her palm rest on the warmth of his chest for a moment before easing out of his reach. 'I'll put the kettle on for tea,' she said and turned to walk out the door, willing herself not to look back because if she did, she wouldn't be able to resist him.

In the kitchen, she filled the kettle with water and flicked the switch to set it to boil. Distance between them was the key, she reminded herself. Once Doc Benson gave Travis the all clear, she would bring their relationship back to the professional level where it belonged.

She couldn't allow her feelings for him to compromise his guardianship of Casey. Any hint of a scandal or relationship between them would put the little girl's future in jeopardy. She couldn't allow personal feelings to get in the way of professionalism, although it seemed it was too late. Both of them had her heart in their hands already.

Travis came through dressed in jeans and a dark T-shirt as she poured the hot water into the mugs for the tea. Ignoring how sexy he looked, she jiggled the teabags until the dark liquid seeped out and mixed with the clear. She watched the swirl of tea sink to the bottom of the mug and felt the warmth of him against her back, his hands flat on her hips.

'Thank you for staying with me.'

The press of his mouth against her hair had her

leaning back into him, her eyes closed as a reply dried up on her tongue. When those hands folded across her tummy, she didn't have words to protest. Warm lips travelled down her cheek as he pressed her back into him.

'You taste so good,' he whispered against her ear, nibbled the lobe and proceeded to press butterfly kisses against her neck.

Heather covered his hands with hers and pressed them closer. Oh God, just to enjoy his touch for a moment longer before facing the cold, hard slap of reality. What harm could it do? She allowed her head to fall back against his shoulder as he let go of her hand and his fingers travelled across her ribcage, grazing the underside of her breasts.

'Travis.'

His name came out on a sigh. She should tell him to stop but the flick of his tongue on her skin felt too good, too damn right. And when the palm of his hand caressed the roundness of her breast, Heather lost the will to protest or pretend she wasn't enjoying every stroke and press of his hands.

His kiss was light on her lips as he turned her in his arms, his tongue teasing a response from hers. She let her hands wander, encounter the growth of stubble along his jaw that scraped her palms, and cupped her hands on his face.

'What if Casey comes in?' Heather didn't want him

to stop but they had to think of the consequences if the little girl wandered in.

'She'll sleep for another hour yet unless I wake her.'

Behind her, he moved the mugs of tea and lifted her up onto the bench so her body was level with his then he stepped between her legs and she felt him, hard and thick, against her.

'Sweet Jesus, Heather, you drive a man crazy,' he lifted his head to whisper, his eyes searching hers.

In them she saw lust, desire, need ... and something deeper. All the reasons to deny him didn't seem important anymore, only this heart-rending urgency to have him inside her counted. To ride the length of him and let go of everything holding them back, to give themselves over to their need for each other at this moment in time, and chase the dark shadows away for a while.

Heather twisted closer, shifted to accommodate him, almost crying out at the rub of his jeans against the junction of her thighs. Then her hands were on his zipper, dragging it down, reaching for him.

He moaned against her lips. 'Fuck. Sweetheart, please tell me you want this?'

'I do. Oh, Travis, I do.' Desperation made her words sound like a sob.

'Whatever happens ...' he murmured, closing his eyes as if he didn't want to face reality either.

'Hush.'

She took control of his lips, not wanting words to come between them. Later they would worry about consequences, but right now in their own little world with no one to witness their spiral into desperate need for each other, all she wanted was Travis.

Her hands eased his jeans from his hips while his worked their way up her skirt to the elastic of her silk panties, touching each sensitive part of her skin as they went, driving her crazy until she wanted to cry from the pleasurable pain.

Then he was pulling her towards him, nudging at her entrance. She wrapped her arms around his neck, her body alive with wanting him, her mind aware of his injuries and the need to be gentle. He lifted her up in his arms and she slid down on him, ready for the width and length of him, surprised as he filled her, loving the feel of him, slick and hot.

'Don't hold back, baby,' Travis whispered. 'A little pain will be worth the risk. You can kiss me better.' He smiled against her mouth and Heather kissed him harder.

Wincing a little, he backed away from the counter and sat on a chair, letting her straddle his lap. He thrust into her and she followed his rhythm, pouring her soul into it because if this was the only dance they ever had together, she'd damn well make it count.

Climax came fast in a flurry of kisses and hands. Heather collapsed against Travis' chest, his hand cupping her head, the other holding her close. Her heart pounded in time with his, the silence stretching between them as each caught their breath.

Heather didn't want to leave the comfort of his arms, not when everything about being there made it feel like the right place to be. She closed her eyes to listen to him gain control over his breathing, ride the wave of the rise and fall of his chest, and absorb the heat of his body under hers. She never wanted to leave this safe haven.

Travis stroked her hair, twirled it around his fingers and gave it a little tug. 'Still awake there, sweetheart?'

She smiled into the curve of his neck, nipping the skin with her lips. 'Barely.'

'I think our tea might be cold.'

'You think?' Heather placed her hands on his chest and eased away from him.

He cupped her face in his hands, a frown on his brow. 'We good here?'

Guilt edged its way into her mind as the euphoria slowly wore off and the impact of what they'd done came crashing down. Even so, she could not bring herself to regret what had happened between them.

'We're good. You'd best let me up now before Casey finds us like this.'

He grinned. 'Wanna shower?'

The teasing light and promise in his eyes almost had her saying yes. 'No. Well, yes, but I should be going home for that.'

Travis sighed. 'You can't leave me alone until Doc Benson gives me the all clear.'

He shifted her on his lap, slipping free from her sheath. Emptiness filled the space inside her and she wanted to call him back. How was it he made her feel whole again, like there was something to fight for if those DNA tests for the Motor Neurone gene proved positive, but still too much stood between them.

She swung her leg back over his and stood up, his hands on her hips for balance. Was it wrong to want him again?

He stood and zipped up his jeans. 'How about I give you some fresh clothes and a towel, and you can take a nice leisurely shower on your own?' The look on his face told her he'd much rather be in there with her. 'You and Mum are about the same size. She left some jeans and shirts behind you could use.'

Heather nodded. 'That would be good, thanks.'

He stroked a long finger down her cheek and looked deep into her eyes before pressing a slow, heated kiss to her lips. Then he grabbed her hand and tugged her down the hall towards the bathroom.

'Fresh towels are in the cupboard next to the loo. I'll leave the clothes outside for you.' He gave her a little nudge to move, his lips pulled in a determined line. 'If I don't, I won't be able to leave you again, Heather.'

And because her heart pounded as she seriously

considered what that would mean, she closed the door on him.

Holy fucking bat shit. Travis raked a hand through his hair as he stared at the closed door. He'd screwed Heather in his kitchen. Guilt came crashing down, the weight of it on his shoulders making him lean back against the bathroom door.

What the fuck was he thinking? Casey could have walked in on them, except he knew her sleeping habits well. Hell, Harry could have waltzed in and copped an eyeful. The only reason he had nothing to fear from the CWA ladies and the rest of the town stopping by at that awkward moment would be because those who weren't asleep were otherwise engaged on their farms. *Hooley Dooley.*

Not just that, but he'd put her in a position that made her job difficult, compromised her professional involvement by making it personal.

He pushed away from the door and walked down the hall to his parents' room where he rummaged around for clean clothes. It should never have happened, but God damn it, he couldn't regret it. The timing sucked to be head over arse for a girl he couldn't have—yet.

On the way back, he checked in on Casey and found her sleeping soundly. Good. That meant he might be able to sneak in a shower too before anyone caught him reeking of sex and Heather — a combination he could easily grow used to.

He dropped the clothes at the bathroom door and leaned his head against it, listening to the water running from the shower, thinking of Heather under the spray. And because that made him horny as hell again, he slapped a palm against the door frame and headed back to the kitchen. Screw the tea. This called for coffee. Strong shit.

Chapter Thirteen

Dressed in her borrowed clothes, Heather listened to the sounds of Travis collecting his things for a shower and sipped the coffee he'd made her. The strength of the brew would put hair on her teeth, but at least it provided the wake-up call she needed. Caffeine swept through her bloodstream. She might not sleep for a week now.

She heard the slam of the bathroom door and the rattle of the pipes as the water pressure built. Every nerve ending in her body could relate as she felt her own blood pressure rise at the thought of Travis naked under the spray.

To keep her hands busy, she unpacked the dishes from the dishwasher, dried them and searched for the places they belonged. As she put the last glass on the shelf in the cupboard, her mobile phone rang.

Frowning, she looked at the number and answered the call.

'What the hell is going on in that town?'

Heather winced as her boss' voice boomed down the line. Elliott Crawford was a straight-shooter who only saw the black and white of the law, never the grey.

'I'm sorry, Elliott. What do you mean?'

'Have you checked your emails yet?'

'Well no, not yet. Why?' Heather placed the mug on the table, unease seeping through her.

'A man named Zac Bannister has come forward. He's claiming to be Casey Bailey's father.' Ice edged Elliott's tone. 'Did you know about this?'

Dread and regret that she hadn't written that damned report yet mixed like concrete in her stomach. 'There is speculation that might be the case but nothing to prove it. He's never come forward before.'

'And you didn't think to mention it?' he yelled. 'Jesus Christ, Heather! Do you understand what this means for the department?'

Paperwork, lots of paperwork. 'I was working on a report, but there was an incident —'

Elliott cut her off. 'Yes, I've been informed about the incident too. Bannister has filed a complaint of misconduct by a guardian.'

Heather snorted. 'How hypocritical of him when he started the damn fight. Elliott, please listen to me. There is more to this story.'

'Well it would be bloody nice of you to tell it to me. I have the director's office breathing down my neck because he cc'd them in on the email. You'd better have a damn good report written up for me with all the details when I get there tomorrow,' he barked.

'I will.' Her hand trembled on the phone. Oh God, how had this spiralled so quickly?

'And, Heather?' His voice was deathly quiet with control.

She shivered. *Sweet Mother Mary*. What else could go wrong? 'Yes?'

'Bannister has laid a complaint against you too. For harassment.'

'You can't be serious!' Nausea grew in her stomach. 'He's dreaming. I'm the one who should be filing the complaint against him!'

'And that means even more paperwork,' said Elliott, not sounding amused by the thought at all. 'He's laid a complaint against both you and Travis Bailey. Apparently the two of you are playing happy families. He claims you stayed overnight with Bailey.'

Anger roared through her. 'Well of course I did. Travis took a blow to the head, delivered by Bannister. The doctor was worried he might have concussion. Would you have preferred I left a little girl alone with a man with a head injury so she could wake up in the morning to find him unconscious or in a coma or worse ... dead?'

'Write it in the report, Miss Penney. Until then, you're suspended from this case due to conflict of interest. I'll be taking over. I have Bailey's address on file, so I'll stop in there as soon as I hit town.'

Heather didn't think her stomach could sink any further. Elliott had not an ounce of compassion. He dealt in policies and procedures with little or no regard for heart.

'Elliott, please don't take me off the case until you've read my report. Please.' Close to tears, she wasn't ashamed to beg.

Her boss' tone softened. 'Heather, we've had enough bad press in the department over the Ferris scandal. If you've compromised the case by becoming personally involved with Casey's guardian, I have no other recourse but to remove you.'

'You can hardly compare this case to two shady politicians using foster kids in an election promise to drum up votes.'

'Bad press is bad press. And the Bannisters appear to have powerful people in their pockets — television stations, newspapers, politicians, you name it. I'm under strict orders from the Director General himself to take over the case. God knows what strings they pulled to get that one right.'

'Zac Bannister is a bully. There are circumstances in this case that are not yet public,' Heather urged. Panic seared through her. If Travis didn't get the chance to prove Zac Bannister murdered his sister before they won custody, Casey's life could be in danger.

'Then why don't I know about it? Why didn't the last social worker in the area report special circumstances?'

'Elliott, we need to talk about this face-to-face. I've only just been made aware of the information. Yesterday's confrontation was a small show of what Bannister is capable of. He's a dangerous man.'

She heard the water pipes shudder as Travis turned the water off in the shower. She'd have to talk to him about Tracy's alleged murder, raise his pain again.

'All you need to do is talk to the people in this town and you'll know he's not a popular man, not the kind of man you want to leave a little girl with.'

'I need more than hearsay, Heather. I need proof. Your report. On my desk. Tomorrow. I'll arrive there around mid-afternoon. Have it ready.'

He hung up, leaving her holding the mobile in her hand and praying that Elliott Crawford couldn't be as easily bought as the Director General.

'Everything okay?' Travis' voice reached her from the doorway.

Heather flexed her shoulders, trying to release the knots. She shook her head. 'That was my boss. The Bannisters have made a claim for Casey.'

'Fuck. My time just ran out. Jesus, Heather, I can't

let that mean bastard take Casey. God knows what he'll do to her.'

The fear in his voice echoed in her mind. Heather heard his footsteps cross the kitchen to where she stood looking out the kitchen window. The farm looked so peaceful this morning with the layer of early morning mist hanging over the creek. If only the water could talk. If only the hills the town got its name from could whisper the secrets they held.

Travis' hands came to rest on her shoulders and she leaned back against him. Nothing mattered anymore except for Casey and the fight to keep her with Travis.

'We have to find a way to prove he killed her. Did your sister keep a diary? Photos on her computer? Emails to her friends? Anything where she may have written what happened at the party that night?' Heather turned to face him.

'Tracy wasn't the girlie type.' Travis sighed and moved away to pour a coffee from the pot. 'She wasn't into snapping selfies or chatting on social media. Her friends were happier talking horses than about dresses.'

'Would she have talked to her friends about what happened that night?'

'After the night of the party, she spoke to no one. Her friends called around but she refused to see them, and eventually they gave up and moved on. She wouldn't even talk to me about it, but I knew deep down what had happened. My gut was never wrong when it came to Tracy.'

'What happened to her clothes from that night?' Heather took the fresh mug of coffee he held out to her.

Travis shrugged. 'The dress was ripped. I guess Mum would have thrown it out.'

Heather sighed. 'Any evidence we'd find on her clothing would only point to the fact that she'd had sex and nothing much else. The DNA would just prove the Bannisters right. So there were no witnesses who'd be prepared to come forward?'

Travis shook his head. 'Tracy's friends admitted to taking drugs that night. They were out of it and don't remember anything. They don't even remember seeing Tracy at the party.'

'Then we have to find a way to prove he murdered her down by the creek that day. You said you found things that pointed to a struggle?'

'Yeah.'

'What happened to those items?'

'I handed them in to Sergeant Riggs. He said he'd put them into the evidence box. There was never a chance they'd reopen the case back then. The senior detective on the case had it all sown up pretty quickly as an accident.'

'Would Riggs reopen the case?'

Travis shrugged. 'If there was enough reason to, I guess. There'd have to be fresh evidence or, God forbid, another death of a similar nature for that to happen. All we have is speculation.'

Heather turned back to the window as Marge Everett's bus rattled down the drive, kicking up dust in its wake. She frowned as Travis leaned over her shoulder to see.

'That's odd,' he said. 'Marge is never out this way this early in the morning.'

Heather grinned. 'Maybe she stayed the night at Harry's.'

Travis chuckled. 'Harry might have got lucky. I wonder if he'll remember.'

Marge got out of the bus and bustled up to the veranda, looking flustered. 'Travis! Travis!' she called urgently.

'This doesn't sound good,' he muttered, reaching for the door that led onto the front veranda and opening it.

Heather followed his long strides, almost jogging to keep up. They met Marge at the front door, her hand poised to knock.

'Oh thank God, there you are!' Her breath came in short gasps as she held a hand over her heart.

'Are you okay, Mrs Everett?' Travis put a hand on the elderly lady's shoulder.

'I'm fine ... but it's Harry, love. He's missing.'

Chapter Fourteen

Travis' heart plummeted. He felt Heather's hand close around his forearm and took comfort from it. 'What do you mean he's missing?'

'Well, I stayed the night, you see.' Her fine-boned hand fluttered to her head, her age apparent in the thickened blue veins and thin skin. 'Oh no, no, you cheeky boy! It's nothing like that,' she said when Travis' eyebrow shot up. 'Harry said to stay in the spare room because it would be too dark for me to drive back after all that palaver yesterday. So I stayed and we had a nice dinner, which I cooked, of course.'

Travis tried hard not to interrupt and tell her to get to the point. His mind raced ahead, thinking of places Harry might have gone, but the truth was these days

Harry seldom got past his front yard before he forgot where he was heading.

'Then when I got up this morning, I knocked on his door to see if he wanted a cuppa. After a few knocks, I pushed open the door and his bed was all neat and tidy like he hadn't slept in it. And Robbie is missing too.'

'Have you checked the yard and his shed? Have you heard Robbie barking somewhere?'

The shed was the most likely place to find Harry these days. He pottered around in there with his orchids or did a little woodwork.

'No, I haven't seen or heard Robbie since last night when Harry let him out to pee. I checked the shed and all the way down to the paddock in case he'd gone down to check on the sheep again. I've searched everywhere, Travis.' Marge teared up, dabbing at her eyes with her handkerchief.

Travis patted her shoulder. 'It's okay, Mrs Everett. I'll saddle up Fantasia and take a ride out. I'm sure he's just gone out for a walk.'

He hoped he sounded reassuring because he definitely didn't feel reassured himself. Anything could have happened to the old man. The brown snakes were rife this summer and a bite from one of them could kill the strongest man in a matter of minutes. Harry wouldn't stand a chance.

'Heather, can you wake Casey and get her dressed? Mrs Everett, could you please go back to Harry's and wait there in case he comes back? Call me on my mobile if he does, okay?'

Travis retrieved his work boots from the shoe shelf outside the front door, pushed his feet into them and laced them up.

'Yes, of course,' said Mrs Everett. 'I'll call the ladies at the CWA and warn them in case we have to send out the State Emergency Services to look for him.'

'Great idea, but let me have a quick look for him first, okay?'

The dread in his gut grew. Even with Alzheimer's Harry knew to always tell Travis if he was heading out anywhere. It was the unwritten code of their friendship and a necessity born out of habit for any man farming alone. He lifted his hat from the peg and pushed it onto his head.

'Heather, can you bring me the first aid kit in the kitchen under the sink and a couple of bottles of water from the fridge, please?'

'Should I call Sergeant Riggs?'

'He's not considered missing until he's been gone twenty-four hours. Give me a chance to look first then we'll ask Riggs to bend the rules. Could you let Doc Benson know so he's on standby in case Harry's hurt?'

'Will do.' Heather turned to head for the kitchen and was back with the kit as he waved Mrs Everett down the drive.

'Thanks,' he said, taking it from her.

'Be careful out there.'

'It'll be fine, you'll see,' he replied with more confidence than he felt.

Travis leaned down to kiss her cheek. She smelled so good. Like wildflowers and coming home, like something he wanted to see every day when he rode in from the field. She curled her fists around the material of his T-shirt.

'You're not really in any condition to ride a horse after yesterday. You'll be no good to Harry if you get hurt.'

He trapped her against him with his free arm and kissed her as hard on the lips as his sore jaw would allow. 'I won't get hurt.'

She released her grip on him and pressed at his chest. 'Go now. We don't know how long Harry's been out there.'

Travis released her and with one last look at her lovely face, jogged down the steps, cursing as the jarring sparked a thump in his head.

In the stables, he moved quickly, throwing the blanket across Fantasia's back and saddling her up. She danced with excitement, her senses on high alert. Fixing the bridle, he tossed the reins over her head and adjusted the straps on the saddle.

He mounted and urged her into a walk out of the stables before increasing the pace to a trot, warming her up to a canter. Over the hills, the sun climbed higher in the sky. Another scorcher of a day. Already the sun had the sting of a snake bite. Wherever Harry was he prayed he'd find him soon.

The horror stories of people lost in the outback with no water or food for days spurred him on. No way would he let Harry die that way. His only hope was that Harry — a man who'd grown up on this land long before the town developed close by and knew every square inch of it — would remember the key survival instincts; keep calm, know how to light a fire and find fresh water because drinking your own urine would never be a good way to survive.

Travis rechecked the house and shed in case Harry had wandered back home then he rode out across the paddocks. Reaching the lookout point on the hill that rose above the creek, Travis scanned the water. With no rain or overflow into it for months Whispering Creek meandered gently down towards Marradong, not deep enough for a man to drown in. Not like the day Tracy died.

'Harry!' he called, the echo of his voice bouncing off the hills across the stream.

Nothing. No answering string of swear words he'd expect from the man who'd been a substitute uncle for as long as Travis had drawn a breath. He turned east towards Ranford and called upstream, cupping his hands around his mouth, his voice tinged with desperation.

'Harry!'

Silence as dead as Wongan Creek's graveyard pierced his heart. Where the hell was Harry? And where was Robbie? The dog seldom left Harry's side. Surely he'd hear a bark or a whimper? But the bush around him remained deathly silent except for the call of the cockatoos and the occasional mocking laugh of a kookaburra.

'Jesus fucking Christ, Harry. Where the hell are you?'

Fear and dread twisted his gut, all tied up with a ribbon of guilt. If he lost Harry ... It didn't bear thinking about, not now when he needed to stay positive.

He should have made Harry stay over at his place. If he hadn't gone into town to sign up for the damn rodeo day events, he wouldn't have had the punch up with Zac Bannister. Nor would he have had the most satisfying, gloriously heady sex with the woman who was fast stealing his heart. Instead, he would have been up early enough to get Harry out of bed himself and see him settled into the day's chores. Again he'd failed the people he loved and it ate a hole in his gut.

Travis turned Fantasia's head back down the hill and rode her up along the creek towards Harry's paddocks. The sun burned his eyes and he wished he'd worn his sunnies. He tugged the brim of his hat lower to shield them then whistled for Robbie. Still nothing, no answering bark of excitement his voice usually wrenched from the dog. Not a good sign.

One excruciating hour later, he'd searched every inch of Harry's land and his own, every nook and cranny the old man might have wandered into, without a trace. Not even a hint that he'd been anywhere this morning.

Travis' gut balled into a solid, stony mass of trepidation. His head pounded, his jaw ached and the cut next to his eye stung like a bitch from the salty sweat dripping down his face. His arse was numb and the muscles in his legs screamed from pushing his weight up in the stirrups to scan the bush for signs of life. He headed back to his house, empty and hurting. Had he failed Harry just as he'd failed Tracy? *Please, God, no*.

On the veranda, Heather and Casey waited for him. He wanted to gather them close and hold them tight because he couldn't bear the thought of losing them too.

Heather rushed down the stairs, Casey following her, expectation in their eyes. Travis shook his head, feeling the pain of failure strangle the words he couldn't force out. He felt the reassuring touch of Heather's hand on his thigh, the stroke of her fingers against the denim.

Casey stared up at him, all hope and hero worship, and it killed him that he couldn't have better news to share.

Travis dismounted when Heather's hand fell away, the warmth of it still seeping into his cold blood. He swallowed the burn and forced out the words he hated having to speak. 'We'll have to alert the SES. There's no sign of him anywhere.'

Tears glistened in Casey's eyes. Even an almost six-year-old knew the death sentence those words might carry out here where the bush reigned with its own set of rules. Not only did she know it, she'd lived it. And that simply added to the pain that gripped Travis' chest.

Her arms wrapped around his thigh and clung tightly, her nose buried in the denim. He let his hand fall on her head and stroke her precious curls for a moment before he bent to hoist her into his arms. She pressed her face into the curve of his shoulder and her arms almost strangled him she clung so tightly to his neck.

Travis patted her back with more reassurance than he felt. 'It's okay, sweet pea, we'll find him. I promise.'

Heather watched Travis' good eye close over the pain she saw there as he hugged Casey closer, his chin resting on the little girl's shoulder. She wanted desperately to reach out and wrap her arms around them both, to let them know she was there for them, but that would only complicate their situation with DOHW, because it wasn't comfort she wanted to offer, it was love.

What a moment to admit to herself she had fallen hopelessly and irrevocably in love with this man, his niece and the people of the small town she'd been assigned to.

Her own heart aching for Harry, she turned from them and walked back up the veranda stairs. 'I'll give Sergeant Riggs a call and let him know.'

At the top of the stairs, she stood a moment to watch as Travis walked Fantasia back to the stable, reigns in one hand, the other firmly supporting Casey clinging to his side. She rubbed a hand at the tightness of her throat and dashed the sting of tears from her eyes. Between a rock and a hard place was a shit place to be.

She dialled the number for the police station, her heart a leaden ball as she waited for Riggs to answer.

'Wongan Creek Police.'

'Hey, Sarge, it's Heather Penney. I'm calling you from the Bailey place. I know I should have gone through the emergency line, but I figured you'd get things moving faster.'

'Heather? Please don't tell me Bannister is making trouble again?'

'No, nothing like that. It's Harry. He's missing.' Even as she said the words, they became a stark reality. The consequences, the possibilities of what might have happened whirled around in her mind.

'Are you sure? You know what Harry's like. He might have gone down to the creek to look for those bloody sheep again.'

'Travis has done a thorough search already. There's no sign of him.'

She heard the tone of Riggs' voice change. 'Then we need to get onto it right away. No one knows that property better than Travis. I'll get a search party together. Sit tight.'

The scrape of a chair, the shuffle of papers and the sound of a drawer opening and closing — he was on the move already. Heather closed her eyes and prayed to the God she wasn't sure existed, the one who'd taken her own family from her. *Please let them be in time to find Harry alive.*

She heard a thunk as Riggs dropped the phone, a rustle as he picked it up again, his voice stern and all business in her ear. 'Heather, you still there?'

'Yes, Sarge.'

'Have you called Doc Benson?'

'Yes, I called him about an hour ago when Travis went looking for Harry. Doc's taking a quick look around town in case Harry's wandered all the way in there.'

'Good girl. I'll call him up and let him know we're organising a search. How's Travis doing?'

She looked out the kitchen window to where Travis sat on his haunches talking to Casey, a hand on her shoulder, his face drawn in tight lines. Her heart ached for them both.

'Not so good right now.'

'Understandable. He's told you about his sister?'

'Yes.'

Riggs sighed. 'Bullshit business that was, but my hands were tied. That doesn't mean I'm not watching Zac Bannister like a hawk. I want you both to know that.'

'That's good to know.' Should she say something about Travis' suspicions? He'd given her the perfect opening. No, right now Harry was more important. 'I have something to talk to you about, but it will keep until we find Harry. Please hurry, Riggs.'

'I'm already on my way.'

Heather put down the phone as Travis and Casey came into the kitchen. She filled the kettle and set it to boil. The next few hours, maybe even days, would be the longest in a lifetime for all of them.

'You okay?' she said, knowing full well he wasn't, but she needed to break the awful, heavy silence that hung between them.

He nodded and sat down heavily in a chair at the scarred wooden table that had likely seen a few generations of Baileys eat there, Casey climbing into his lap.

Her heart squeezed at what might be going through the little girl's mind. Not long ago her mum had gone missing too. Now Harry was gone and soon the long, sometimes cold and unfair, arm of the law might steal away the only man who came close to being the father she needed because of a mean, bullying, possibly murderous arsehole.

Heather squashed down the anger that fired up in her belly at the thought. Somewhere between now and tomorrow, she had a report to write — before Elliott came crashing into their world to tear them apart. Now when their whole world had tilted again, life had thrown another curve ball into the park and ripped open all their wounds.

And amidst all that was the letter in her purse, the reminder of the death sentence that hung over her own head that begged for an action she couldn't bear to face. The one that might put a limit on the time she had left to love the man who sat before her, already devastated by loss.

Chapter Fifteen

A sea of orange jackets spread out in the back paddock as the SES volunteers grouped together for a briefing, tested communication and call signs, distributed ration packs, first aid kits and area maps. A surreal sense of urgency had descended on the farm.

In the shade of the veranda, the ladies of the CWA set up tables filled with bottled water, sandwiches and energy snacks. Across the fence in Harry's daisy field, tents and shelters were raised to give the rescuers a shady resting place on their breaks, their bright orange canvas adding a touch of contrast to the yellow flowers.

Heather sat at the table to write up her report and tried not to think about Travis, out there in the blazing sun, injured and hurting. Doc Benson had tried to talk him out of going, but he'd swallowed two painkillers, slapped on his hat and ignored the good doctor's advice.

In the chair next to her, Casey sat colouring in her book with her tongue poking out the corner of her mouth as she concentrated on keeping within the lines.

Heather rubbed a hand over the little girl's head and received a wan smile in return. 'Okay there, honey?' she asked.

'Yeah. Will Harry be okay?'

'Of course he will, you'll see.'

Casey picked out a purple crayon and shaded the princess' dress with the uneven strokes of a child still growing into her motor skills. 'And Uncle Trav?'

Heather sighed. The pain etched into Travis' face when he'd left had been clear. The best she could hope for was that Doc Benson would keep a close eye on him and send him back if he looked like collapsing. Right now he was driven by a stubborn streak and sheer willpower.

'He'll be fine too, sweetheart. Doc Benson will take good care of them both.'

'I'm scared. What if they don't come back?' The little girl didn't look up from her scratching on the paper. The crayon jerked over the lines, the only indication of her distress.

Heather covered Casey's tiny little hand with hers. 'They will. You have to believe that.'

She turned her gaze on Heather. 'Will you stay with me if they don't? I'm afraid of the man.'

A cold fist clamped down on Heather's heart as she saw the raw fear in the little girl's eyes. There was more to it than just being afraid that Travis and Harry wouldn't come back.

'Are you afraid they won't come back like your mum?' Abandoning her report, she pushed her chair out from the table and turned the little girl's around to face her.

'Yes, and I'm afraid of the man.'

'What man, darling?'

'The man from the shop, the one who hurt Uncle Trav.'

The chill that gripped her heart spread to her bloodstream, raising goosebumps on her skin. 'Why are you afraid of him?'

The child scampered off her chair and scrambled up on Heather's lap. She wrapped her arms around Heather's waist and hugged her close. 'He took my mum. I don't want him to take Uncle Trav and Harry too.'

Black spots danced in front of Heather's eyes as the bitter taste of fear snagged her stomach. *Holy Mother Mary.* 'What do you mean he took your mum, sweetheart?'

'He said I'd get into trouble if I told. He said he'd come and get me.'

Her senses on high alert, she held the child close. 'You won't get into trouble if you tell me, I promise. You haven't done anything wrong. Only naughty people get in trouble.'

'He said I was naughty that's why he took my mummy and he said he'd throw me down a dark hole and throw sand on top of me if I told anyone.'

Oh dear God, could this be a horrible figment of Casey's imagination or was there some truth in it? It certainly seemed like something Zac Bannister was capable of. 'When did he say that?'

'The day he came to the house. Nanna and Pop were out working. Uncle Trav went away to the place where they do the rodeo championships. It was just me and Mum.'

No, oh please, no. Her heart didn't want to hear what happened next, but she knew if she stopped the child from talking now, she might never talk about it again.

'He hurt Mummy. I saw him. She told me to go so I ran away and hid under Nanna's bed. I heard Mummy crying then he shouted those things to me.' She buried her teary face against Heather's shirt, her body shaking.

Heather soothed her for a while, alternately wanting her to finish telling the story and not wanting to hear how it ended. After a moment, she asked, 'What happened then?'

Casey looked up, those eyes as beautiful as her

mother's and uncle's, even greener with the sheen of tears. 'He took her away. It was quiet. I waited forever then I came out to look for her, but she was gone forever.'

The child couldn't have been more than four years old at the time, for God's sake. What kind of monster did that to a baby? And too often she'd seen police dismiss statements from children in cases of domestic violence as insufficient evidence, when a child's story was likely more truthful in its innocence than an adult's. Would Sergeant Riggs prove the same?

'Did you tell your Uncle Travis?'

'No. I'm only telling you cos I'm scared.' She pushed her face into Heather's shoulder. 'He said if I told anyone, he'd come back for me. Please, Heather, please don't let him take me. I don't want him to take any more people away.'

'I won't, sweetheart.' She cradled the little girl against her as she leaned back in the chair and prayed for Travis to come home.

How could she tell him his niece had witnessed his sister's abduction? That the murder theory was now even more likely to be a reality? How could they possibly protect her against the monster that was Zac Bannister? They had to find a way to prove him guilty, but was the evidence of an almost six-year-old witness enough to stand up in court?

As Elliott Crawford's tall, broad-shouldered frame appeared in the doorway a day earlier than promised, Heather realised she'd run out of time.

Chapter Sixteen

Frustration tanked through Travis as the sun headed west to bed. With the light fading fast in the bush, they'd soon call off the search. The SES volunteers had split into teams and combed every inch of both properties on foot before crossing the creek into the dense bushland that meandered up the hills. Twelve long, fruitless hours of searching with no sign of Harry or Robbie. He wanted to howl at the injustice of it, except that would make his headache worse.

Doc Benson eyed him warily. He wondered if the doctor saw what he was feeling. Stars danced in front of his eyes and he tried to blink them away. A cold sweat followed the shivers he fought to control. The pounding in his head and nausea in his stomach reminded him of the bruise on his face and the cut next to his eye.

When he got home and murdered his headache, he'd go looking for Zac Bannister, rip his head off and shove it up his arse like he'd promised to do for putting him in this vulnerable state.

'You should go home. There's not much more you can do.'

If he could nod without his head falling off his shoulders, he would. 'I know.'

'I'll go back with you. An injection might work faster than pills.'

Travis took off his hat and wiped the sweat from his brow with his arm. Could it dull the pain and guilt of losing Harry? Another death on his conscience.

'He's not dead yet, Travis. Harry's tougher than you think.'

'Get out of my head, Doc.'

'I don't need to be in there to see what you're thinking, son.' Doc took his arm. 'Let's go home. These guys will give it another half an hour before they pack it in until tomorrow too. We still have to walk back and we've come a fair way today.'

Travis didn't want to think about how many kilometres they'd covered through the dense bushland and red dirt. It made him all too aware of how far Harry might have wandered. 'Yeah, you're right. I was just kinda hoping ...'

'We all were.'

Travis knew he wouldn't sleep a wink worrying about Harry, unless the painkiller injection came with a double dose of knockout. Was Heather still at home with Casey? God, he hoped so. He had to straighten this out. Tell her what had happened between them was a mistake.

No, not a mistake. The timing just sucked. His focus needed to be on the three people who mattered in his life — Tracy, Harry and Casey.

He followed Doc home along the trail the teams had marked to indicate the areas they'd already searched. Each thud of his boots on the ground made the hammering in his head more intense until he felt like his spine had sharpened to a spear that was gouging a hole in his skull.

Outside on his veranda, the ladies of the CWA ladled soup into bowls and handed out freshly baked bread rolls. Behind them the lights of the homestead were on, not quite bright enough in the fading sunlight yet to be a welcome home. No welcome celebrations tonight. Not without Harry.

He made it up the steps with Doc's help, exhaustion and pain weighing him down heavily. Low voices reached his ears — one definitely Heather's beautiful dulcet tones, the other male and unfamiliar.

Apprehension joined all the other emotions controlling his steps. Who the hell was in his house and where was Casey?

'Easy, kid,' said Doc as Travis stumbled in his haste to get to the kitchen.

There was Casey, curled up in Heather's arms, her face buried in Heather's shoulder. She lifted her head and eyed him warily, the way she did when she'd done something naughty. It wasn't a look he saw often, so it started an unsettled feeling quivering in his gut. His heart softened and he smiled at her, letting her know that whatever it was, it would be okay. Whatever she'd done couldn't be worse than Harry going missing.

His heartbeat picked up pace as his gaze fell on Heather's face. She looked tired, her eyes puffy, her skin pale. And she looked like she'd been crying.

His eyes flicked to the man beside her, wincing as the movement made them feel like they were about to fall out of the sockets.

The city suit looked out of place against the well-loved kitchen table. Shiny black shoes and a black silk tie. Why did DOHW superiors always need to dress like funeral directors?

So Heather's boss had made it to town in record time, but then again they were only two hours from Perth. He wondered whether it was the Bannisters or the Director General who'd put the wind up his arse.

The man turned a cold, ice-blue gaze his way. Somewhere in his mid-thirties, if he smiled, he'd be a hit with the ladies of all ages in Wongan Creek. This stern, he made Miss Turner look like Aphrodite. He uncrossed his long legs at the ankles and stood, darkly handsome, tall and broad-shouldered.

Travis stamped down on a twinge of jealously that this man had been alone in his kitchen with Heather for God knew how long. Then he reminded himself she wasn't his. Could never be his.

'Travis?' Heather's voice held a glimmer of hope, one he hated that he couldn't fulfil.

He scrubbed a hand over his face, feeling the gritty addition of sun and windburn to his growing list of injuries. 'Nothing.'

Heather's hand fluttered to her mouth. 'Oh no.'

'I'm not giving up yet.' He turned his gaze to the man who looked like he'd stepped right off the pages of some fancy fashion magazine. He'd bet his canola crop those shoes never got as much as a fleck of dust on them. 'Travis Bailey.' He held out his hand for a shake.

'Elliott Crawford, Head of the Department of Health and Welfare.'

The man's handshake was at least firm and decisive. There was nothing Travis hated more than a half-hearted, limp handshake.

'This is Doc Benson.' Travis drew the doctor forward to introduce him.

While the two men shook hands, he walked past them to where Heather sat with Casey on her lap. God, she was beautiful. Even tired and teary, she looked like an angel.

He wanted to gather them both tightly against his chest and hold them there in case they too went missing like Harry. But with Crawford's cold eyes on them, he couldn't risk it, so he put his heart in his eyes instead and said, 'Thanks for looking after Casey for me.'

Heather chewed on her lip. His hands itched to reach out and stroke it. There was nothing he wanted more right now than to spend the night with her wrapped in his arms, knowing both she and Casey were safe. He reached for Casey instead and lifted her gently out of Heather's arms.

'Uncle Trav,' Casey murmured. 'Did you find him? Is Harry okay?'

The pain, disappointment and frustration of the day seeped into his bones. 'Not yet, but he will be. We'll be up early tomorrow to search for him again.'

Her hand came up to cup his face. 'You'll find him, Uncle Trav. I know you will.'

He wished he had her faith. 'Harry's a tough old goat, sweet pea. He'll be all right.' But the words felt as empty as Harry's house tonight where the lights couldn't be seen glowing in the distance from Travis' kitchen window.

Bella bustled in with a tray of soup bowls and a pile of bread buns. 'You'll need this, all of you.' She cast Elliott Crawford a warning look. 'And you lay off your business at least until Travis has had a chance to eat and clean up. You city folk have no idea how much a search and rescue takes out of a person here in the bush.'

A reluctant grin tugged at the man from DOHW's lips, and Travis gave him brownie points for that.

'Well, I hope then that one of those bowls of soup is for me because it smells pretty good.'

Bella almost beamed until she remembered in time that Elliott Crawford was the enemy in town. She looked at Travis. 'Nothing but the best for these guys.' She looked back at Crawford, hands firm on the tray. 'You haven't asked, but I'll tell you anyway because out here we're all family. If you want the truth about how much Travis Bailey loves his family, you come and ask me before you believe any whispers you hear on the grapevine. Got that?'

In the process of lifting the tray from her hands, Crawford said, 'Got it. I've promised Miss Turner the same thing. I wouldn't dare do otherwise.'

In that moment, Travis wondered if they at least stood a small chance against the Bannisters.

Travis put Casey down onto a chair and put a bowl of soup in front of her. 'Here we go, sweet pea, eat up.'

He took the seat next to her, opposite Heather. With the table between them, he wouldn't be tempted to reach for her hand and the comfort it offered. With Eagle Eye Elliott watching their every move, he couldn't afford to slip up. Neither of them could.

They went through the motions of eating, silence

hanging heavily in the air as the sombre mood embraced him. Even Casey's usual cheerful chatter was stilled as she sipped her soup from a spoon with one hand and clung to his shirt with the other.

He had no appetite for Bella's delicious minestrone, usually his favourite, but knew the importance of sustenance in a search and rescue, so he ate on auto pilot.

Occasionally, he cast a quick look at Heather from under his lashes and saw she kept her gaze glued to her plate. Just as well because he wouldn't be able to stop himself from reaching for her if she looked him in the eye.

Wiping his lips on the paper napkin next to his plate, he pushed back his chair and stood. 'Excuse me, I need to clean up. Casey, stay here with Heather, okay?' With Harry missing, he didn't want Casey out of his sight, not for a minute. 'I'll read you a bedtime story when I'm done.'

'Okay, Uncle Trav.'

He gently eased her fingers from the death grip she had on his shirt and gave her hand a reassuring pat. 'Good girl.' He ruffled her hair. 'Finish your soup then.'

With a quick nod to Elliott and Doc, and a glance at Heather's beautiful face, he left the room.

Ten minutes later, showered, fed and medicated, Travis strode back into the kitchen on a waft of shower soap and citrusy scent. Heather inhaled appreciatively. He had more colour in his cheeks now the ashen shade of pain had receded.

'Hey, Riggs.' Travis greeted the police sergeant who'd joined them in the kitchen. 'How did your group go on the east end?'

Riggs shook his head. 'No luck. We've got backup coming in from Collie and Williams to search the foothills tomorrow.'

Travis rubbed a hand over his face. He looked so drained. Heather ached to put her arms around him and hug him tightly, reassure him Harry would be found alive and well, but even she knew that the longer he was out there, the less of a chance of survival he had.

He turned to her. 'Thanks for tucking Casey in. I popped in to say goodnight and she was almost asleep.'

'You're welcome. She couldn't keep her eyes open anymore. We read one of her favourite stories together while she waited for you to come in and say goodnight.'

His tired smile tugged at her heart. '*Billy Bailey goes Walkabout*. She brings that one out every time someone goes missing in the outback. She swears Billy is a real descendant of ours because he has such great survival skills.'

Heather stepped forward and gave his arm a quick rub of sympathy, the closest she could get to being personal with her boss watching on, but wanting to do so much more.

'Travis, we need to talk about Casey.' She kept her gaze on his, willing him to understand. 'I know the timing isn't great, but this whole thing with Harry has raised a memory for Casey we're not sure you're aware of.'

A frown creased his brow and dread gripped her stomach at the thought of what they had to reveal. She was glad the police sergeant was there.

She'd had to tell Elliott what the little girl had said she'd seen, but she'd hesitated to tell him what Travis had told her. That was a story for him to tell, but what Elliott would confront him with now would be hard to hear. Surely with Casey's confession and Travis' suspicions there would be enough reason to reopen the cold case on Tracy and stop Zac Bannister in his tracks forever.

'In light of what has happened with Zac Bannister over the last few days, I think it might be wise if Sergeant Riggs hears this too.'

She prayed he could read the pleading in her eyes, the message that it would be okay despite the horrors Casey's confession would uncover.

He nodded slowly, his eyes narrowing. What she would give to see those crinkles at the corner of his eyes the result of laughter instead of concern, to be able to hold him as the events leading up to Tracy's disappearance unfolded and to stroke that frown away from between his eyes.

The laughing light she normally saw in his green eyes was out and in its place a dark sadness she wished she could change.

With a gentle nudge, she pushed him towards a chair. 'Sit before you fall down.'

'Takes a lot to topple a Bailey.'

He attempted a grin but it formed a grimace. Heather knew him too well, she realised, as she acknowledged his tired attempt at humour with a soft smile of her own.

Elliott Crawford's voice pierced the warm glow in her heart and Heather felt the slice of his words. 'Don't let me interrupt the moment here, but I believe it's been a long day for all of us and I'd like to get this out of the way.'

Blushing, Heather moved away, sat and pushed her case folder over in front of Elliott. 'As you know from this morning, I've been removed from the case due to a report from the Bannisters which suggests a conflict of interest.' For Riggs' benefit, she added, 'I stayed the night to take care of Casey and Travis after the fight yesterday and it's been suggested that Travis and I are in a relationship.'

Riggs snorted but made no comment.

Heather dragged her gaze back to Travis' face. 'So, Elliott will be handling your case from now on.'

She didn't add that Elliott had filed a transfer for her

out of Wongan Creek, a move that would see her sent back to Perth and moved into the aged care sector. He'd thought it best after hearing Heather's side of the story about the incident on the mine site with Zac.

Even though her heart was breaking at the thought of leaving Travis and Wongan Creek, she knew she had to do what was best for all of them. Already she was in way too deep.

Travis eased his chair back, stretched his legs out and crossed his arms over his chest. His actions reminded her of a graceful stallion, every move carefully executed and deliberately controlled. She could see the muscles in his shoulders tense and his jaw set stubbornly against what was to come.

'Travis,' Elliott began, flicking open the cover of the manila folder neatly labelled in Heather's handwriting. 'Has Casey ever spoken to you about what happened the day her mother went missing?'

Travis shook his head. 'She was barely four years old when it happened. All she could say at the time was that her mummy was gone. We didn't think she understood the reality.'

'When you arrived home that day, where was Casey?'

Travis frowned. 'I drove back from Newman as soon as I knew Tracy was missing so I arrived here two days after they found her. Mum told me they found Casey hiding under their bed.'

'Did you find that unusual?'

Travis drew in his long legs and sat up straight in the chair. 'Not really. We figured she was scared being left alone in the house and that was the place she felt safest. What was unusual was that Tracy had left her alone here to go down to the creek. Tracy never left her unsupervised. She'd never do that. Even now, I make sure there's always someone to stay with her if I can't.'

The defensiveness in his tone raked at Heather's heart. How unfair it was that he felt he needed to justify his and Tracy's actions when there was a man on the loose with murderous intent on his mind.

'Did you tell that to the police?' Elliott frowned and scribbled a note inside the folder.

'Yes. The investigating officer didn't think it was important. We still don't know why she did that day. Tracy would never have gone down to that creek alone. She seldom left the house unless I was with her.' Travis raked a hand through his hair, tiredness dragging at his shoulders.

Elliott put down his pen, leaned forward on the chair and laced his fingers together on the scarred wooden table. 'Casey told Heather she saw a man take her mother away. Were you aware of that?'

Travis paled under the sun and windburn of the day. 'No.'

The word came out on a choke and Heather wanted to hold him against the pain she heard there. She watched the horror etch his bruised and battered features, adding to the hurt he already carried as Elliott relayed what Casey had told them.

He dragged both hands through his hair, his shoulders hunched against Elliott's words. Heather felt the tears sting her eyes again. She'd lost count of how many times she'd cried for him today.

Riggs slapped his hands against the table, making Heather jump. He pushed his chair back and stood. Walking around to Travis, he squeezed his shoulder. 'I'll look into this, son. That's a promise.'

Travis didn't appear to have enough energy to do more than nod. With another quick tap on the back, Riggs left.

Elliott closed the manila folder. 'I'll work closely with Sergeant Riggs on this, Travis. If what Casey has told us proves to be true, you have a strong case for retaining custody. Until we have more information and decide on the best way to proceed, I'm leaving her in your care.'

Travis nodded again, his hands clutched so tightly between his knees that his knuckles bloomed white. Heather ached to hold him close.

Her boss pushed back his chair and stood. 'I'll make my way back to the hotel now and be back tomorrow. Heather, we'll talk about your transfer in the morning. I know you're officially off the case, but I think Travis here might need your help with Casey until Harry is found. You have my permission to stay and assist in your former capacity as their case worker.' He looked over at Travis. 'Unless you want to make other arrangements, Travis?'

Travis shook his head, his eyes firmly on the track shoes he'd pulled on earlier. His voice was quiet and sad in the room. 'If Heather's okay with that, so am I.'

She sensed his withdrawal, felt the walls go up around him and hated that what they had was over before it had a chance to blossom. 'I'll see you out, Elliott.'

'Thanks. I'll catch up with you in the morning.' He opened the kitchen door and stepped out onto the veranda.

As Heather followed, she stopped to look back and saw Travis' shoulders tremble. The strong, beautiful country boy she'd fallen in love with was now a broken man.

Chapter Seventeen

Travis spent the night in a chair next to Casey's bed, keeping watch over the little girl as she slept. He knew he should get some sleep, be rested for the long day ahead. Another day of searching for Harry as around him his world crumbled.

He heard Heather moving around in the room next door. Tracy's room. Knew she was just as restless as he was. He tried to process Elliott's words about a transfer but his mind was clogged with what Casey had seen.

His heart ached with guilt and regret that this small, beautiful, innocent child had witnessed such horrible things. It explained so much. How hard she tried to please him and her grandparents. How determined she was to behave, the number of times she'd put herself in the naughty corner. The fear in her eyes every time she came face-to-face with Zac

Bannister. All because of a threat made by a man who did not deserve to be alive. And then there was the guilt that ate away at his soul. He'd left them at the mercy of the heartless mongrel.

Anger and hatred for Zac Bannister ate into his guilt. The longer he thought on it, the more determined he became to bring the bastard to justice. So many things had happened in quick succession after Tracy's body was found and Casey's welfare had become a priority, so perhaps even he had overlooked some of the clues that pointed to Zac's involvement. Like what had happened to Tracy's dress from the party.

He remembered the boxes Mum had packed in the shed. Tracy's things she hadn't had the heart to give to charity. Were there clues in those boxes? Evidence that might point in Bannister's direction? Now that Riggs had a new lead on the case, anything to support a conviction could be reviewed as evidence.

As the sky began to lighten with the approach of dawn, Travis eased out of the chair, kissed Casey's forehead and decided to head out to the shed.

As he passed through the kitchen, he found Heather putting the kettle on to boil. Outside the windows, in the tents spread across his land and Harry's, camping lights started to glow, indicating that the volunteers were stirring to prepare for another day of agonising search.

He stopped and let his eyes rest on her for a moment. 'Hey.'

'Hi,' she responded, her voice barely above a whisper.

'You okay?' Puffy, tired eyes, crazy hair and all, she was still the most beautiful vision he'd seen. All the more reason she should get the hell out of town away from the threat of a madman in Wongan Creek. A transfer out of town was the best thing for all of them. He'd be able to take better care of his people if there weren't any distractions.

Heather nodded. 'I'm okay. Are you? You didn't sleep much last night.'

'Too many things going on in my head. Can you stay with Casey again today? She trusts you. So do I.' He hooked his fingers into the belt loops on his jeans and stared at the floorboards.

'Of course, I'll be here for as long as you need me. Where are you going now? Please don't go out there alone without the rest of the team.'

The fear in her voice was tangible, the danger a reality. Not just Harry going missing but also what Zac Bannister was truly capable of and when he'd strike again.

'I'm going down to the shed to look through Tracy's things. Maybe there's something in there that will help with the case now Riggs has opened it again.'

'Oh, Travis.'

Heather took a step towards him and reached for him. He read the need to comfort in her eyes and stepped back, hating himself for changing that look to one of hurt.

Not trusting himself to speak, he turned away, opened the door and walked away from the woman he'd fallen in love with. Closing the door behind him, he focused on the shed at the bottom of the garden and willed all thoughts of Heather from his mind.

Even when this was over, his focus would only be on Casey and Harry, if they found him alive, because he wouldn't let them down again.

Heather's heart clenched as she watched Travis walk down the path to the shed and ply the door open. In the quiet early morning with only the call of the birds at dawn, the hinges squealed with the sound of a rusty door that hadn't been opened for years.

Gone was the larrikin she'd grown to love. In his place was a man destroyed by the darker side of humanity. And she'd lost him before she'd had him. She should be thankful. Wasn't that what she'd wanted? No commitment, no happy ever afters? His withdrawal shouldn't hurt so much, but it did.

She sat at the table, her hands wrapped around a mug of steaming tea, a pot of coffee brewing for Travis and any early risers from the tents outside. Soon the paddocks would be crawling with volunteer rescuers once again.

God, she hoped they found Harry today and that he'd be safe and well despite the odds. One positive thing for Travis to hold on to. As soon as the search was over, she'd be packing her bags and leaving Wongan Creek. It shouldn't hurt so much, but it did.

Watching Travis deal with what he had these last few weeks, she knew she had to pluck up the courage to face her own fears. It was time to know for sure whether or not she carried the gene that resulted in MND, whether the result was good or bad. She had nothing left to lose. You couldn't lose something you never had.

An hour later as the paddock came alive, Travis trudged back inside, his arms empty and his face creased with disappointment. Heather's heart broke a little more as he swept past her without a word, totally closed off to the world.

When the breakfast rush was over and the search teams left for the day, Heather went through the motions of getting Casey up and dressed. Another long day stretched ahead of them, one she prayed would end on a happier note.

Keeping Casey entertained was easy, even though the little girl seemed more withdrawn this morning. The ladies from the CWA helped, getting her involved in preparing lunches and giving her clean up jobs to do.

Heather helped out too. She'd miss this when she

transferred to Perth. The community spirit was different in the city. People were busy with life and work, the hustle and bustle of urban living. And she'd miss Casey ... and Travis. But a broken heart could mend. All she had to do was focus on what lay ahead.

Midday rolled around and the first team came back in from the field, and the relay team went out. They were kept busy with handing out food and drinks, and desperately tried to keep up hope for Harry.

Chapter Eighteen

Travis shaded his eyes against the sun and searched the upward slope of Whispering Hills. He whistled for Robbie and listened to the silence that greeted him.

Goddamn it, where were they? A whine reached his ears and his heart rate picked up. 'Robbie!' He whistled again.

'Over there,' said Doc Benson, pointing towards the thick scrub to his left.

They walked between the growth of eucalypts, calling for Harry and Robbie. As they got closer, Robbie edged out of the scrub, his front left paw off the ground as he limped towards them.

'Hey, boy.'

Travis knelt down and held out his hand to Robbie.

The dog barked twice then whined again as he nudged Travis' hand.

'Where's Harry, boy? Let me look at your foot.' He lifted Robbie's paw and checked the pads underneath. They were raw and aggravated as if the dog had been digging for a while. He pulled out a thorn and set Robbie's paw back on the ground. 'Is that better?'

Robbie barked.

'Where's Harry, boy?' Travis asked again, letting the dog drink from his water bottle.

Robbie nudged his hand and turned back into the scrub, limping on three legs. They followed him. Doc radioed the team coordinator.

'We've found Robbie. He's okay. He has a sore paw and might be a little dehydrated, but he's leading us upstream towards Pearson's Bridge.'

'Copy that,' came the response. 'I'll relocate a team to follow. Keep us posted, Doc.'

'Copy that.' He flicked the switch and reattached it to his belt, jogging to catch up with Travis. 'How's the head?'

'Okay. Better.'

'Good. The side of your face is a lovely shade of purple.'

'You get that.'

Travis watched as Robbie weaved in and out of the scrub and headed back to the creek bank. Pearson's Bridge loomed in the distance. It was a hell of a long walk for a man in his seventies with arthritic knees. He hoped to God Harry had survived it. Even in summer the nights could get chilly when the wind blew off the hills across the creek.

Robbie ran on, nose to the ground, picking up his pace.

'He's got something.' Travis lengthened his stride, ignoring the sharp jabs of pain through his still aching body from the impact of his feet hitting the ground.

Robbie veered off to the right and up past the bridge pylon into the bush. He stopped a few metres up, pawed the ground and whined. Travis caught up and knelt down next to him.

'Good boy!'

He rubbed the dog's head and offered him a piece of jerky from his ration pack. Half a metre ahead was a hole in the ground about two metres wide.

'Who the hell would dig a pit like that out here in the middle of nowhere? Bloody hell, the scouts are out in this bushland all the time. Someone could get hurt.' Doc Benson peered into the dark hole.

Robbie whined and barked, pawing at the ground again.

'Is Harry down there, boy?' Travis shone his torch into the hole. 'Harry? Harry!'

A soft groan reached his ears and Travis' heart soared. 'Oh thank God. Harry, answer me, you old bastard.'

Harry's voice reached him, weak and thready. 'Took you long enough, you little sod. Get me out of this bloody hole.'

Travis didn't know whether to laugh or cry, so he did both. 'Are you hurt?'

'Broke my bloody arm when he pushed me into the hole. Think me ankle's gone too.'

'Who pushed you down the hole? Robbie?' The euphoria at finding Harry slid like concrete into the pit of his stomach.

'No, that bloody mongrel Zac!' Pain etched Harry's voice.

Travis looked at Doc. 'We need to get him out of there. I don't like the sound of that.'

'Me neither,' agreed Doc. He stood to pull the radio from his belt.

'Okay, Harry. Stay still. Help is on the way,' Travis reassured his friend.

'Righto, mate. You better get the coppers on it too.'

'Why's that?'

'There's some strange shit down here.'

Travis caught Doc's frown and answered it with his own. 'Do you think he's delirious?'

Doc shrugged. 'Could be.'

'I'm not delirious! I've got me torch here and there's some strange stuff down here. Look!'

A beam of light landed on a pile at the bottom of the

pit. Travis' heart froze and the hair on his arms rose on a wave of goosebumps. 'Fuck.'

'They found Harry! He's okay.' Marge Everett pulled Heather into a tight hug as a cheer went up around the veranda.

Relief flooded her as she received one hug after another and returned them happily. For the first time since she'd broken her silence about the day her mum disappeared, Casey smiled too and that made Heather's heart swell with love.

She swung the little girl up in her arms and did a happy dance along the veranda. Casey giggled and hugged her tightly.

'I love you, Heather. Will you stay with Uncle Travis and me forever?'

Heather missed a step in her dance, stopped and lowered Casey to the ground. The child clung to her hand, her eyes round and pleading.

'Please, Heather?'

'Oh, darling —'

Pain gripped her heart and squeezed. How could she tell this sweet little kid that she had no future here or anywhere? That each moment in time was a step closer to reality, a place where happy ever afters didn't exist. At least, not for her.

Her transfer had come at a good time because she'd already lost her heart to the town, Casey and Travis.

An unbearable ache enveloped her as she looked down at the sweet pixie-faced Casey. She'd never have a child of her own. What good would it do to love this beautiful little girl? She would only lose another loved one when the monster called Motor Neurone Disease took control and stripped away any life they might have together, any chance of being a happy family.

Casey's attention swung to the arrival of the search teams. Weary, grubby but happy with the outcome, they celebrated with backslaps, coffee and bottled water as each team returned to base.

She bounced on the toes of her boots. 'Where are they, Heather? Where's Uncle Trav and Harry?'

'They'll be along soon, sweetheart. If Harry's hurt, they'll need a stretcher. Why don't we go inside and get some blankets and things in case Harry needs them?'

'Okay,' agreed Casey.

It felt like days but in reality it was closer to a couple of hours before Travis appeared with the last search and rescue team to arrive. He carried Robbie in his arms, carefully supporting a bandaged paw.

An intense ache speared through Heather as she watched him walk towards the house. His face was pale against the bloom of the purple bruise along the side of his face and jaw. All she wanted was to hold him and ease his pain.

Casey clutched her hand tightly, looking up at her for reassurance and the ladies of the CWA watched her reactions closely. Heather knew it was definitely time to leave the town. She couldn't bear it if everyone got their hopes up about a relationship between her and Travis.

Travis put Robbie down carefully. Blood pounded through Heather's veins as Travis' eyes searched her face. Tired, grubby and frowning, he walked slowly towards them as if each step caused him pain. Robbie limped along beside him.

Casey ran down the stairs towards him and Heather watched as he held out his arms to scoop her up. Her throat closed around the love that rose from the depths of her soul.

Mrs Everett nudged her gently. 'Go on, girl. That man needs a hug.'

She shook her head. 'I'm sure there'll be plenty going around for him.'

'But he needs one from you, Heather.'

'Mrs E ...' she protested.

Travis walked up onto the veranda and headed straight for her, his eyes burning with a pain so deep she didn't think she could resist the temptation to hold him if she tried. What the hell had happened out there to etch such devastation into his face?

'Travis?' Her words came out on a whisper, trepidation churning in her stomach.

His lips stiffened into a grim line as he held out his

free arm. She stepped into the circle and wrapped her arms around both him and Casey. His grip on her tightened, pulling her close until she could feel the heat from his body permeating through her.

'Just hold me, baby,' he mumbled into her hair, pressing a kiss to her scalp. 'Just hold me.'

'I can do that. Where's Harry and Doc?'

'The RAC chopper should be here shortly to airlift them out. Doc's going into Perth with Harry. They want to do a CT scan and we don't have those facilities at our hospital here. Doc's worried about internal bleeding and fractures. Harry's not a youngster anymore.'

Heather nodded. 'Is he badly hurt?'

'He's a bit battered and bruised. His arm is broken and his ankle might be fractured,' said Travis, his tone grim. 'Riggs will be back as soon as the chopper arrives. He's going to want to talk to me, so I'll have to head into town to the station later.'

Heather's unease grew, but questions were best kept for when Casey was out of earshot. The atmosphere around the team who'd brought Harry in was tense, unlike the heady euphoria of those who celebrated his rescue.

Something was horribly wrong. Beneath her hands, Travis' body was tense and clammy. A frown marred his features and his eyes had a haunted look she badly wanted to erase. She hated that he looked so defeated. He should be happy. Harry was alive.

Travis removed his arm from around her and set Casey down on her feet. He turned to the group of ladies who had gathered around them.

'Bella, can you take care of Casey for me? I need to talk to Heather alone for a moment.'

'Of course, Travis. Come along, Casey. Benji and his mum are on their way here. Let's go and get some cookies and tea ready.'

'Thanks.' With a hand on her back, he steered Heather inside, through the kitchen and into the lounge room, but he seemed too wired to sit and paced the floor instead.

She let him walk it off, watching his every move, waiting until he was ready to talk. With every stride of those long, beautifully sculpted legs, every twist of his hips as he turned and every rub of his jaw with a shaky hand, she watched him suffer.

'Travis, let me help you.'

His footsteps faltered and he stopped. 'I don't know if you can help me. This has gone too far.'

'Then talk to me. What happened out there that has you so spooked?'

She stepped forward and placed her hand over his heart. It pounded against her palm. He covered her hand with his, squeezing her fingers against his chest. Then he dragged her against him and held her tightly.

Heather waited, listened to his heart beat as she

wrapped her arms around his waist. His hands stroked her hair in a shaky rhythm.

'We found Harry in a pit in the dense bush up past Pearson's Bridge. We don't have the full story yet because Harry's recollection of what happened is sketchy. It sounds like he was pushed.'

'Oh no! Who'd do that?' Heather lifted her face to his.

'He says it was Zac Bannister.'

Heather shivered against him and tightened her hold. 'Oh God.'

'Harry says he saw lights across the creek last night, so he went looking early this morning. He thought it might be someone trying to steal those damned sheep of his. He doesn't remember how he got to Pearson's Bridge but he remembers running into Zac. Sounds like the bastard decided it was the perfect opportunity to get rid of Harry.'

'With Harry out of the way ...' Heather shuddered. She didn't want to think about what could have happened to the old man.

'It would give them the opportunity to claim his land at auction when it came time to settle his estate. Riggs will take him in for questioning. This time though there's evidence.'

Heather pulled away so she could see his face more clearly. 'Evidence? Is that why there's a forensics team on the way?'

Travis nodded. 'This time we have him. We can make it stick. But oh God, Heather ... what was down there ...'

She pressed her face into his chest and tightened her hold as his hands rubbed circles on her back. Chills followed the movement of his fingers on her skin.

'We found human remains, a WCM shirt with Bannister's name on it, covered in blood, and Tracy's mobile phone. I didn't even know it was missing. How did we not realise it was gone sooner?'

Heather shivered. Remains. Not Tracy's because her body had been found, so someone else had met their fate at the hands of Zac Bannister.

'Maybe the phone will hold some clues in Tracy's case,' she murmured.

'We're hoping. It looks intact and we're hoping the battery is good so it can be charged. I want this to end. I want him locked away for good.'

'Then let's hope there's sufficient evidence against him this time. Riggs won't waste time getting the facts now.'

'Yeah, thank God we have him back in charge of the case. He won't let Bannister walk away from this a second time.'

Heather looked up at his face. 'You're exhausted, Travis. You need some rest. Why don't you clean up while I help the ladies clear things away?'

'Stay with me tonight. I need to know that you're safe in case they let Bannister go.'

Heather's heart stuttered. 'Travis ... I can't.'

'Please. I need you, Heather. I've never said that to anyone. I need to hold you.' He tipped up her chin. 'After all that's happened these last few weeks, I've realised life is too short for regrets. I love you and I need you to stay. I can't lose you too.'

Euphoria mixed with regret and churned in her stomach. Fate was cruel in the hand it played. A man who had lost so much deserved more than yet another loss, another heartbreak. To stay with him, sleep with him—and she knew it would come to that—would be selfish, knowing she'd be leaving soon. But what girl would pass up the chance to spend the night in Travis' arms and take with her one last beautiful memory to keep her warm when the days grew cold and dark. And, God help her, she loved him back even if she couldn't keep him.

Chapter Nineteen

ravis sat in Riggs' small office at Wongan Creek police station. He'd cleaned up and then come straight down to give Riggs as much information as he could on what they'd found and the events leading up to Harry's disappearance. He hadn't wanted to leave Heather or Casey alone. Not having almost lost Harry. But he owed a debt to Tracy that needed to be paid. He'd waited long enough for answers and maybe now he had them, he could lay Tracy's ghost to rest.

Travis wanted to scream his frustration at the slow turn of the wheels of justice, but he knew Riggs had to tread carefully around the handling of Tracy's case to achieve the outcome they wanted — Zac Bannister locked up forever. So he tried to be patient and still the distress of rehashing the circumstances surrounding

Tracy's death. To cooperate as much as he could while they waited for the battery on her phone to charge up enough to switch on.

He wanted a shower, to call the hospital and check on Harry, and to go home and crawl into bed with Heather curled up against him and Casey safe in the room next door. But first he owed it to his sister to finish this.

Across the table from Travis, Riggs clicked away at his computer with the mouse, calling up the database of missing girls he needed to match the remains to, the bloodied clothes had been sent to Perth for DNA testing and the battery indicator on Tracy's phone moved at an annoyingly slow pace from red to green.

They'd rehashed every moment of the night of the party, the day she went missing and the excruciating pain of the condition they'd found her body in. Even though a trial could go on for years, they needed to make the charges stick. Already, John Bannister had his most expensive lawyers on it, although Travis guessed that even he couldn't deny the evidence pointing to the fact that his grandson was a murderer.

'That's it for tonight, Travis. Go home. Get some rest. HQ are sending out two of their finest detectives tomorrow and we'll at least have a good file ready for them.' Riggs linked his fingers and stretched his arms out in front of them, his knuckles cracking.

'Not the same ones from the original investigation, I hope.'

'No, mate. These two are deep in an investigation into the bikies linked to Zac's name. I know them well. They're fair, unbiased and thorough. I have complete faith in them getting a conviction. Now go home to those girls of yours.'

Travis stood and stretched. 'I'll sleep easier knowing you have enough evidence to keep Bannister in custody.'

'And that's where he'll stay. I can promise you that. I don't care how much noise his grandfather makes. Although, I think you'll find he won't be quite so chirpy either this time around. Not with all the evidence piling up against his precious grandson. Go!' Riggs ordered.

'Going,' said Travis, a ghost of a smile touching his lips for the first time since Harry went missing.

The drive home down the dark road that wound out of town into the countryside seemed endless, but eventually the lights of the homestead shone a welcoming light across his paddock. Peace had settled in his front yard for tonight at least. Tomorrow would bring more upheaval, but tonight he planned to celebrate one small victory and Harry being found alive.

The front door opened, spilling light onto the veranda as he pulled up outside the house and killed the engine. Robbie bounded out the door and down the steps, barking excitedly. Heather and Casey stepped into the light of the doorway and waved. His heart beat a little faster. She'd stayed. He wasn't sure she would. Bella, Mrs Everett or even Benji's mum would have taken Casey. But Heather had stayed and that meant ... he wasn't sure what it meant exactly.

Travis got out of the ute and closed the door, pausing to give Robbie's head a quick rub.

'Hey, boy. How's the paw?' He examined the bandaged paw Robbie held up. 'You'll be chasing frogs and bunnies again before you know it.'

With the dog walking close to him, he walked up the veranda steps. His girls looked so beautiful standing in the doorway together. Could he hope that Heather loved him back? That she'd stay and be a part of their lives now that no court in their right mind would award custody to a suspected murderer? Now that all aspects of conflict of interest had been removed.

Casey clung to Heather's hand, her little face screwed up in a frown. The events of the last few days had unsettled her, stolen her confidence with the resurgence of one awful memory. If it took a lifetime, he'd do everything he could to restore that confidence and erase the terror she'd faced.

'Hey, sweet pea,' he said, taking the steps two at a time. He scooped her up and hugged her tightly. 'I thought you'd be asleep by now. It's late.'

'I couldn't sleep. I was waiting for you. It's not Heather's fault. Please don't be cross with her.'

Tears of uncertainty glistened in her beautiful green eyes so like Tracy's. He remembered seeing that same look in his sister's eyes every time he'd tried to talk to her after the party, through the months of silence as her body grew with the baby she carried but wouldn't talk about. No one in his family would ever feel unsure or unsafe again. He'd do everything he could to make sure they didn't.

'I'm not angry, sweet pea. Not with you or Heather. It's hard to sleep when there's so much going on. Why don't we have some hot chocolate out here under the stars and we'll read a story together? Then maybe you'll feel a little sleepier.'

Casey nodded and buried her wet face in his neck. He patted her back soothingly for a moment before turning to Heather and pressing a kiss to her cheek.

'Thanks for staying.'

She reached up to touch his face, her eyes unreadable in the shadows, her skin warm and soft against his. 'I'll put the kettle on.'

Travis cupped her hand to his face with his free one then turned it over to press a kiss to her palm. She closed her fingers around it.

He watched as she walked inside, loving every sway of her hips and every stride of her shapely legs. If all they had was this one night, he'd make it count because tomorrow wasn't promised.

Travis set Casey on her feet on the old sofa. She scurried into the corner as he sat to remove his boots.

'Will Harry be okay, Uncle Trav? He'll come back, won't he?'

'He'll be fine, sweet pea. Harry's tough. It'll take a while for his arm and leg to heal, but you know Harry, nothing keeps him down.'

'Will he come live with us now?'

'I'll do my best to make sure he does. He'll need someone to take care of him for a while.'

Travis settled back against the sofa and put his feet up on the rail. Casey curled up into his side. He hoped he could protect her from some of the ugliness a case against Zac Bannister would flush out. They'd get through it, he'd make sure of that because it meant he got to keep at least one of the girls close to his heart.

Heather came out with a tray of mugs filled with hot chocolate, leftover cookies the ladies from the CWA had baked, and Casey's favourite book. She put the tray down on the wide ledge under the window and handed Casey her mug.

'I put a little cold milk in it for you, sweetheart, so it won't be too hot to drink right away.'

'Thank you, Heather.' Casey took the Disney princess mug with both hands and sipped. 'That's yummy.'

Travis tugged on the leg of Heather's jeans. 'Sit.

You don't have to wait on us. It's been a long couple of days for all of us.'

She sat on his other side, leaving their drinks on the tray to cool. Her leg brushed his, her warmth chasing away the chill he'd felt since finding Harry and the bones, but she was as stiff as a board next to him.

Travis reached for her hands, clasped together tightly in her lap. He pried them apart and entwined his fingers with hers, giving them a little squeeze. She smiled and nerves danced in his belly.

'I'm finished! Can we read the story now?'

Casey held out her mug to Travis. He let go of Heather's hand and took it from her. 'Of course, my princess. Do you want me to read it or Heather?'

'Both! You do the boy bits and Heather can do the girl bits.'

Travis smothered a smile at Heather's blush. He gave her a little wink that made a grin tug at her lips. Things would work out just fine. Together they read the story and it didn't take long for Casey to nod off against Travis' arm.

'I'll put her to bed,' he said quietly. 'Don't go anywhere, okay?'

'I won't.' Her words carried a soft promise that was music to his ears.

～

Heather swallowed the nervousness lodged in her chest and willed the butterflies to stop fluttering in her tummy. Common sense tried to sneak in and she pushed it away.

One night. That's all. One night before she left Wongan Creek and the people in it. One last, precious night with the man she'd grown to love but couldn't have. He deserved someone nice and healthy like Janet, who could have his babies and grow old with him. She couldn't promise him that.

His footsteps sounded on the polished jarrah floorboards a moment or two before the fly screen door opened and he stepped out onto the veranda. Her breath caught at the sight of him—the width of his shoulders against the light, the taper of his hard body and the jeans that hugged his hips.

The black T-shirt he'd changed into before going to see Riggs moulded his arms and chest. Her hands itched to feel those muscles flex under her hands again. Soon she would.

The cushions dipped under his weight. Travis' old sofa was fast becoming one of her favourite places to be. She rubbed the clammy palms of her hands on her jeans.

He leaned his head back against the sofa and sighed. Every curve and angle of his body was downright sexy. She studied each precious inch of him, committing the vision to memory for those dark days when she'd be alone with only the ticking of the clock for company.

'Does Riggs know how Harry ended up in that pit?' Best to focus on what was. It made what could be easier to forget.

'Harry doesn't remember anything except Zac sneaking up on him and us finding him. We can only guess that he wandered off. That's one of the consequences of Alzheimer's. They get confused easily with direction. Riggs will know more after he's questioned Zac, who won't talk until he's lawyered up.'

Heather shook her head. 'Why would he hurt poor Harry?'

Travis shrugged and rubbed a hand over his face. Tiredness showed in the dark circles forming under his eyes. 'What was Zac even doing up there? Harry must have surprised him, caught him doing something nasty. Maybe he saw the opportunity to get rid of Harry so they could make a play for Murchison's Run. Given what we found in that pit, I'd guess he didn't want any witnesses. He didn't bank on Harry being a stubborn old bugger.'

A sad smile tugged her lips. 'I'm going to miss Harry. I'll miss everyone.'

'You're still taking that transfer? You don't have to leave, Heather.' His voice was low against the night sounds of the bush.

'I have to.'

'Why?'

Because she'd lost her heart. How could she explain

that to him? He'd already lost so much. What simmered between them had the potential for forever, except she might not have a lifetime to enjoy it.

She rolled her shoulders against the tension building there and sat back, side by side with Travis. The chill in her soul warmed a little with his heat. Her gaze fell on his hand where it lay against his thigh — tanned, long-fingered and callused by manual labour. Tonight wasn't for talking, it was for celebrating. Harry was alive and Casey's future was secure.

She slipped her hand under his, palm up, and felt the squeeze of his fingers as they entwined with hers. 'Let's not talk about it now, okay?'

Resting her head on his shoulder, she snuggled closer. They sat in comfortable silence for a while, the night sounds of the bush easing the friction between them.

'What will happen to Harry now?' Heather asked quietly.

'As soon as they give him the all clear, he'll come back to Wongan Creek Hospital for a while. We have basic facilities here for minor surgery, maternity and non-life threatening cases. When they release him, I'll convince him to move in here with us.'

'And Zac?' Not that he'd be a threat to her any longer when she left, but she cared about the people of Wongan Creek.

'Riggs has enough to keep him in custody until a

court hearing. He'll be transferred to a Perth facility tomorrow.'

'Will they have enough for a conviction?' What if they didn't? It didn't bear thinking about. If they released him, he'd be out for blood — Harry's, hers, Travis'.

'They have enough. Riggs will make it stick this time. John hasn't even argued against Zac's arrest. I don't think he realised how sick his grandson really is.'

'It's kinda sad though, isn't it?'

'Don't feel sorry for them, baby.' He lifted their joined hands and kissed her knuckles.

Heather shivered against him as the feather-light touch of his lips brushed her skin, sending the butterflies in her tummy spiralling.

'John knew Zac had a problem. He just didn't know how bad it was,' he continued, studying their entwined fingers. 'He could have done something about it a long time ago, before it got to this, but he ignored it.' Reaching over with his free hand, he cupped her face and brought her lips within inches of his. 'I don't want to talk about the Bannisters anymore tonight. Right now, this is about you and me.'

Heather drew in a breath against the surge of need that pulsed through her. With his lips a whisper away, all she wanted was to feel them on hers, to erase the evil of the day and replace it with goodness. To spend this one night with Travis and to know every inch of him.

Then his mouth was coaxing hers, sending spirals of heat through her blood, chasing away thoughts of murderous intent and crime. And he tasted like promises and dreams, sun and blue skies, forever and white satin. All the things she couldn't have forever but would enjoy for just one night.

She kissed him back, putting her heart and soul into it. She'd make this last night count, make it so unforgettable that it would last through the dark days ahead.

Heather let her fingers slip under his T-shirt, explored the contours of his abdomen, blazed a trail higher towards his heart. It thumped unsteadily under her palm.

His tongue danced with hers as he eased his fingers out of her grip and stroked a hand across her hip, drawing her closer. He eased her up onto his lap so she straddled him, their hips aligned.

His mouth left hers to travel over her face with sweet kisses that set fire to her blood. Then his teeth nipped at her earlobe and she curled into him, feeling the hard ridge building between them.

She let her head fall back, exposing her neck to his mouth. With each flick of his tongue and press of his lips, her skin grew hotter.

'Travis,' she whispered, squirming against him. Her fingers found his nipple and she rolled her thumb over it, whimpering as he moaned against her.

And then his hands were touching her, tracing the length of her spine, the curve of her hip, over her tummy and up until they brushed her breasts. He tipped up her chin and she met the heat in his eyes.

'Let's take this inside. Hold tight, sweetheart.'

He shifted her off his lap, stood and swept her up into his arms. Heather linked her hands around his neck, depositing soft kisses along his jawline as he walked towards the door. Travis nudged the fly screen door open with his foot and let it close behind them then he pushed the front door closed, pausing a moment to hear it click shut behind them.

As they reached his bedroom, he let her slide down the length of him, keeping her anchored there with his hands caressing her hips. His eyes were closed and exhaustion etched his face. She reached up to ease the frown lines from his forehead.

'Love me, Travis,' Heather whispered.

His eyes opened and the heat of his gaze slammed into her soul. 'I already do.'

Then his hands were busy easing her shirt from her shoulders, his thumbs caressing her skin, his lips following the trail. Heather eased the hem of his T-shirt up and let her fingers play across his body, feeling the muscles clench under her touch.

His movements were unhurried as if he wanted to absorb the feel of her, save it to memory. They had all night. Then he peeled her jeans over her hips, taking her underwear with them in one smooth move. She stepped out of them as his hands cupped her bottom and drew her closer.

Heat, beautiful and liquid, flowed through her as she pressed against him, feeling his desire hard and rigid at her belly. She reached between them.

'It's only fair I get you out of these.' Heather nipped at his bottom lip.

He smiled against her mouth. 'No argument here, sweetheart.'

And then he was kissing her, his tongue dancing with hers, the pressure of his mouth so sweet she wanted to cry out but couldn't. Her hands gripped the waistband of his jeans, frozen with pleasure. Only when he lifted his head, did she draw his zipper down while he eased his T-shirt over his head.

At last there was nothing between them but heated skin. Travis gathered her against him and she gloried in the feel of his nakedness against hers. She let her hands explore every inch of him, a favour he returned. Her knees buckled at the sensations each stroke and caress yielded.

He lifted her in his arms, kissed her breathless then lay her down on the bed. 'You're beautiful, Heather.'

His gaze raked every inch of her, leaving a trail of fire in its wake. Then the mattress dipped under his weight and he was there with her, his length aligned with hers, his hands making magic on her skin until at last he covered her body with his. His hands clasped hers, raised them over her head and together they rode the age old rhythm of love.

He filled every inch of her, thrusting, withdrawing, making her spine arch, letting go of her hands so her fingers could dig into the flesh of his backside. She'd lied when she'd told him Miss Turner's donkey had a better rear. His fitted her hands perfectly.

Then his mouth was on hers, giving her a taste of something that beat the best chocolate on the planet, and his hands fine-tuned her body to match his rhythm.

'Come with me, baby,' he whispered against her ear, his breath hot, the words urgent.

'Yes,' she answered, closing her eyes and giving herself up to the magic of loving Travis Bailey.

Chapter Twenty

Heather watched Travis sleep, dawn creeping through the half-closed blinds, the first rays of the morning sun streaking across his face. Her heart twisted in a knot. Every time he'd turned to her in the night, she'd fallen a little deeper, a little further in love.

His lashes fluttered open and a satisfied smile stretched his lips. He reached out a hand to caress the curve of her hip. 'Hey.'

'I should go.'

'Stay.'

His fingers trailed up to her waist, playing in the dip before moving up her arm and over her shoulder. She shivered as delicious tingles followed in their wake. If she stayed any longer, it would be harder to leave.

The cold pre-dawn had brought with it the reminder

that she'd only committed to one night. There was no future for her and Travis and prolonging the goodbye would only make it more unbearable.

Travis sighed. 'I don't like the look of that frown, baby. What's on your mind?'

He'd been honest with her all along. He'd trusted her with his secrets. Didn't he deserve the truth? Heather sat up and swung her legs over the edge of the bed. Pulling on her discarded shirt, she stood and walked to the window to peer through the blind at the morning sun. It bloomed warm against the clear sky, climbing slowly to what would be another burning hot day.

She heard the rustle of the sheets as he pushed them aside, the sound of his feet hitting the wood floor with a slap then he was next to her, naked, hard-muscled and gorgeous. Her heart broke a little more.

'Heather, honey, I think after last night you can trust me with what's going on in that busy head of yours.' His arms came around her and he drew her to him, his forehead against hers. 'Spill it.'

She couldn't look him in the eye, see the pain when it came, so she closed her eyes. 'I have to go. If I stay, I'll only end up hurting you. And Casey. I can't do that, Travis.'

'Hurt us how?' He pressed her head to his chest and hugged her tightly.

'I can't put you through that pain.' Against her ear,

his heart beat steadily, his warmth reaching in to ease the chill in her own. Each soothing stroke of his hand on her hair made her heart ache more.

'Talk to me, sweetheart.'

'You've lost so much already. Now you have Harry and Casey to care for. I can't be a burden to you too.'

'Heather, you're a strong, independent woman who has brought so much happiness to this town. How can you even think you'll be a burden?'

'Because I might have Motor Neurone like my mother had. I can't give you forever. I won't have children. And when it comes to the end, I'll be totally reliant on you, completely incapacitated. I can't put you through what I went through with Mum.'

His hands traced soothing circles on her back. 'Last time I checked loving someone meant taking the good with the bad. Sickness, health, richer, poorer — isn't that what the vows say?' He pressed a kiss to her head. 'We'll see this through together. You said you *might* have MND. What if you don't and you walk away now?'

Heather pushed out of his arms. If she didn't go now, he'd wear her down, make her believe in happy ever afters. She started picking up her clothes from where they'd landed the night before, the memories of a night in Travis' arms whirling in her head. If all she got to keep was those memories, she had to be content with it.

'The preliminary blood tests showed a gene anomaly. Doc Benson has referred me to a specialist in Perth.' She stepped into her underwear and pulled on her jeans. Going through the motions. It's what she had to do every day from now on.

'I'll come with you. You don't have to do this alone.'

'I *do* have to do it alone.' Her words caught on a breath. 'It happens fast or it happens slow, Travis. Either way, everyone suffers. You deserve better than that.'

She looked at him standing at the window, gloriously naked and strong, a frown etching his brow. Her soul ached with loving him, but she'd rather break his heart now before she got too deep.

'So you sleep with me and then decide it's over.' His voice was dangerously quiet in the room, the edge it carried razor sharp. He raked a hand through his hair. 'Did what we shared last night mean absolutely nothing to you? I have too much at stake as Casey's guardian to treat relationships like one night stands, Heather.'

His words sliced her soul, guilt eating into the wound. She shook her head. 'It meant everything to me.'

'So why are you running away?' He walked towards her, placed his hands on her arms. 'If the tests are positive and you are ill, I'd rather enjoy a few precious moments *with* you than live a lifetime *without* you. I love you, Heather.'

The honesty in his words, in his eyes, shattered what was left of her resolve, but she dragged her willpower to the fore. 'I can't stay, Travis.'

His mouth hardened, the light in his eyes dimming, every muscle in his body stiff as he stepped back. 'Then go. Go now before Casey wakes up. She loves you, Heather. I had hopes of us being a family, but I can see loving you isn't enough to keep you here.'

'All the more reason for me to leave. I never wanted to get anyone's hopes up. I never planned on having a family.'

Travis walked over to the bedroom door and opened it. 'Don't let me stop you then. Run away, Heather. Run away from the people who love you, who want to stand by your side. Harry won't remember, but Casey will. And if you think leaving now won't hurt us, you're wrong.'

Heather picked up her car keys and purse, her feet heavy as she moved to the door. She stopped in front of him, searched his face, but he kept his gaze on the wall.

'I'm sorry,' she whispered, the ache in her heart so strong she thought it might actually break. She watched the mask descend on his features, cold and distant, and knew she'd lost him forever.

Elliott was sitting at Heather's desk when she walked into the office after a shower and change of clothes. She'd hauled her suitcases out of the cupboard and had already started throwing her belongings into them, her mind closed to the pain the thought of leaving raised.

'How soon can I leave, Elliott?'

Her boss sat back in the chair, his eyebrows raised. 'I didn't think you'd want to leave. It's pretty clear you have a thing for Bailey, Heather. The Bannisters weren't wrong on that account.'

'They are wrong. The Baileys were clients just like every other case I've worked. You were the one who took me off the case and arranged this transfer. I want it to happen. The sooner the better.'

Elliott's gaze narrowed on her thoughtfully. 'That's not the impression I got yesterday. You don't seem to realise how well you fit into this community.'

'It's my job. Now it's done and it's time to move on.'

'Hmm,' Elliott muttered. 'This wouldn't have anything to do with those blood tests, would it? Are you throwing all this away because of an illness you're not even sure you have?'

She'd had to tell Elliott about the testing, declare any hereditary illnesses on the health check required for her job application. Heather tipped up her chin and ignored his question.

He picked up his pen and tapped it on the case folder in front of him. 'Did I ever tell you about my wife?'

Heather frowned. Elliott was married? She'd never heard rumours of a wife or seen proof of one since he joined the department.

'No,' she replied, taking a seat on the opposite side of the desk.

'When I met her, she was nineteen, just starting out her career as a runway model. Two years later she was diagnosed with breast cancer. Sadly it was too late already. The cancer had spread and was aggressive. We got married in the spring that year and less than six months later she was gone.'

Heather shifted in her seat. 'I'm so sorry.'

'I'm not. We had two and a half beautiful years together. There was anger, pain, suffering, yes. But there were a multitude of very happy moments too and I wouldn't change that for anything. You get my point?'

'Loud and clear, Elliott. I'm sorry for your loss, I really am, but I need to deal with this my way. I'd like to leave as soon as possible.'

'You might be needed to give evidence in the Bannister case.'

'Then I'll be there when I'm needed.'

'I got the impression you are needed ... right here. You're cleared on the conflict of interest complaint. The townsfolk were quite happy to go in to bat for you. I have a file full of glowing recommendations and character references.' He dropped the pen and steepled his fingers. 'Maybe you should think about that for a moment.'

'Elliott, now is not the time for you to see things in technicolour.' Heather fidgeted with the cup holding her array of pens. She had to harden her heart against this damn town that had woven its magic around her, made her feel like there was something to live for after all, only to have it ripped from her again when the time came.

He chuckled. 'Sometimes a man has to play hard ball. I know you think I'm a black and white man, Heather. Mostly, it's true. In this case, I'm prepared to colour outside the lines.'

'I'll send you a colouring book so you can embrace your inner child and explore your newfound talent.' She smiled grimly. 'Great to see you're human after all, but you won't change my mind. I can be packed and out of here in a couple of hours.'

Elliott sighed. 'If you insist, I can't stop you. Your first job when you get back to the city is to check up on Harry. He'll be in hospital there for a few days more. I need an assessment on his state of health, both physical and mental, so we can add him to the visitation list for when he comes home.'

'Who'll be filling my position?'

'I hear Martha Wallace wants to come back to Wongan Creek.'

'Oh, Elliott! You can't do that to these poor people. She's a terror!'

He cocked an eyebrow at her, a grin tugging at his lips. With a shrug, he turned and tucked the folder into the filing cabinet. 'Choices, Miss Penney. They always have consequences.'

Half an hour later, Heather tossed her cases in the boot of her four-wheel drive. No matter how guilty she felt about leaving the town to the mercy of Martha Wallace, it was the best for all of them. Of that she was certain. Elliott had it wrong. The town didn't need her and everyone there had their own problems without her adding to them.

She stood in the doorway and took a moment to look around the house that had been home for the past six months. It echoed the emptiness in her heart. For all its pretty cottage décor and warm, welcoming feel, it had never really been home for Heather.

There were none of her precious knickknacks on display. She'd never unpacked her box of crystals or the small collection of Royal Dalton statues her mum had treasured. They were the only things her mum had kept as a reminder of Heather's grandparents. She'd destroyed all photographs and correspondence, and all traces of her heritage — even her Irish passport once she had her Australian citizenship. Now the little she'd left behind gathered dust in a storage unit in Perth along with all their memories of life in Darwin. All Heather had arrived with was her clothes, and that was all she'd take away with her.

When she'd come to this small town, she hadn't bargained on finding friendship with the ladies of the CWA or forming a bond with a lonely old man and a family she'd grown to love. It had never occurred to her that she might want to stay.

The realisation made her chest ache, but even so Heather knew it was time to face her demons away from the emotional ties no matter how tempted she was to stay. She'd be taking her suitcases, but be leaving her heart behind.

Heather closed the front door and locked it then got in the car and drove the couple of streets up to Main Street. Outside the real estate agent's office, she dropped the key through the brass slot in the front door. The flap clanged shut with a finality that made her realise another part of her life was over. More memories to hold close to an empty heart.

The town was stirring slowly and she met the 'good mornings' with a little wave of her own. She'd miss them all, but such was life. With one last look, she got into the car and drove away, ignoring the tears that rolled down her cheeks.

Chapter Twenty-One

'Why the hell have I got a cast on my arm?' Harry tapped on the plaster of Paris mould with his knuckles. 'And why is my ankle strapped up tighter than a virgin's chastity belt?'

Travis sighed. 'You had a run in with a hole and a bad guy.'

Harry snorted. 'That only happens in the movies. You taking me home?'

'Yep.'

'Good. The food here is shit.'

'Yes, but the nurses are prettier.' Travis patted his shoulder. 'I heard you asked one to marry you.'

'She had painkillers and I needed them. I'm not as tough as I used to be.'

'You're a hell of a lot tougher than you think. Come

on, Hotel Bailey has a room ready for you.' Travis helped him up out of the chair next to the hospital bed.

Harry held up his plaster cast. 'You gonna wipe my arse too?'

'That's your left hand, you old bastard. Your right one works just fine.'

Harry chuckled. 'Still got your spark even though that face is pretty miserable. What's got you looking so sorry for yourself?'

Travis rubbed the scar on his eye. The stitches were out and it had healed nicely. The bruises he'd got thanks to Zac Bannister had faded to a tinge of yellow and his jaw no longer ached when he chewed. If only his heart wasn't battered and his dreams weren't filled with Heather, he'd be just fine.

On the upside, the DNA testing on the clothes found in the pit matched Zac's, Tracy's phone had held video and sound she'd taken as he'd chased her down to the creek. The cocky fool had let her film the whole thing, then taken over as he'd held her head under water and watched her drown, never thinking the phone would survive to give evidence.

The remains were identified as a girl who'd gone missing while hitchhiking from Perth to Kalgoorlie. He'd confessed to indecent assault and murder, and now waited in a maximum security prison for sentencing. Prison had its own kangaroo court and Zac had pissed off a few people when he'd given up the names of a few of his bikie mates. Shower time for him would be an interesting party.

Justice was served and Travis should be happy as the town came to terms with having harboured a murderer. He had the answers that had plagued him since Tracy's death. Casey was his forever and his plea for adoption had been approved thanks to Elliott. Harry was coming home, Robbie's paw had healed and the sheared sheep were happily grazing in the newly harvested and turned canola field. But victory wasn't as sweet as it could be.

He'd read up on the effects of Motor Neurone Disease, researched the care a patient would require, and realised it was all useless if the person who needed it didn't want to be cared for. So he'd sucked it up and tried not to think about her every time he sat on the sofa with his feet up. Or remembered to put the toilet seat down. Or when he ran the firebreak on Fantasia's back hoping to see her four-wheel drive pulled up on the side of the road so she could pretend she wasn't checking him out and give him shit about his arse. His arse missed the grip of her hands and the rest of him hankered for her too.

'Is that pretty little social worker gonna take care of me when I get home?'

Harry so remembered the wrong things at the worst times. Couldn't he remember the things that didn't make Travis' heart ache?

'I'm not sure Elliott would like you saying he's

pretty,' replied Travis, his gut squeezing at the thought of Heather.

'Who's Elliott?'

'Heather's replacement.' Travis picked up Harry's bag and watched the nurse help him into a wheelchair. He followed them out into the hallway as she wheeled him to the lift.

'Who's Heather?'

'The pretty little social worker.' He stabbed the elevator button a little harder than intended.

'I thought she was Eileen, you know. You shoulda asked her to marry you.'

'Yeah, thanks, Harry.'

'Is that what's got your Y-fronts in a knot? She turned you down?'

The nurse giggled as she wheeled him into the elevator.

Travis grimaced. 'Something like that.'

He wondered if he'd ever stop hurting. It had been over a week since she'd left town. A week of fielding questions from Casey, frowns from the ladies at the CWA and the occasional casserole showing up on his doorstep.

At least Robbie had brought home a stray kitten that kept Casey occupied until bed time when she'd ask for the story Heather used to read. It was damn hard for a man to keep it together sometimes.

'Hey, Travis?' Harry's voice interrupted his thoughts

as the elevator stopped with a bump and the doors swished open.

'Yeah, mate?'

'I've been thinking ...'

'That's dangerous.'

'Smart arse. You know how Bannister wants to buy my land?'

Travis' heart missed a beat. 'You're not thinking of selling out, are you?'

'Do I look like a fool?'

'With a bright green cast on your arm and a moon boot on your foot, you want me to answer that question?'

'That's what made me think. What if we build a seniors' lifestyle village on my land? You know, for the ageing population of Wongan Creek since that bloody gold mine seems set to stay around for a while. We can do a bowling green, a pool and a gym. Some of those cottages where you can still be independent but help is on hand if you need it. Then I can stay and still see the sun rise over the creek.'

Travis thought about it as they walked towards the ute. 'That's not a silly idea, Harry. I'd rather have an old age home next door than a gold mine or a housing estate.'

'Lifestyle village,' Harry grumbled. 'You could lease out your land to the village and start a hobby farm. The residents can potter around in it. Start a Grower's Market.'

'Now we're talking. I'd support a Grower's Market and we might as well put the land to good use. We can look at what else would grow well with the canola crop so we don't cross-contaminate. I'm liking the concept more and more, you clever old bugger. Why don't we run it by Doc Benson when we get home?'

Travis opened the ute door and helped Harry inside. He'd been thinking about what to do with the empty paddocks not filled with canola ever since he'd sold the cattle, but with raising Casey and taking care of Harry he'd had enough to juggle. Harry's suggestion opened up a whole string of possibilities.

'We'll talk more about it on the way.'

If he could keep Harry's mind focused on the topic for long enough, he might remember it when they got home. The more he thought about it, the more the idea grew on him. Maybe it would keep his mind off the one perfect person to run the facility.

Heather fiddled with the zipper on her purse and tapped her foot nervously. She hated hospitals and waiting rooms. The smell of antiseptic and old magazines set her nerves on edge. They reminded her too much of the hours spent in and out of hospital with Mum.

At least the blood tests were done. Waiting for the results was the killer. Visiting Harry when he'd been recovering in hospital had made her realise the need to get her own affairs in order. She had no family to care for her. Still, she'd need a will to leave the little bit she had to a charity if the DNA tests proved positive for the mistake in the gene code that caused MND.

Over the last week, she'd been prodded and poked, attached to electrodes and had her muscle responses recorded, and transcranial magnetic stimulation to measure the activity of the upper motor neurones in her brain. And now the wait for all those results so she could take charge of her own destiny. The specialist had warned that the chances were high given the severe case her mother had.

'Miss Penney?'

Heather looked up at the receptionist. 'Yes?'

'Mr Loudon will see you now.'

Heather's heart pounded as she stood. God, she wished Travis was here now. That she'd said yes to him coming with her. That she hadn't walked out on him a month ago. She missed him and Casey so much. The stars in the city were dimmer and the night sounds were nothing like the bush. She'd much rather listen to the chirping of cicadas than the constant whine of sirens.

She walked up the stark white hallway with its fluorescent lights and blue and red patterned carpet, her footfalls soundless. With a quick knock, she pushed open the door.

Perry Loudon smiled warmly at her. His wispy grey hair, round cheeks and frameless glasses made him look like a kindly professor from a fairytale movie, a wizard with the power to make or break her dreams.

'Come in, my dear.'

Heather closed the door behind her and clutched her purse tightly to stop her hands from shaking. She smiled weakly at him as he invited her to sit. Her mind raced with the possibilities of the outcome of this appointment. The things she'd have to arrange if the results were positive, the life she could rebuild if they were negative. She couldn't allow herself to hope just yet. Since meeting Travis and Casey she had reason to hope because her life without them was miserable.

'How have you been? I hope all those tests weren't too stressful for you?'

'A little scary. I'm glad they're over,' Heather admitted.

Being hooked up to the machines had terrified her, but sitting alone in the waiting rooms preparing to take the tests had scared her the most. That was when she'd wished she'd had someone to hold her hand through this journey.

'I'm sure you are. Well, I'll get straight to the point then. You'll be pleased to know that the TMS scans came back normal. The MRI was all clear. Now, that doesn't diagnose MND, but we do like to check for any pre-symptom damage just to make sure.'

Heather let out a little sigh of relief, although her fingers were white from the pressure of clenching them. 'So that's good, right?'

'Very good. The nerve conduction study and Electromyography results were equally as pleasing. Your nerves and muscles are all reacting normally. Very well indeed. So that rules out any premature muscle and nerve degeneration.'

Knowing the studies were all clear was comforting but it was the blood test results she feared the most. They were the ones that counted. She placed a hand on her tummy to try and still the churning.

Mr Loudon smiled kindly at her. 'I know this is hard for you, my dear. We're almost there. Now the blood tests ... these are what you're waiting for. I'm very pleased to tell you that this round of tests came back absolutely clear. They ruled out the mutated gene completely. You do not carry it and therefore you cannot pass it on to your children.'

Relief flooded her body and mind, followed by not knowing whether to laugh or cry. Heather did both as Mr Loudon handed her the tissue box. The months — no, years — of waiting, wondering, worrying were over. The life she never thought she'd have now stretched emptily ahead of her. She had a chance to change that.

'It's quite okay to cry, my dear. As long as they're tears of happiness.'

'Thank you.'

'You're welcome. I'm very pleased with the outcome. Not many people are given a second chance when it comes to genetic illnesses. Now, I hope you'll go on to make the best of life, my dear. We only get one go at it. And if you ever have any concerns again, please be sure to consult your GP. I'm certain you won't need to.'

Heather paid her bill, her mind still spinning with what could be, and left the specialist's rooms. She was free, but all she felt was relief. She had a future, a long one. So where was the elation to fill the emptiness in her heart? She got into her car and drove home, stopping along the way to pick up a bottle of champagne. Maybe when the good news penetrated the fog she'd lived in since leaving Wongan Creek, she'd be in the mood to celebrate.

An hour later, the champagne flute filled with bubbles and a plate of cheese and crackers in front of her, the people she wanted to share her good news with were almost two hundred kilometres away. Her two-bedroom rented apartment with a view of the city echoed with the fizz of bubbles going flat in the glass while her unpacked boxes taunted her from their lonely corner.

Chapter Twenty-Two

Harry peeled back the dusty lid of a weather-beaten storage box and Travis coughed.

'Jesus, Harry. There are more moths in here than in your wallet. Apparently you open this box almost as often.'

'Smart arse,' grumbled Harry. He picked up a battered red folder and opened it. 'The title deeds to Murchison's Run. You and Doc Benson are the only two I trust with them.'

Travis took the folder from Harry's unsteady hand and patted the old man's shoulder. 'You're doing the right thing, mate. It's the perfect solution to keep you on your land. The town council love the idea. This will be the perfect tree change for retirees.'

Harry stared into the box and frowned. Reaching back into it, he pulled out a fat yellow envelope. He lifted the flap, his fingers tapping the paper inside. 'What's this then?'

Doc Benson stepped forward and peered at the envelope. He chuckled. 'Come on, Harry. You know what that is. We looked at it together about six months ago. Go on, have another read to refresh your memory.'

Harry pulled out the contents and two photographs fluttered to the floor. Travis leaned down and picked them up. 'Who is this, mate? An old flame?' He held out a sepia photograph of a pretty young woman for Harry to see while he studied the other one of the same woman holding a toddler in a frilly dress.

Silence fell in the dusty shed as Harry read the letters in the envelope. He stroked a finger across the flowing writing on the powder blue paper and sighed. 'Eileen.'

Travis looked at Doc and raised his eyebrows. Doc grinned. 'Harry's little secret. I couldn't say anything before — patient confidentiality — but I think now you're officially Harry's guardian, you need to know that there is another stakeholder in the lifestyle village development.'

Harry held out the letter to Travis. 'You'd better read it, son.'

Travis read, but the words blurred as he struggled to take it all in. He turned over the photograph attached to the paper with a rusty paperclip, a colour print of a young girl holding a baby girl. His heart pounded in his chest as eyes the colour of hot chocolate stared back at him. 'Far out, Harry. And you let her walk away?'

'I had to. I gave her the opportunity to come back and she chose to walk away instead.'

'I'm not talking about Eileen.' His heart pounded as reality set in. He'd heard some bizarre tales of lost love in his time, but Harry's was a stretch of fate he was struggling to comprehend. And it had struck twice in the same place causing loss and broken hearts.

Doc put a hand on Travis' shoulder. 'Easy there, lad. It's taken us years to piece this jigsaw together ourselves. Eileen passed on about five years after they arrived back in Ireland. We had trouble finding her daughter — Harry's daughter — because she'd changed her name by deed poll. Unravelling fifty odd years of red tape and sealed records is quite a challenge, but we got there six months ago.'

Travis shook his head. 'Why didn't you tell me sooner? Why didn't you tell her?' he asked his old mate.

Harry sighed. 'I thought I did.'

'How did she end up in Wongan Creek?'

Doc Benson took the letter from his hands, folded it and pushed it back into the envelope. 'I worked closely with Elliott to have Heather fill the position so she could be close to Harry but I didn't want to take any chances with his health or his property. You can't trust anyone these days, so I needed to make sure she was the real deal and wouldn't take advantage of him.'

Travis raked his hands through his hair. 'She was the real deal.'

'Yes, she was.'

'And we let her walk away.'

'Heather had her own demons to face, son. You know that. It didn't seem fair to lay this on her until she had. She needed time to sort things out.'

'How long?' Travis wanted to get in the car and bring her home right away. If not for his own sake, then for Harry's.

'She told you about the MND?'

'Yes.'

'As soon as the report from her specialist lands on my desk, I'll be contacting her. We need her name and signature on the title deeds for Murchison Run Lifestyle Village. Then the CWA will contact her with an offer to run it.' Doc grinned.

'She doesn't want to be a burden, Doc. She made that quite clear.'

'None of us do. But she deserves to know the truth and this way there will be enough money to take care of any medical expenses if she needs it.'

Travis would rather take care of her himself. Every moment she was away, he missed her more. Every second he waited was another shaved off the time they could be spending together. 'What if she doesn't want to come back?'

'Then I guess you'll be the one who will need to

give her good reason to.' Harry pulled the lid back on the box. 'It's about time you put that charm to good use.'

The old school oval was alive with the annual Wongan Creek Rodeo activities as Travis pulled into the grounds and parked his ute next to Elliott's four-wheel drive. The town council had delayed the rodeo until the police investigation was wrapped up and the media attention linked to Zac's case had died down.

Travis smiled. It didn't look like Elliott was in any hurry to leave Wongan Creek and if the whispers were true, he and Janet might just have a budding romance on the go. So far, his quest to fill Heather's position remained fruitless. The ladies of the CWA had very quickly stepped in and voted against Martha Wallace returning to the community. Apparently they didn't need any more dragons in town. Miss Turner was quite content to hold onto the title.

'Look, Uncle Trav! They have a merry-go-round and everything.' Casey's excitement was barely contained as he opened her door to let her out of the ute.

The air around them was filled with the delicious smells of sausage sizzles, hot beef rolls and hamburgers, except when you stood downwind and got a whiff of the steers, horses and pop up animal farm for the kids. Travis wrinkled his nose.

'Come on then, we'll go find Benji and see if he wants to spend some time down Sideshow Alley.'

She held his hand tightly and led him through the market stalls. The ladies had outdone themselves this year. He could tell that, come the end of the day, the back of the ute would be full of home-baked pies and cakes. And no doubt, Casey could be tempted by the quilted princess bedspread the ladies at the quilting society had made.

He was glad the threat of runaway mickies had been removed when John Bannister sponsored some decent fencing to keep them contained to the arena. The need to have the markets at the Town Hall had been eliminated and they were back in the thick of activity where they belonged.

'There's Harry and Mrs Everett.'

Mrs E, bless her, had picked Harry up in the bus along with some of the other seniors. Harry's idea for a lifestyle village had been a hit with the town council and planning for the facility had begun. So the CWA was doing a trial run of activities to be rolled out as soon as the facility opened.

'Travis.'

John Bannister put a hand out to stop them as they walked past the Wongan Creek Mining market stall. Behind him the advertising banners all carried a white ribbon to show support for victims of domestic violence. In the past, Travis might have thought it an empty show of support to boost the Bannister profile as a community player and gain popularity votes, but the outcome of the gruesome find in the pit out in the bush had changed that.

It looked like the man had aged a hundred years in the last weeks. Gone was the cocky businessman and in his place a broken old man who'd lost everything, including his pride. The downward slope of his shoulders and the extra lines etched into his face showed the scandal over Zac's arrest had hit him hard.

'Bannister.'

'I want you to know that Harry's development has my full approval and financial backing if he wants it. I won't stand in his way.' He kept his eyes downcast, shaded by his wide-brimmed hat.

'That's good of you. I'm sure Harry will appreciate it.'

'I owe it to him after what happened with Eileen. It's time to bury the old hatchet. And for what it's worth, son, I'm really sorry about what happened to young Tracy. I should have paid more attention to what was going on. I've set up a trust fund for the little one. You'll receive the details from my lawyers soon.'

'We don't need your money.'

'I know, but it's only fair. I won't fight the adoption either, but I would like to see her from time to time. She is my great granddaughter, after all.'

Travis held out his hand. 'I'm sure we can arrange visitation under supervision.'

After a small hesitation, John Bannister shook Travis' hand. 'Thank you.'

With a smile, Travis patted the old man's shoulder then followed Casey down the row of stalls. Elliott called out to him.

'Hey, Travis!'

'Elliott.' He eyed Janet's apron tied around Elliott's waist with amusement. 'I must say, you're fitting in well here. Pink roses suit you.'

'Very funny. Hey, have you heard from Heather lately?'

The mere mention of her name had his heart beating like a drum that echoed the emptiness of it. He missed her so much he was still considering a trip to Perth to find her and bring her home kicking and screaming if he had to, but Doc Benson had told him to wait a little longer and give her some space.

'No. You?'

Elliott shook his head. 'I had hoped to hear from her yesterday.'

'Is there something wrong?'

'Well ... you know about her mum's illness, right?'

'Yeah, she mentioned it.' And it still hurt that she'd think he wouldn't stand by her through it if she had it too.

'She had her tests last week, so I was hoping she'd ring me ... or you. You know, since you two are close.'

Travis grimaced. 'We're not close.'

Elliott eyed him squarely. 'That's a shame. Maybe you should ring her.'

'She made it quite clear what she wanted when she packed up and left, mate.'

It pained him to say the words when he still cared so deeply. How many times had he picked up the phone to call her, only to press the red button to end the call before it finished dialling?

Elliott shrugged. 'Just saying.'

'I heard, thank you. See you later. I promised Casey a ride on the merry-go-round. I had wilder horses in mind to ride, but Doc Benson wouldn't clear me for the rodeo this year. I don't think he realises how hard my head is.' Travis grinned.

'You're not the only one who's bloody hard-headed,' muttered Elliott.

'What's that, mate?'

'You heard me. Here, Casey ...' He handed her a shiny dollar coin. 'The first ride is on me. Choose the wildest horse for your uncle.'

Casey giggled. 'They're all the same. Some just go higher than others.'

Elliott ruffled her curls. 'Don't lose those boots when you go on the jumping castle.'

'I won't.'

'Let's go, sweet pea. We might catch the next round if we hurry.'

Travis took her hand and led her towards the merry-go-round. He didn't want to think about Heather or the empty void his life was without her. She'd made her choice. He had to remember that.

They waited in line for a few minutes until the ride cleared then Travis put Casey up on the saddle of a unicorn. He took the horse next to her on the outside. She giggled as his legs still touched the floor even as the merry-go-round moved and the horse reached its highest point.

Travis loved hearing her laugh again. It would take a while for her to push back the memory of the day Tracy was taken, but at least she was getting there knowing she was safe and that the threat had been removed.

She had fewer nightmares and was sleeping better. The kids who'd teased her at school had stopped taunting her when Miss Turner told them Casey had a daddy who was going to adopt her, and if she heard them calling Casey awful names again, she'd remove party pies from the school canteen menu and make them all eat celery sticks.

As the horses turned and the tinny showground music tinkled, he looked across at the queue of people watching along the fence line. His heart skipped a beat as he spotted Heather leaning on her arms on the fence. She gave him a little wave he wasn't sure how to return.

Chapter Twenty-Three

Heather smiled at the picture Travis and Casey made on the merry-go-round. Her heart melted a little more. She saw the moment he spotted her, took in the look on his face before the carousel turned and she got a view of his back.

She remembered that back well. The last time she saw it, it was naked and hot under her hands. How had she ever thought she could live without him? Not when the sight of him had her blood roaring through her body and her lips eager for his.

Travis the lover was sensational. Travis the man equally hard to resist. Would he take her back? Or would he move on? Could he forgive her for being weak and running away?

'Took you long enough. I was hoping you'd show up.'

'Excuse me?' Heather turned to look at Harry, comfortably seated in a wheelchair next to her, the bright green plaster cast on his arm covered in black marker pen drawings she suspected was Casey's art work.

'What were you thinking leaving our boy like that?'

Heather sighed. 'You know, sometimes I think you're faking your memory loss, Harry.'

'My what?'

'Never mind. How's the arm healing?'

'Better than that bloke's heart.'

Heather rolled her eyes. 'Are you behaving yourself for Elliott?'

'Yes, but he's not as pretty as you.'

'Okay, flattery wins.'

'There's something I need to show you.' Harry pulled a fat yellow envelope out of the pocket of his flannel checked shirt. He opened it up and pulled out some old photos and letters, spreading them out on his lap, his arthritic fingers tapping the sepia images. 'Found these when young Travis and I were looking for the title deeds to the farm. I'd forgotten about them. I remembered when I pulled the photos out.'

He picked up one of a young woman in a vintage style dress and handed it to Heather. She took it and studied the girl's pretty features. 'She's beautiful.'

'Yes, she was. Do you recognise her?'

'No. Should I?' Heather looked closer but nothing about the woman's face recalled any memories. 'Who is she, Harry?'

'Her name was Eileen. I was in love with her. A lovely Irish lass who came here as a nurse. We were going to get married but I was called up to fight in 'Nam.'

'What happened to her?'

'She dumped me for John Bannister while I was away. She was pregnant, you see. Didn't think I'd make it back from the war. Bannister was three years younger than me, Eileen the same age as him. It didn't last long because even back then Bannister was a hothead. Not as bad as young Zac though, the bloody mongrel.' Harry held the letter in his hand, the paper fluttering in his unsteady grip.

'Did she leave him?'

Harry nodded. 'Long before the baby was born. Only stayed with him a month or so. She sent me a letter from Darwin a year later to tell me she'd had a baby girl and married a fellow countryman.'

Unease crept up Heather's spine and she shivered despite the heat. She looked at the photo again, taking in the shape of the young woman's lips and eyes, the same high cheekbones her mother had. Harry handed her the second photo, the one of the woman and her baby girl taken around the age of three. The resemblance had her stomach tying itself in knots.

'Recognise the baby?'

'Harry, this is impossible … it can't be. This can't be my mother.'

'Nothing's impossible, girl. Not when fate has a hand in things.'

He handed her the third photo and Heather's blood ran cold. Her hands shook on the faded colour photograph. This one she knew. It was the same as the one her mother had sent to her parents when Heather was born. The first and last time she'd mentioned them and the only photo her mother had kept a copy of.

'How did you get this?'

Harry tapped another letter, this one written on powder blue paper but in the same handwriting as the other. 'Eileen asked me to look out for you and your mum. She and her husband had gone back to Ireland. He didn't want anything to do with the girl when she fell pregnant. He blamed Eileen. More fool him.'

Numb, Heather stared at the photo and then at Harry. 'Why didn't you go back for Eileen?'

Harry shrugged. 'By the time I got back from 'Nam it was too late. She seemed happily married and she didn't want anything to do with me. I offered financial support but she didn't want that either.'

'Why didn't you come looking for us?'

'I did, lass. But I couldn't find any trace of you.

Your mother changed her name. In those days records were sealed so tight you couldn't crack 'em no matter how hard you tried.'

Heather's heart ached. There was so much she didn't know, so much her mother never had time to tell her before she fell ill. So much they'd all lost. But this … it defied all logic.

Harry tucked the photos and letters back into the envelope and pushed it back into his pocket. 'You can read these another time. Fate works in funny ways because Doc found you in the end when you weren't even looking.'

'I would have if I'd known.'

'Course you would have. Don't let that boy get away, Heather.' He waved at the merry-go-round where Casey waved back at him. 'Don't let history repeat itself. Life is a funny thing. Every now and then it gives us a second chance.'

'Harry, this is insane.' Heather leaned down and hugged him. The impact of his revelation had yet to sink in and she had no idea what she would do when it did.

Harry patted her back with the awkwardness of an old man not used to receiving or giving affection. 'Not as insane as you think. Doc Benson traced you and your mum through the old Darwin hospital records. How do you think you got the job here in Wongan Creek?'

Heather laughed. 'I'd like to think it was through good references and excellent qualifications.'

'Well, that too.' Harry shrugged. 'You can call me Poppy. Or Pop.'

She kissed his forehead. 'Poppy it is. I still think this is insane.'

Harry chuckled. 'What's insane is that you haven't run over there, hit the emergency stop on that damn merry-go-round and dragged your man off his high horse yet. He knows. I showed him the letters and the photos. It's fate, I tell ya.'

Heather laughed and hoped that Harry would remember all this in the next five minutes, grateful he'd remembered it at all. Even if he didn't remember, she knew she'd found her home and her family. All she had to do was convince Travis. Looking at the dark expression on his face, she'd rather wrestle a two-headed hungry crocodile.

The tinny music stopped and the merry-go-round slowed to a stop. She watched Travis and Casey make their way towards the exit. His long, jeans-clad legs ate up the distance as Casey skipped along happily beside him.

A dark blue T-shirt stretched across his broad shoulders and clung lovingly to the contours of his hard muscles. And oh God, those arms ... those beautifully sculptured arms that made a girl feel so safe and secure. Right now, she'd give anything to have them wrapped around her again.

'He hasn't given up on you. Be nice to him.' Harry

looked at her sternly. He spoiled the look with a twinkle in his eye.

'I promise I will be.' She turned as Casey came running up to her, her little boots sending up tiny puffs of red dust.

'Heather! You came back!'

Casey's sweet face lit up with a smile. She threw her arms around Heather's waist and squeezed hard.

Heather hugged her back, but her eyes were on Travis. He'd lost weight, but the bruises had faded from his face at last. The tiny white scar near his eye a reminder of the close call they'd all had with Zac. At least there was one thing they could put in the past.

'Heather.' His nod was cool, his eyes unreadable.

'Travis.' Tangible strain rode in waves between them.

'You two need to be alone. Try not to be idiots about it. Casey,' said Harry. 'Give us a push over there to Mrs E, would ya? I'll help, but I can only do one wheel, so push straight.'

'Okay, Harry.'

Casey took the handles of Harry's wheelchair. Heather watched them make slow progress to where the group of CWA ladies huddled together a few feet away, trying hard to pretend they weren't watching and listening to every word.

Bella stepped forward and with a wink and a thumbs up for Heather, took control of Harry's chair. Mrs E clasped Casey's hand securely in hers, chatting away cheerfully.

Travis ran his thumb along the length of his nose and stared at his boots. 'Subtle as a brick, our Harry.' He folded his arms across his chest.

Heather laughed. 'Good to see he hasn't changed.' She placed a hand on his forearm where it crossed over the other. 'Travis, I'm really sorry about what happened between us. My head was a mess after what happened with Harry.'

He lifted his gaze to hers, the green almost emerald as he stared right into her heart. 'You knew you could trust me. I've always been true to my word.'

She stepped closer, pleased when he didn't step away. With both hands on his forearms she eased them apart until he dropped his defensive pose. The barrier removed, she could feel the delicious heat of his body.

'I made a mistake, Travis. I've never had anyone to talk to before. No one I could tell about the fear that built inside me. My whole life revolved around Mum. Any friends I might have had wandered away when things got complicated and Mum's care took up all my time. Friendship is like love, it needs to be nurtured. I never learned how to grow either of them.'

He stared over her head, the walls around him impenetrable, his hands fisted at his side. Her hopes began to fade.

'I took the tests.' Her words fell like rocks between them.

'I heard.'

Heather chewed her lip as his gaze came back to meet hers then travelled to her mouth. Her heart fluttered. 'I got the all clear.'

A small flicker of light in his eyes. 'That's great. I'm happy for you.' His fists uncurled and he placed his hands on his hips. 'You'll be able to get on with your life then.'

The weight of sadness and rejection built in her stomach. She only had herself to blame. She'd dumped him after the most amazing sex a girl could dream of having. After forming a bond of friendship and trust, she'd not trusted him with her own fears. She'd fallen in love and thrown it away.

'Yes, I guess so.' She swallowed the hurt and blinked against the burn of tears. She'd cry them later when she was far away from the place that had once felt like it could be home.

'Why did you come back, Heather?'

She dropped her gaze to her hands where they worried the brim of her hat. 'I don't know. I guess I hoped ...'

'What? That now you know you're genetically perfect we'd welcome you home with open arms? Do you honestly think we didn't love you the way you were? Wouldn't have supported you when you needed it?'

She swiped at her cheek where a tear escaped her lashes, couldn't bring herself to look at him as her hopes shattered and her heart ached. She'd found her family but was losing the man she loved.

'Instead you chose to walk away. And now it suits you to walk right back. You're going to have to do better than that.'

Heather dashed the tears away, smearing her mascara. She looked at the black streaks on her fingers then wiped them on her jeans. 'You're right. Again, I'm sorry. I'll go.' She turned to walk away.

'Oh for God's sake, Travis Bailey, swallow some of that damn pride before I shove it up your arse.' Harry yelled from far enough away to be out of their space but close enough to intervene when needed. 'I swear, boy, if my ankle was strong enough I'd come over there and tan your hide with my cane.'

'Shut up, Harry,' Travis shouted back.

Heather felt the warmth of his hand encase her arm, stopping her from taking a step away. She turned her head to look at him, let her gaze travel over his face, committing each curve and contour to memory for later.

'Do we mean anything at all to you, Heather? What do you want from us?'

What did she have to lose? Everything she'd dreamed of, hoped for was already lost.

'I don't want anything from you. I want to give back to you, to the community of Wongan Creek, because without you, I am nothing. I'm just a lonely, miserable city girl living out each day until I die, which now is a hell of a lot longer than I expected to.'

She turned and stood boot to boot with him, her chin raised stubbornly. 'I want to watch Casey grow up, be there for her when she has to choose her first ball dress or go out on her first date with Benji or whoever else it might be. I want to sleep next to you every night and wake up to your charming personality in the morning.'

'Ha! She's got you there, mate!'

'Shut up, Harry! And then I want to make love to you until you have no strength or desire to get out of bed to look for Harry's sheep which aren't even missing.'

'Oh my!' Mrs E covered Casey's ears, but she was too busy playing football with Benji to notice.

'I want to drink my apple juice out of a doll's tea set every night, maybe even my wine too. I want to have your babies and spend the rest of my life making up for being so stupid as to let you go in the first place. I love you, you ... *arsehole*. Is that enough for you?'

Travis' hands fastened on her hips and he tugged her closer. 'Could you say that again? Without the arsehole bit.'

She raised her hands to cup his face. 'I love you, Travis Bailey. I can't imagine another day without you. I sat in my apartment with a bottle of champagne going flat and no one to share it with, and I realised I'd thrown away the greatest gift of all. You and Casey.'

'So, let me get this straight ... you only love me because of Casey.'

Heather tugged hard on his ear.

'Ouch.'

'I love you because of you.'

'That sounds terribly Irish.'

She stood on her tiptoes and pressed her lips to his. 'Then let me speak a language you understand.'

She kissed him until the stiffness left his spine, let her hands trail down his chest and brush his hips until his arms encircled her waist. His mouth softened against hers and he kissed her back until both of them were breathless. When his arms tightened around her and held her close, she knew she'd won.

He lifted her up and she wrapped her legs around him. Pressing his forehead to hers, he said, 'I might take a little more convincing.'

She cupped the back of his head in her hands and kissed the tiny white scar at the corner of his eye. 'I have a lifetime to try.'

Behind them Harry let out a whistle and Robbie barked excitedly.

'Well, I guess I'd better start designing a wedding cake,' said Bella.

Virginia Turner sighed. 'Great. A whole new

generation of Baileys to terrorise the classrooms.' Her smile said she didn't mind the challenge one bit.

'Oh my goodness,' murmured Mrs Everett, her hands clasped under her chin and her faded blue eyes damp. 'I'd better order in more wool. I'll have to start knitting booties and beanies soon.'

Travis grinned against Heather's mouth and lifted his head. 'You know what you're taking on, right?'

'Yes. I wouldn't have it any other way.'

Then he was kissing her again and her mind wandered far away from the festivities.

Chapter Twenty-Four

Travis hugged Heather closer and pressed a kiss to the creamy skin on her shoulder. He couldn't believe his luck. She'd come back. To stay. And she was Harry's granddaughter.

Could it get any better than that? He'd woken up every morning for the last three weeks and thanked her for coming home — Travis Bailey style — with his heart and his soul.

She'd loved the plans for the lifestyle village and was full of ideas for the running of it. They'd agreed to adopt Casey as a couple and she hadn't hesitated to put her signature to the papers which made him love her even more. Casey's smile was even bigger, and life was great.

Heather stretched against him and sighed so he let his hand play on her hip and trail over her thigh then make lazy circles on her stomach. She snuggled closer and he knew exactly how to wake her up. He nibbled her ear and when she yelped and turned her head towards him, he pressed his lips to hers.

'Morning, beautiful.'

She smiled. 'Hey.'

God, he loved her smile, her face, every inch of her body and soul. 'I missed you when you were gone.' He told her that every morning in case she forgot and didn't realise how thankful he was she'd come back. Hopefully she never got tired of hearing it because God help him, he meant every word. He'd never thought it possible to love someone so deeply.

Heather cupped his face in her hands. 'I missed you too.'

'Can I show you how much?'

'I think you showed me well enough last night. And the night before.'

His hand travelled up her belly to her breast. 'I need a reminder.'

She turned her body to align with his. A perfect fit, his body agreed, so he continued his exploration with his lips. 'Was that a purr?' he asked against her throat.

'A little one.'

He covered her body with his. 'I like it when you roar.'

Heather laughed and dragged his head up to kiss his mouth hard. He was happy to reciprocate but just as things were getting interesting, Heather stiffened under him.

'Travis, is that Mrs Everett's bus coming up the drive?'

Robbie barked out a friendly rap from his spot on the veranda outside the window.

Travis sighed and rolled away to find his boxers. 'And here I was hoping it was your engine running on high revs.' He pulled them on and pushed the blinds aside with his finger. 'Ah, shit.'

Heather propped herself up on her elbows and he turned to look at her. 'Who is it?'

'It's my parents. This could be good or it could be very bad.' He ran a hand through his hair and searched for his T-shirt. He found it near the bedroom door, picked it up and dragged it over his head, shoving his arms through the sleeves.

Heather got out of bed and pulled her clothes on. 'I'll put the coffee pot on and wake Harry and Casey.'

Travis pulled her closer and kissed her hard. 'Sorry, baby.'

'Don't be sorry. Go out there and welcome them home.'

Her encouraging smile said she had his back — and his front — so he squared his shoulders and made his way through the house onto the veranda. He pulled the fly screen closed behind him just as the campervan pulled up in front of the house. He waited as his parents climbed out and received a warm welcome home from Robbie who danced in circles and peed himself with excitement.

The first thing that struck him was how beautiful his mum looked with her short, greying hair cut in a bob and the healthy colour to her skin. The second was how much his dad had aged since he'd seen him last.

Travis stamped down the disappointment that it had taken them so long to come home. He'd tried to call them to let them know about Zac but they were out of mobile range. So he'd left a message and hoped they'd healed enough to come back for the trial.

'Hey, guys, you're home!' It would always be their home, no matter how much they tried to avoid the sad memories the farm raised. He walked down the steps into his mother's open arms, wincing as she hugged him tightly. 'Jeez, Mum, have you been working out?'

Barbara Bailey laughed. 'Got to get rid of the bingo wings somehow. It's good to see you, son. The place looks great.'

'Thanks. Hi, Dad.'

'Travis.' His father's features remained stony.

Great. Nothing had changed. There'd be awkward silences all through breakfast, lunch and dinner as usual. When would he ever forgive Travis for screwing up?

'Oh come on, Edward. You can do better than that,' Mum scolded. 'For God's sake, lighten up.'

His father scowled but moved forward to give him

an awkward man hug. His mother smiled and then her gaze rose to the veranda.

'Oh, who's this then, Travis?'

Travis looked back over his shoulder and smiled. 'Mum, Dad, this is Heather.' He walked up the stairs and put his arm around her shoulders, drawing her into him, seeking her warmth and comfort before pressing a kiss to her temple. 'She's going to be my wife.'

'Are you asking me or are you telling me?' Heather nudged him in the ribs.

'I propose to you every morning, sweetheart. Every night too. And sometimes in the middle of the day when we get the chance.'

'But I like words, Bailey.'

Heather smiled at him and his heart melted a little more. If she wanted words, he'd give her every single one in his vocabulary until she kissed him to shut him up. 'I'll give you words. And actions.'

His mother walked up onto the veranda with his dad close behind her. Her gaze flicked between them, taking in Travis' arm around Heather's shoulders and the look on his face he knew would tell her all she needed to know. He loved Heather with everything left in him to love.

'Well, this is a wonderful surprise. Lovely to meet you, dear.'

'She's also Harry's granddaughter,' added Travis.

'Harry's granddaughter?' Edward's eyebrows got lost in his hairline.

Heather smiled and held out her hand for him to shake. 'That's right. Harry and Eileen's granddaughter.'

'Oh my!' gasped Barbara. 'So the rumours *were* true then!'

'Close your mouth, Barbara. Things like that happened. Even back then.'

'Oh shut up, Edward. See what I have to put up with?' She hooked an arm through Heather's and drew her away from Travis' side. 'I hope you've got the coffee pot on, love. I think I'll need a strong one to hear this story.' With her hand on the fly screen door, she turned and said, 'Edward, you be nice to Travis now while Heather and I catch up. If you're good, I might even save you some coffee.'

Travis tried hard not to chuckle and failed. He muffled it with his hand as he caught the warning in his father's look. 'Sorry.'

Edward placed his hands on his hips and watched his wife disappear into the house. 'Don't be.' He turned his head to peer out over the paddocks. 'You sold the cattle.'

Travis rubbed his nose. Was that an accusation or an observation, he wondered. He'd never quite known with his dad. 'The south-west is Angus beef country now, Dad. The cows didn't like getting gold dust in their teeth.'

'You always were a smart arse, Travis. You're growing canola.'

'It's the new gold.'

Edward nodded. 'Looks good. Why are Harry's sheep in our paddock?'

'He keeps losing them. This way I know where they are. And he and Robbie are living with us for a while.'

'Fair call. He's bad then?'

Travis sighed and rolled the stress from his shoulders. 'He has good days and bad days. Now we have Heather, it helps. He might not remember who you are though, so be prepared.'

Edward nodded again. 'Heather seems like a nice girl. Eileen's granddaughter, hey? Go figure. Your mother has a sixth sense about these things and I can see she likes her.' He looked around. 'You kept the sofa.'

Travis patted the worn arm. 'It has good memories.'

'I used to sit out here and read stories to you and Tracy, show you the stars.'

'I know, Dad. I remember.'

'It was hard. Losing her. Twice.'

No one knew that better than him, so Travis kept his mouth shut.

'It wasn't your fault, son. Not what happened at the party and not when she ... went missing.'

'Did Mum tell you to say that?'

Edward ran a hand through his hair. The white patch

of fringe used to be gold like his son's. It stood out against the grey streaks in his dark hair. 'No. I just realised I never said it when I needed to.' He tossed the campervan keys in his hands. 'I never meant to make you feel like it was your fault. I should have listened to you that night. Let you go to that damn party and bring her home. Your mother and I should never have let her go in the first place. I heard they put him away.'

Travis sat down on the sofa and put his feet up on the rail. He didn't need to ask who his father was referring to. 'We nailed him, Dad. He'll be paying his dues for a very long time. I'm sure he's a favourite with the inmates already. Hopefully they'll let him live long enough to stand trial.'

Edward sat next to Travis and toed off his running shoes. 'Good job, son. You stuck to your guns on that one.' He put his feet up on the rail. 'I heard Harry's building a retirement home next door.'

'Lifestyle village.'

'Will they play canasta on Fridays?'

'Canasta, chess, play dates — whatever.'

'I think I might buy one of those cottages for your mother and me. What do you think?'

Travis raised an eyebrow. 'Does that mean you're hanging around for a while?'

Edward shrugged. 'Can't run away forever. I'm sorry I did. I shouldn't have left it all up to you.'

'Maybe it's what needed to happen, Dad.'

Edward held out his hand to his son. 'Are we good?'

Travis looked at the hand shaped so like his own. 'We're good.'

They shook on it and spent a few quiet moments staring out over the creek at the hills rising above it.

'Trav?'

'Dad?'

'Why does Harry have a daisy field where his canola used to be?'

Travis grinned. 'So he still feels like a farmer.'

Harry pushed through the fly screen door. 'Where the hell are my bloody sheep?'

Travis laughed hard and rubbed his eyes, his fingers coming away damp, happiness bubbling in his gut. 'Shift up, Dad. Make space for the old bastard so he can see his sheep.'

Harry squeezed into the tight gap on the sofa and stretched his legs out as far as his arthritic knees would allow. 'Ah, there they are. My little beauties.' He looked at Edward. 'Who are you?'

'You don't remember me? Edward Bailey. Travis' father.'

Harry grinned. 'I remember you. Just making sure *you* remember who you are. Took you long enough to remember where you lived.'

Travis shook his head. 'Harry, you really have to learn to play nice with the other children.'

Edward sighed. 'He's right. I can't argue with that.'

Casey came padding out, her princess pyjamas wrinkled and her red curls tangled. She climbed onto Travis' lap and stared at the man next to him. Frowning, she looked at Travis.

'What's up, sweet pea?'

'I'm confused, Uncle Trav.'

He smoothed her curls down and watched as they sprang up again. 'Why are you confused?'

'Well, when you marry Heather she'll be my new mum because you're my new dad and then Harry will be my new poppy so what do I call my old poppy?' She took a breath and let it out on a sigh.

Travis chuckled. 'That's a good question, sweet pea.'

Edward ruffled her curls. 'Sounds like one we need to figure out over coffee. Should we go inside and work it out?'

'Might wanna put some pants on first, young bloke,' said Harry, pointing down the drive and reminding Travis he still only wore his boxer shorts. 'The cavalry's arrived.'

Through the dust kicked up by the tyres, Mrs Everett's bus appeared, followed closely by Doc Benson's four-wheel drive and Riggs' police wagon.

'Oh man,' grumbled Travis as all hope of being alone with Heather any time soon evaporated. 'Casey, go warn Heather to clear some space in the fridge. I see casseroles and apple pie coming.'

The bus pulled up to a stop and as the door opened, the ladies of the CWA poured out, arms laden with goodies.

'Heard you and Barbara had come home, Edward,' said Miss Turner. 'About time too.'

'It wasn't like I had a choice, Virginia. I believe your instructions were quite clear. Something about getting my backside home to Wongan Creek or I wouldn't be able to sit for a month? I guess it was just as well we were on our way home already.' He turned to Travis. 'We had no mobile signal for a while and only got your message about Harry going missing and Zac's arrest when we got to Darwin.'

Travis shrugged. 'Doesn't matter, Dad. You're here now.'

Edward squeezed his son's shoulder. 'It's where I want to be.'

Doc Benson and Riggs joined the crowd on the veranda and there was a bit of back-slapping and man-hugging before they all filed into the kitchen through the fly screen door. The noise level rose as the ladies reunited with his mum.

Travis spotted Heather at the kitchen table, her hands cupped around a mug of tea. He walked behind her and wrapped his arms around her shoulders. She patted his forearms with one hand and kept a hold on her mug with the other.

'It might be a while before we get the place to ourselves around here,' he whispered in her ear.

She turned her head and smiled then pressed a kiss to his lips. 'We can always sneak over to Harry's old place,' she whispered back.

'It's a date.' He sealed the deal with a kiss before pinching Heather's mug out of her hand but kept his face close to hers.

'Hey!' She made a play to get it back. 'What are you doing?'

'Take a look around you.' He let his gaze follow hers around the table.

Mrs Everett sat at the table with her knitting out and showing Casey ... *Oh my God, is that a pink baby beanie?* The thought made his heart pound. The kettle and coffee pot were getting a workout with the ladies of the CWA gathered around the kitchen bench. His dishwasher would be pretty busy cleaning all those cups and mugs Ms Turner had taken out of the dresser.

Mum reached into the fridge for bacon and eggs. Dad and Riggs argued at the back door of the kitchen over who could cook them best on the barbie, and Robbie sat next to Harry's chair all dopey-eyed from an ear scratch.

He watched Heather's face as she saw what he did

— the smile that spread her lips, the light in her eyes as she took in the scene around them and the kiss she pressed to his cheek that almost made him forget the point he was trying to make.

He raised her mug in a toast. 'Say hi to your new family, sweetheart.'

THE END

Secrets (Wongan Creek Series Book 2)

Want to know what happens next in Wongan Creek? Join Tameka and Harley in their fight to save their farms as long-buried secrets rise to the surface.

Secrets (Wongan Creek Series Book 2)
by Juanita Kees

Still waters run deep in Wongan Creek …

Harley Baker stands to lose everything when spray drift from his neighbour's toxic herbicides destroys his crop. But arguments are tricky when it comes to Tameka Chalmers. Financial ruin is only a small part of the nightmare that keeps him away from the woman he's always loved.

Tameka Chalmers knows that her father's farming methods are outdated, inefficient, and even dangerous.

There's so much she would like to do differently, but her father's rule is absolute, and she must do as she's told or be prepared for the consequences.

When Harley confronts her about the damage to his crop, the interaction triggers an unexpected chain reaction that throws everything she's ever known into question. As long buried secrets rise to the surface, everything they believed to be true will be challenged. Can they rise from the ashes of lies and betrayal when each step they take brings danger closer to their door?

Chapter 1

Tameka confiscated the rope Harley's dog had destroyed along with three hundred square metres of her newly sown barley field.

'Hooley Dooley, Loki, what have you done?'

Oh, Harley Baker would pay for this, for sure. She paid no attention to Loki's attempts to claim her attention even though twenty-three kilograms of Catahoula Leopard dog leaping at her torso wasn't easy to ignore.

'Sit down!' Tameka said sternly, surprised when Loki obeyed and looked at her with his melt-your-heart eyes. No-one melted her heart. Not Harley Baker and not his dog either. 'Bad dog.'

Loki gave a short bark and offered up a reconciliatory doggy grin.

'Don't smile at me.'

She looked over the dog's head at the destruction in his wake and ignored the paw that scratched at the leg of her denims in a bid for attention.

Her neatly ploughed and planted rows of barley resembled a churned-up dirt bike track after the annual fair in the wake of Loki's destruction, the almost empty container of liquid concentrate mix she'd used for spot-spraying and hadn't had time to put away yet overturned in the soil.

Now there was Loki's health to worry about too. If he'd ingested some of the herbicides her father insisted on using, he could be an extremely sick dog and that would break her heart. No amount of pushing towards using organic herbicides could sway Louis Chalmers away from chemical poisons.

But then no amount of hard work and dedication could make him believe she was worthy of his praise either. No, her dad would be far happier if he'd had a son instead of a daughter.

Loki's adventures in the barley would only prove him right that she was an incompetent farmer and manager who couldn't even keep the gate between the two farms shut — no matter whose fault it was that the dog had chosen her field as his playground.

She set the container upright and checked that the lid was still securely screwed into place as the low gear warble of a four-stroke engine reached her ears. That'd be Harley coming to look for his dog. No four-legged horses for that farm boy. His were all steel-framed, power-hungry two-wheelers as sleek and sexy as he was.

She shivered inside her sheepskin-lined jacket and tugged her beanie down around her ears. A sexy pain in the arse who once had owned her heart.

The 200cc Trojan appeared out of the remains of the morning fog, and Tameka sucked in the cold air, letting it burn down her throat and into her lungs as she watched the bike progress down the firebreak.

When dealing with Harley, she needed a heart of ice, or he'd get under her skin and make her remember what he felt like under his flannel-checked shirt and denims. A distraction she couldn't afford when it made her long for the friendship and love they'd lost.

Oh, she knew exactly what he looked like under those clothes thanks to a dare when they'd been young and stupid. He'd been eighteen and filling out in all the right places when he'd lost his bet about her father letting her manage the farm. She'd made him do two laps of the firebreak around Bakers Hill on his damn bike — naked, wearing only his boots — in the middle of winter. And then there was that one time in his ute … At least he had clothes on today. It would make it much easier to stay angry with him.

He pulled up at the fence, and she let the rhythm of the engine throb through her, itching for a ride. Her father wouldn't have bikes in the field. That's what utes were for. And where the ute didn't go, you walked. She looked at Harley's face under his red beanie. Not only was he wearing clothes, he was also wearing an incredibly angry face. Good, because she was angry too and spoiling for a fight.

'Your bloody dog just wrecked all my hard work. Churned up my field and made it his damn playpen.' Raising her voice over the engine noise, she threw her arms wide across the scene. The culprit sat centre stage for a split second before his brain kicked into gear and he pounded across the field of destruction to greet his owner.

'Sit. Stay,' Harley commanded.

The dog sat his butt in the churned-up soil and peered through the fence, head cocked to one side, ears pinned back and a questioning whine in his voice. Harley cut the engine and pushed down the stand. Denim clung to his thighs as he swung his leg back across the seat.

Tameka tried hard not to appreciate the view while she ignored the hitch of breath in her throat. Watching Harley move had once been her favourite way to spend the day. It still was, except now she did it from the other side of the fence. On the odd occasion they did speak it was as if they were strangers and had never been lovers or even good friends, their conversation polite, stilted and all business.

The easy stride of those long legs, the way he

dragged a hand through his hair when he was annoyed, embarrassed, or simply irritated. His smile and easy laughter, how he used to make her feel — special, wanted, loved — were all happy memories she kept locked in her dreams to chase away the monsters at night.

Today his flannel shirt was red and black, just visible under a black puffer jacket, his footy scarf wrapped around his neck to ward off the morning chill. West Coast Eagles — another reminder of what they'd once had together. Through thick and thin, she'd always be a Dockers fan. Purple would always clash with yellow and blue.

But right this minute it wasn't about the good-natured football rivalry they'd once had between them or the times they'd spent cheering for opposite teams, finding reasons to kiss and make up. That was in the past. Today was all about the partially ruined rows of barley crop she'd have to re-seed.

Harley pushed through the open gate in the fence between their farms. A pang of regret nudged Tameka's heart. She missed the days when he'd come through that gate for reasons that didn't cause a scowl on his face. When they'd been on speaking terms — on kissing terms — except on Derby Day. Back in the years when the competition between her and Harley had been about who could climb the highest in the old gum tree down by the creek or who could sow a row faster.

The only purpose the gate served these days was when Loki nosed it open to chase the birds out of the trees around the dam, or like today, kill and bury his rope for resurrection later.

'I'll come down and weld that bloody gate shut.' He stopped with his boots inches from hers, and she could smell the remnants of his shower soap and toothpaste as he called, 'Loki, heel!'

Loki obeyed, his ice-blue gaze full of apology as he leaned against Harley's leg and begged for an ear scratch.

A pang of regret filled her heart at the way Harley stood so close, his body heat warming her personal space. There'd been a time when she could reach out and tug at his beanie or steal his scarf. Or lean up against him and kiss the spots of colour the cold morning put in his cheeks.

'Might be best.' She raised her eyes from his mouth to his face and caught the grim expression there, her heart sinking at the annoyance in his eyes. 'Who stole your sunshine and rainbows this morning? I'm the one with the churned-up field.'

He whipped off his beanie, shoved it in his jacket pocket and blew out a warm, angry breath that tickled her face.

'That'd be you, Tameka.' He reached inside his puffer jacket, his arm brushing across her chest, and pulled out a cutting with wilted leaves. 'Looks like we're even over Loki's mess because your infernal preference for phenoxies has destroyed almost my entire crop on this side of the fence line.'

Shit. Tameka took the cutting from his hands, stepped back and studied it. Her heart plummeted. Deformed leaves hung limply from the stunted stems; misshapen, brittle, and burnt. Damn it, hadn't she warned her father about spray drift? Harley's towering hops would have copped a good portion of it. With his bines climbing at over ten metres high, there'd be little chance of them avoiding the damage phenoxy spray caused to broadleaf crops. No matter how careful she was about spraying.

Harley shoved a hand through his toffee-coloured hair. 'Long-term, *preventable* herbicide damage. How many times do we need to have this conversation?'

'My hands are tied, Harley.' Anger pushed her heart back up where it belonged. Of course he'd blame her. Everyone would.

'Bullshit. You're the farm manager on Golden Acres. You call the shots.'

And if he believed that, he was dumber than she'd given him credit for. Her father would never let go of the reins completely for as long as he breathed in this life. But Harley wasn't done lashing out at her yet. She would bear the brunt of it — his anger and frustration — knowing he had every right to feel that way, powerless in that there wasn't a damn thing she could do about it, no matter how hard she tried. She stayed silent and let him offload his grievances to the top of her head while she studied the mud.

'Every year I lose crop I can't afford to because you continue to use chemical weed killers. As if the water shortages aren't doing enough damage. Damn it, Tameka, you have no idea the council hoops I have to jump through to get approval to use recycled water until I can get my dam built.'

She shook her head and bit her tongue. As if she hadn't already explored alternatives to phenoxies and tried to convince her dad to use them. And the lack of rain affected her crop as much as it did Harley's, even with their dam as back up.

When she didn't buy into the argument, he continued. 'So, do you know what? Your churned up rows don't quite cut it compared to three hectares of stunted growth that produced little or no damn crop this year.' He closed the gap between them until they stood boot to boot once more.

No, of course they didn't. The back-breaking hours she'd spent on and off the tractor towing the archaic box air seeder with its failing air hoses, tilling the soil, fertilising, checking, measuring, only to have her father inspect it, find it lacking and make her do it all over again — none of it counted. Anger made tears sting her eyes. She fought them back. Tameka Chalmers didn't cry and screw Harley Baker for making her want to.

'Take your dog and your dickatude and get off my land.'

She raised her hands and shoved him hard, catching him off guard so he stumbled back and fell on his arse in the soil. She bent and picked up the tortured remains of Loki's rope and lobbed it at his chest. Then she turned and walked away.

Damn him for invading her space and making her want to spill her guts to him like she used to before. To tell him exactly what she had to do to keep Golden Acres up and running. And the rest. The whole horrible, God damn *miserable* story.

'Tameka, wait.'

She hesitated at Harley's shout but didn't stop or turn around.

'I'm sorry I yelled at you, okay. It's been a bitch of a day, and it's only just bloody started.'

As if every day was freaking paradise for her. He could rot in hell along with his damaged crop. She didn't care what he had to say.

'It's not just the phenoxy damage. Some of the cones on the north-side bines have developed downy mildew. My harvest is down fifty percent thanks to all the damage, and my profit with it. The bank is threatening to foreclose on my loan if I can't make payment. If they won't grant me an extension ...'

The desperation in his tone almost had her turning

around, but nothing should make her feel sorry for Harley Baker.

'I'll lose everything.'

Except that. Her heart plummeted to her boots and stopped her in her tracks at the thought of what that meant for Harley and Bakers Hill. She wouldn't wish that kind of ruin on her worst enemy because she knew the cost of it all too well herself.

Whispers, Secrets and Shadows (Wongan Creek Series) can be purchased from your favourite bookseller. If they don't have it, ask them or your local library to order it in for you.

Dear Reader

This book has been written and edited using Australian / UK English grammar and punctuation conventions because the story is set in Australia. For more information on the differences between UK and US language and punctuation, please consider reading this article: https://tinyurl.com/56tkbh6a

If you enjoyed this book, please consider leaving a review on BookBub, Goodreads or the platform you purchased it from. If you would prefer to email me, please visit the contact page on my website at https://juanitakees.com/contact/. I do love to hear from readers and welcome your feedback.

Kind regards

Juanita Kees

Other Books by Juanita Kees

Wongan Creek Series

Whispers

Secrets

Shadows

Unfinished Business

Exposed

Tagged

Silenced

Bindarra Creek

Home to Bindarra Creek

Promise Me Forever

The Calhouns of Montana

Montana Baby

Montana Daughter

Montana Son

Contemporary Romance

Finish Line

Paranormal Fantasy

The Gods of Oakleigh